D0426280

THE
AGENCY

THE AGENCY

Rivals in the City

Y. S. Lee

CANDLEWICK PRESS

Copyright © 2014 by Y. S. Lee

First U.S. edition 2015

Library of Congress Catalog Card Number 2014944913
ISBN 978-0-7636-5914-1

15 16 17 18 19 BVG 10 9 8 7 6 5 4 3 2

Printed in Berryville, VA, U.S.A.

This book was typeset in Palatino.

Candlewick Press
99 Dover Street
Somerville, Massachusetts 02144

visit us at www.candlewick.com

To H, our constant delight,
and to N, who shares it all

One

Saturday, 13 October 1860

The streets of London

It was a miserable day for a walk: sleety, frigid, dark. Nevertheless, Mary Quinn and James Easton, Private Detectives, were out for a ramble about Bloomsbury, bundled against the penetrating drizzle, straining to distinguish people from lampposts in the dense fog that swamped the streets. Mary's skirts were soaked to the knee and much heavier than when she'd first set out. Their boots were thick with mud.

Mary smiled up at James, squeezing his elbow. "Isn't this delightful?"

He laughed. "Unalloyed bliss, apart from the rain, the wind, and the bitter cold. Can you still feel your fingertips?"

She wiggled them experimentally. "A little. Could you tilt the umbrella toward me, please? It's dripping on my shoulder." James complied, and they paced on, passing a sodden, shivering boy wielding a broomstick taller than he was. "Wait a moment, James." But James was already turning back, pressing a coin into the crossing sweeper's unresisting palm. He murmured something and gave the child a gentle pat on the shoulder.

Mary watched the boy stumble away, a slight figure swallowed by the dark smog. She shuddered. It was like a heavy handed morality play to which there could be only one conclusion.

James returned, offering his arm once more. "Where were we?"

"You were complaining about the weather. Not for the first time." She smiled at him again, teasing now. "Are you quite certain you don't want to come up to my flat for tea and toast and scandal?" As her future husband, James wanted their marriage to be respectable. It wasn't for his sake, particularly, although she suspected he cared about reputation more than he would acknowledge. No, it was for Mary: in order to bury her past and allow her a fresh start, they had agreed to behave with Utter Propriety. No matter how hypocritical and inconvenient the conventions of etiquette, it was worth observing them for the social invisibility it would afford their marriage. These cold and uncomfortable walks about town were a perfect example of their new courtship: How else could an unmarried lady and gentleman hold a truly private conversation, unchaperoned and uninterrupted? James's logic was inarguable. And yet, after twenty years of freedom, Mary desperately resented these superficial social restrictions. Was this the moment to propose her little escapade?

His reply wiped all thought of it from her mind. "I'd love to. Let's just pop into the next church and get married first."

She puffed with amusement and saw her breath in the air. "Of course you've a marriage license in your pocket."

"Do you doubt it?"

"I'd no idea you were on such intimate terms with the Archbishop of Canterbury."

"There are common licenses, you know. One can be obtained from any vicar."

She halted and stared up into his dark eyes. They glinted with mockery, and something else, too: a challenge. Her mouth dried. "A-are you—in earnest?"

"I'm asking you to declare yourself. We could be married within the hour, if you so chose." His expression was neutral, his tone maddeningly even. He might have been offering her his seat on the omnibus.

She was suddenly at the edge of a precipice, fascinated and terrified in equal measure. Of course she wanted to marry James . . . someday. But now? Here? "I—I don't know what to say," she confessed, unable to meet his gaze.

"That is an answer in itself." He sounded calm, but there was no missing the undercurrent of hurt in his voice.

She spun to face him fully, taking both his hands in hers. "I'm sorry, James. I love you, truly. And I want to marry you."

"But not yet."

"I'm just learning a whole new way of being. Can you

picture yourself in my place?" Mary closed her eyes briefly, knowing that James certainly tried. He was deeply sympathetic to the horrors of her childhood on the streets, her life as a juvenile housebreaker, her unexpected escape from the death sentence. She'd never been free to explain exactly how she'd been rescued by the Agency, but he knew enough. "After a childhood such as mine, I'm suddenly a woman of means. I can choose what to do with my days. I answer to nobody. Can you see why I might want a little more time for such selfish liberty? This is my first taste of true independence, the closest I'll ever come to perfect freedom." She paused. "It *is* selfish; I have no illusions that it's anything else. But it's a giddy, dizzying sort of freedom, and I want more time to explore it."

After a few moments, he squeezed her fingers. "I think I do understand." She felt limp with relief. "It's too easy for me to forget. I answer only to George, and that's as a business partner. Although he is my elder brother, I am very much my own man."

She smiled. "That you are. And you've chosen a willful, stubborn, scandal-ridden disgrace of a fiancée."

"Only the best for me."

"James." Mary pulled him close—too close for perfect propriety. "Thank you."

His finger glided against the curve of her cheek. "I can't say 'My pleasure.'"

She smiled. "I do want to belong to you one day. And to claim you as my own, as well."

"I very much look forward to being claimed." He glanced around furtively, then dipped his head to hers, kissing her—all too briefly—on the lips. "Perhaps I'll have your name tattooed on my arm so there's no doubt as to whom I belong," he said, tucking her hand into the crook of his elbow and resuming their steady walking pace. "What would you say to your initials in Gothic letters, surrounded by scrolls and hearts?"

"No need," she said with a laugh. "Once you're mine, I won't permit you to forget it."

They walked on in a daze, utterly distracted by each other and by visions of their future. It wasn't until they heard church bells ringing the hour—it was already eleven—that Mary returned to the present. "Ought we to talk business?" she suggested with a slight sigh.

"Sadly, yes. What news of ailing Mr. Colfax?" It was the last—and, admittedly, only second—item on their list of current cases.

"I'm afraid it's bad: I've traced the purchase of three substantial amounts of arsenic over the past year directly to his wife."

James whistled. "I thought it was supposed to be difficult to buy arsenic now. There was all that administrative reform after the Bradford tragedy." Less than two years earlier, there had been an accidental mass poisoning in the north, when arsenic was mistakenly included in a batch of peppermint sweets.

"In theory, yes. But all one need do is tell the chemist

5

what it's wanted for—everybody in the world wants it to kill rats—and sign the ledger."

"Did she sign in her own name each time?"

"For the first lot, yes, which makes me wonder if the idea only came to her after the fact. But for the second and third purchases, which are more recent, she took care to use a false name and address. I'm certain it's her, though. Not only does the handwriting match, but the chemists—she used a different shop each time—remembered her and described her with accuracy."

"What's next?"

"We still don't know exactly how she's doing it," said Mary. "She's not suffering from any sort of digestive upset, and neither are the domestics. It must be in something he alone consumes. Dissolved in the whiskey, maybe, or perhaps he's the only one who likes sugar in his coffee."

"I'll ask him to consider what it might be," said James. As the male partner, he was also the public face of their fledgling detective firm—a concession to convention that seldom failed to irk Mary, if she dwelt upon it. "And perhaps he ought to take a short holiday. It would be useful to confirm that he doesn't suffer these digestive horrors when he's on his own; only when dear Mrs. Colfax presides over the menu."

Mary nodded. "In the meantime, I doubt Mrs. Colfax is a threat to anybody but that very heavily insured husband of hers."

They plodded on, contemplating the faithlessness of modern love and marriage. Their client had been a frail and rather elderly bridegroom for three years—a doting husband until, after too many sudden and agonizing gastric attacks, he had slowly begun to suspect the worst. Before their marriage, Mrs. Colfax had been a lively young widow, handsome and sociable and absolutely penniless. Their marriage was just the sort of thing Mary had been taught to eschew at the unconventional Miss Scrimshaw's Academy for Girls. The thing was that with just a little more patience, the fortune would pass legally to Mrs. Colfax. Yet she seemed reluctant to wait for it. Money had a way of spoiling people's judgment.

Had it done the same to her? Mary thought half guiltily of her own fortune, the gift of a grateful and generous Queen Victoria after Mary had averted an attempt on her life. That lump of capital, while a tiny sum to the queen, had changed Mary's life entirely. It had made her a woman of some means, a person with the power to shape her own future. It would also mark her as a potential target for small-time fortune hunters if word of her independence got out. Of course, when she married James, her money would become his property. . . .

"What are you brooding about?" asked James. "You're not planning to poison me with arsenic, are you?"

That raised a smile. "If anyone's buying arsenic, it's your precious housekeeper."

James grinned. "I thought Mrs. V. had thawed toward you a bit."

"A *very little* bit. You know, she might be the main impediment to our marriage."

He shivered dramatically. "Absurd. The real impediment is that I'll be a solid block of ice before you give me a definitive yes."

"So much whining!" Mary laughed. "Are you really about to collapse from the cold? We could take a turn about the museum now that our confidential business is concluded."

"I wish we could," said James, "but I've got to get back to the site. It's payday for the men, and I don't like to be late. Next time, certainly. Or better yet, we'll end in a coffeehouse."

They turned and walked briskly toward Mary's small flat in Burton Crescent, picking their way carefully through the muck churned up by passing horses and carts. As always, James waited for her to extract her door key, then unlocked the front door and returned the key to Mary's upturned palm.

This was the moment. She had to speak now. She tilted her face up to his and said, "I've a proposal to put to you."

James batted his eyelashes and spoke in a quavering falsetto. "Darling, I thought you'd never ask."

"You may regret saying that when you hear just what it is."

"Is it so very dull?"

"Quite the reverse. Not to mention thoroughly unlady-like and far from respectable."

"We've waded through sewers, dangled from a bell tower, and stumbled out of a burning building together. Can you top that?"

"Possibly." Mary fumbled in her reticule and produced a torn half sheet of paper. "I found this yesterday."

"This" was a handbill for "Mr. Ching, a Chinese pugilist of noble extraction, closely related by blood to the Chinese Emperor," who challenged "the sportsmen of England, Britannia's athletes, all of Her Majesty's skilled and subtlest fighters, to best him in an unarmed fight," with the winner to receive a prize purse of one pound. For the semiliterate, there was even an illustration of a determined-looking Chinese man, wearing loose robes and facing the reader in a fighting stance.

Curiosity lit James's eyes. "'Mr. Ching claims the superiority of Chinese hand-and-foot fighting,'" he read, "'and promises ocular proof of such. Not only will Mr. Ching fight: he will take on all who present themselves.' Are you planning to challenge the distinguished Mr. Ching, Mary?"

"No," she admitted. "But I would dearly love to see him fight."

James's brows drew together in a frown. "The address is in Leicester Square. 'Hazardous' doesn't begin to describe the place. . . ."

"Hear me out," she said quickly. "The notice made me think of my father. After I saw it, I suddenly remembered watching him practice these very complicated chains of hand and foot movements when I was a child. He claimed that when used at speed, they were more effective than most weapons. He promised to teach me, when I grew older." She paused. "Then, of course, he disappeared."

"I've heard of such a style of fighting," allowed James. "But setting aside questions of safety and propriety for the time being, how will seeing this Mr. Ching affect you, do you think? Is it wise to revisit this sort of memory?"

"I've never claimed to be wise," said Mary. "And I've no idea what the effect might be. Quite likely, it will be a crashing disappointment. . . ."

"But you want to go. No. You *intend* to go."

"Yes." She drew a breath and looked up at James. "It's tonight."

His expression was scrupulously neutral. "The only women in the vicinity will be prostitutes. You'll be in danger from the moment they see you."

"I'll go as a boy, of course."

"The return of Mark Quinn?" He considered. "Still risky. You make rather a handsome lad."

She hesitated. "Aren't you going to scold me for doing something so inappropriate? We've been so thoroughly dull and forbearing for months now, and I'm jeopardizing all our hard work."

"And what good would scolding you do?" His smile

was crooked. "Besides, is that how you think of me, Mary? A stuffy killjoy, obsessed with what respectable people might think? A fusty old man who can't quite understand how your mind works?" His mouth twisted further. "Perhaps that's why you don't want to marry me."

Mary was genuinely alarmed. "James, that's not it at all. I know you want what's best for me. For us. As for being a fusty old man . . . well. I've never once thought of you as either fusty or old." She smiled up at him. "Believe me, I thoroughly appreciate your manliness."

He permitted himself a small smile at that, then lowered his voice. "Has it occurred to you that if we married now, you would be infinitely freer to do as you please?"

She blinked. "It hadn't." She paused, then spoke more slowly. "But now that I think of it, it's only partially true. You can go to a boxing den at any time, on your own or with male friends. But if it was ever hinted that I'd gone, too, such a rumor could still threaten our social reputation as a married couple, or that of your family firm."

He considered her words. "So it's a larger problem we face. You will always want to exceed the limits of respectable feminine behavior."

She thought about it seriously. "Yes, I think I will. Sometimes, at least." A pause. "And you? Will you always value propriety and a spotless reputation? Are those so dear to you?"

He was already shaking his head. "I respect those things for their utility. They make daily life smoother and

11

easier, and I want your life—our life together—to be as free and pleasant as possible. But they are not paramount to me—" He was interrupted by the chiming of the nearby bells of St. Pancras Church. It was half-past eleven.

"You had better go pay your laborers."

"Yes. But we need to finish this conversation, Mary."

She nodded. "As for tonight, will you come with me?"

"I suppose there's no dissuading you."

"No. I'll go alone, if you prefer not to come."

"Then how can I possibly refuse?"

She looked at him. "You ought to, really. You shouldn't let me coerce you with threats of danger and scandal."

"What if I just want to see you in breeches again?"

She smiled and raised an eyebrow.

"I'll call for you at eight."

"Better if I meet you at the corner of Russell Square, I think."

"Right." Usually, James took his leave by kissing her hand and murmuring some tender endearment. Today, however, he chucked her under the chin. "Cheerio, Mark."

Two

Mary's rooms were on the top floor, up three flights of stairs. The flat was inexpensive because of the inconvenience, but to Mary this was one of its great appeals. It had small, high windows, with views of the rooftops, and seemed almost to press against the low gray sky. It was practical, too: she never had to listen to neighbors' tramping footsteps as they passed her door on the way to their own flats, and this veneer of solitude pleased her immensely.

Unlocking her front door seldom failed to give her a thrill of satisfaction. This was her own home, the one she'd chosen and for which she paid a quarterly rent. It was small: a postage stamp of a hall linked to a cozy sitting room, beyond that a bedroom, and, finally, a tiny bathroom. There was a shared kitchen buried in the depths of the building, to which Mary never ventured. Instead, she dined out once each day. The new class of coffeehouse or restaurant that deigned to serve unaccompanied ladies sequestered them in a separate dining room, to be sure, but they were offered hot, competently cooked meals none-theless. At other times, Mary boiled an egg and toasted bread over the sitting-room fire or nibbled on fruit and tea. This never struck her as subsistence. Rather, it was freedom from the tyranny of three square meals a day, of sticky porridge and spattering chops, and the ordeal of washing up that followed. Mary also had a daily maid, a girl who came in each morning to clean.

In all, Mary was as free and private as a young woman could possibly be. James had seen her flat only once, before she'd moved in. Nobody else visited. When she closed the front door behind her, she was the creator and sole inhabitant of her own small world.

Mary shed her rain-heavy cloak, lit a small lamp, and stoked up the fire in the sitting room. She balanced a kettle on its tripod over the bright fire.

She had just exchanged her walking dress for a dry woolen gown when her doorbell rang. *James.* She skimmed down the steep flights of stairs, unlocked the front door, and threw it open with a broad smile—a grin that slack-ened into astonishment when she beheld the thin, neat, middle-aged lady standing before her.

Several long moments passed. Mary knew she was gaping, yet couldn't quite summon the appropriate greet-ing. Eventually, she settled for a weak "Miss Treleaven?" Her first, panicked thought was that Anne had seen James depart. It was more than likely.

"Hello, Mary." The Agency's past and present manager, Anne Treleaven, smiled sedately. "May I come in?"

It wasn't really a question. Mary nodded, stepped aside to let her in, and assumed something approximating a serene expression. "Of course. How lovely to see you, Miss Treleaven." It wasn't a lie; she was extremely fond of and grateful to Anne, who, with Felicity Frame and the rest of the Agency, had rescued, educated, trained, and supported her for so many years. Mary owed them, quite literally, her life. Yet this unannounced visit was disconcerting, to say the least.

She led Anne up the stairs at a much more conventional pace than her usual two by two. She needed the time to gather her thoughts. Inside, Anne removed not only her cape but also her hat and gloves, confirmation that this was no fleeting social call. As if there had ever been a chance of that.

As Mary showed Anne into her small sitting room, she became intensely aware of its spartan appearance. She'd rented the flat unfurnished, preferring not to live with others' bits of cast-off history. Yet, Mary had discovered, shopping was tedious. Once the initial flush of novelty had worn off, she could think of half a dozen things she'd rather do than browse mediocre furnishings in Tottenham Court Road. As a result, the sitting room was oddly bare—a single sofa, a low table, a rug—calling to mind her simple room at Miss Scrimshaw's Academy for Girls rather than a lady's parlor.

They perched awkwardly on opposite ends of the small sofa and spoke of safe things at first: Mary's new life as mistress of her own flat; the fierce public debates that had raged all through the summer and autumn over Mr. Darwin's incendiary book *On the Origin of Species*; the capture of Beijing yesterday by British and French forces and its repercussions for the opium trade; school life at Miss Scrimshaw's Academy, which covertly housed the Agency in its attics and where Anne was head teacher.

Mary poured boiling water onto fragrant tea leaves and discovered two remaining biscuits in the tin.

Anne made no mention of her former fellow manager, Felicity Frame, and her departure, which had fractured the Agency. Mary understood the divide in terms of ideology. Felicity had wanted to employ male sleuths and expand the Agency with the help of her new, high-ranking contacts in government. Anne thought the Agency should concentrate upon its specialty, placing female detectives in discreet situations. But Mary couldn't imagine what Anne's new reality must be like, having worked for so long and so intimately with Felicity. She was both anxious to ask and reluctant to hear the answer. But before she found the right opening, Anne leaned forward and came to the point.

"I am here to ask if you'd consider one more job for the Agency," she said, taking charge of the teapot. A not-so-subtle power play, wondered Mary, or was Anne showing signs of nervousness?

Mary permitted herself to look surprised, but said nothing.

"You've a comfortable life here, that's clear. I also realize you're disappointed in the way things ended between Felicity and me. . . . You're not the only one," she added.

"Disappointed" failed to come close as a description. Anne Treleaven and Felicity Frame had been much more to Mary than the managers of the Agency; they'd been closer to stepmothers, an unlikely and extraordinarily effective duo whom Mary had tried to emulate in all things. Their falling-out nine months ago had torn apart the Agency and, with it, Mary's life. She had lost both her surrogate family and her home.

Mary silently offered Anne a biscuit, but neither woman took one. The tension was already too high.

"But I've come to you first, because you're the best choice for this task," said Anne at last. "Do you wish to hear more?" This was the same phrase that Anne had always used when offering Mary a chance at an assignment. From this point on, all they discussed would be in strictest confidence. Mary searched her face for a sign, but Anne's spectacles were as good as a mask.

Faced with this familiar challenge, Mary felt a peculiar swirl of emotion: intense curiosity, a surge of suspicion. Why couldn't an Agency member do the job just as well? Above all, though, she had a sudden, powerful desire to be on assignment for the Agency one last time.

It had been nine months since the events at Buckingham Palace that launched her independence. Nine months since the rift in the Agency. Nine months since she and James had founded their own fledgling detective bureau, Quinn and Easton. She didn't actually need the Agency anymore. But just as surely, she missed it, in the way one might long for a childhood home.

Mary leaned forward in her chair and nodded. "Yes, please."

There it was: a gleam of satisfaction in Anne's steel-gray eyes, distinct even behind the spectacles. An instant later, it was gone. "You recall, of course, the Thorold family."

How could Mary ever forget? Her time with the Thorolds had been her first experience of detective work: a routine exercise that had suddenly ballooned into a swift and deadly criminal plot. "Naturally. Mr. Thorold admitted his guilt with regard to insurance fraud and was sentenced to life imprisonment. Mrs. Thorold fled the country."

Anne nodded. "Henry Thorold stoutly denied any involvement in the piracy scheme, and his denials rang true: there was no logical reason for him to be involved in attacks on his own merchant fleet. Scotland Yard views his wife's flight as an admission of guilt, and she remains their prime suspect for the acts of piracy and the deaths of so many Lascars. The sheer scale of Thorold's marine losses over the years—dozens of ships sunk, dozens of

Lascar crews dead, extremely valuable antiquities never recovered—points to somebody with inside knowledge of the vessels' routes and cargoes. The circumstantial evidence is compelling: Mrs. Thorold had both means and opportunity to commit those crimes.

"There is also her attempted murder of James Easton, and the suspected murders of two others. As you know, Mr. Easton's testimony will be conclusive. Yet until Mrs. Thorold returns to England, our police are powerless to arrest her."

Mary nodded. This seemed obvious enough. "So much for the parents. What about Angelica? She announced her intention to study music in Germany. Did she do so in the end?"

Anne nodded. "She studied first in Germany, where her music teacher had connections, and later in Vienna. She has never returned to visit her father in jail, until now. Henry Thorold is dying, Mary. As his next of kin, Angelica was notified of this. She embarked on the journey from Vienna to London last week."

"Was Angelica never regarded as a suspect? Why seek the mother but not the daughter, who also promptly fled for the Continent?"

"Angelica was interviewed by the Yard and judged to be profoundly ignorant of the family business. You must remember that she'd been away at boarding school for several years before coming to live at home again that spring."

Mary frowned. "And Mrs. Thorold?"

Anne's smile held little amusement. "Scotland Yard's best guess as to her location is 'somewhere in Europe.' But you're right. They are very interested in the possibility that she may return in order to see her husband one last time."

"Why on earth? It's not as though they were fond of each other, what with Mrs. Thorold using pirates to raid her husband's merchant ships."

"Yes, but if she could persuade him to make a deathbed confession . . . ?"

Mary sat up, scalp prickling with the possibility. "Thus clearing her name, and freeing her to return to England?"

"Precisely. The police ensured that the news of Thorold's illness — a cancer, it seems — was well known. He has suffered a slow decline, but the prison physician believes he now has only a few days to live. We — the Agency — have been asked to watch for Mrs. Thorold's return."

Mary swallowed hard: a difficult gesture, given the lump in her throat. Her first thought was of James, whom Mrs. Thorold had very nearly murdered. Her second was a fervent prayer for his safety, in this moment and those to come. "She'll be in disguise," she managed to say. "You're watching all the ports?"

Anne paused, clearly surprised to be questioned in this way. "Yes. But she's extremely practiced in changing her appearance, as you know, and very few members of the Agency have actually met her face-to-face."

"What about the banks? She must have left a nest egg somewhere, under a false name."

"The name is Mrs. Fisher, actually, and the bank's been notified." Anne looked amused. "Anything else, my dear?"

Anne was treating this like a game. Didn't she realize how deadly the situation was? "Another house, under a third name?"

"Not that Scotland Yard is aware of."

"What about former associates? She had a junior partner in the piracy scheme." Mary's mind raced ahead. Someone else who could set the stage, even before Mrs. Thorold was on English soil . . .

"Ah, yes. He confessed to everything, but most unhelpfully died before his trial. We're not aware of any other assistants."

Mary nodded as the scene emerged clearly in her mind. "So you're asking me to watch the prison, since Mrs. Thorold will need to make personal contact with her husband."

"Yes. You're the most likely to recognize her, having lived in her household."

"She played the invalid matron to perfection throughout my time there. It was a genuine shock to see how she really spoke and moved when she thought herself unobserved."

Anne nodded. "She is a formidable adversary." The two women fell silent as they remembered Maria Thorold:

accomplished dissembler, unhesitating murderer. Such a vengeful woman was unlikely to have a short memory. After a pause, Anne finally acknowledged what was only too evident. "I realize, of course, that you'll be in an extremely hazardous position if Mrs. Thorold learns you were the cause of her initial downfall. Mr. Easton is also at risk, of course." Anne inclined her head. "I believe you are in frequent contact with him?"

Mary nodded. More silence. Finally, she asked, "Where is Thorold being held?" Her thoughts went to Pentonville or Millbank prisons, so-called model jails, recently built on humanitarian schemes. They were tidy and orderly and clean. Nothing like her own brief experience of incarceration.

Anne's hesitation prepared Mary for the answer. "Newgate," said the older woman at last. "He's in Newgate." She leaned forward and touched Mary's arm with a light, hesitant hand. "I'm sorry, my dear. I am deeply reluctant to ask this of you, but Mrs. Thorold is an exceptionally dangerous criminal who remains at large."

Mary nodded, her blood suddenly roaring, nearly too agitated to be contained by her veins. Of course it was Newgate. Where she had narrowly escaped hanging, after an ill-judged attempt to steal a piece of gold plate from a deceptively well-guarded house. Unbidden, the stench of its corridors suddenly entered her nostrils: dung and filth and fear. She forbade herself thoughts of the jail, blinded herself to memories of its dank cells. She tried, at any rate.

And after several moments, a measure of logic asserted itself against terror. "Surely not Newgate?" she finally managed. Her voice was loud in the quiet room, but she didn't care. "Newgate holds prisoners who haven't yet been tried."

"And those awaiting deportation," said Anne, "neither of which is the case for Mr. Thorold. I, too, thought this highly unusual and looked into the matter. He's being held under a relatively obscure classification, as a person convicted of offenses on the high seas."

Logic had its limits, and Mary found this explanation of little reassurance. Fear still clawed her insides at the very word "Newgate," and her memories of its dark interior remained vivid. She held herself as still as possible so that she didn't curl into a ball. She tried to breathe slowly, focusing on the high, wide window of her parlor, the warmth of her own fireplace. She was her own woman. She was free.

When she recovered herself, Anne was saying, "I should count it as an enormous favor, Mary, if you were to accept this assignment. I know there's nothing now to tie you to the Agency . . ."

Except gratitude, thought Mary. And memories. And very real affection for this woman, who'd rescued her from jail and changed her life beyond recognition. Everything in the world still tied her to the Agency . . . except her loyalty to James Easton, and their hopeful new partnership. She cleared her throat, and Anne instantly became attentive. "Before I can give you an answer, Miss Treleaven, I must discuss the matter with Mr. Easton. He is my business partner now."

Something very like regret compressed Anne's features, but she quickly smoothed her expression. "Naturally."

It was only in that moment that Mary realized what else was wrong about the conversation: Anne's use of "I." When Felicity Frame had been part of the Agency, she and Anne had always spoken as "we." Mary had always thought they meant the Agency as a whole, the collective of clever and unconventional women to which she was privileged to belong. But Anne's use of "I" suggested otherwise.

"I realize this is an urgent matter and shall endeavor to give you an answer as quickly as possible."

"Tonight?"

"Tomorrow," said Mary firmly, and rose. It was impolite of her, of course, all but demanding that Anne depart, especially with a cup of tea unfinished. But what was decorum compared to the problems she and James now faced? Her mind whirled. James was Mrs. Thorold's primary adversary in England, the essential witness in any case against her. Mary's anxiety on his account was reasonable in its foundation but distorted by emotion: it was unlikely that Mrs. Thorold was already on his trail, ready to do him harm. It would be excessive to interrupt his work with a message, and she would see him in a few hours. Logical as her thoughts were, they offered little comfort.

"I shall await your reply," said Anne, recalling her to the present moment. "At any hour of the day or night."

Mary nodded. "Thank you."

She saw Anne down the zigzagging flights of stairs and into a hansom. The rain had stopped; the dank chill subsided. But as Mary closed the front door behind her, she shivered.

Three

The same evening

Near Leicester Square

The venue, if one could grace the place with such an exalted name, was a public house near Leicester Square, and it was called, improbably, the Crown Inn. It stood a few doors down from the notorious Cambrian Stores, arguably the rowdiest and most violent pub in all of London. The Crown Inn was several degrees grottier.

Even from the street, James had the measure of the crowd: poor, male, drunk, aggressive. All about them, people simmered with pent-up frustration, a ferocity both tempered and stoked by their Saturday wage packet and a grim determination to make the most of the weekend. It was an obvious powder keg, an exceptionally foolish place to be on a Saturday evening. They should never have come. James glanced down at Mary, noted the determined line of her jaw, and said nothing.

Her boy's costume was nearly perfect: the jacket and breeches well-worn, the boots just a few miles from falling to pieces. The only flaw was her hair. Instead of cropping it short again, she had covered it with a tattered cap. He hoped it wouldn't get knocked off her head. On any other night, he'd have quietly insisted upon leaving. But something was different about Mary this evening. She was generally intense, focused—qualities they shared. But tonight, she was drawn as taut as a violin string. Tighter, possibly.

For Mary, this was clearly more than an irresponsible escapade. It was a compulsion that seemed to include an element of homage to her father, the paying of a debt. He could understand that. She'd concealed her family history for so long. Would have to continue to do so, at times. But this evening, it was time to explore it. His role tonight was simply to accompany, to acquiesce, to help her however he could.

There was a burly man at the door, taking money. "How much?" asked James, trying to peer inside.

"Tanner." The man glanced at Mary with bored eyes. "And half price for your brother."

James was genuinely surprised. "Steep, that, innit?"

The doorman shrugged and gestured with his chin at the seething mass of bodies packed into a stripped-down room. "House rules. Take it or leave it."

James dug into his trouser pockets—he'd left his billfold at home, along with his bespoke boots—and counted out ninepence. "Better be worth it," he muttered.

Inside, their shoes scuffed against the packed sawdust

that had been thrown down to soak up beer and blood. The Crown Inn wasn't so much a pub as a boxing den that sold indifferent mugs of ale at inflated prices. It had nothing to offer beyond a large sparring ring, a few tiers of benches against each wall, and a ceiling that amplified the spectators' jeers and roars. The spirit within was heady. It reminded him of the festival atmosphere outside Newgate on a hanging day, come to think of it.

Boxing matches, both amateur and professional, were difficult to avoid in London. It was a city of casual brawls, where men—and the occasional woman—seemed to glory in stripping to the waist and locking horns. Boxing was a way to settle disputes, entertain one's mates, earn a little money, and let off steam, all at the same time. At the Cambrian Stores, the retired bare-knuckle boxing champion Nat Langham held prizefights at least once a week. The sight of professional fighters sparring for a cash prize often inspired patrons to fisticuffs of their own.

Thus far, Mr. Ching's idea was far from original. What set him apart, however, was his unapologetic use of Chinese fighting techniques, and—the truly reckless aspect that made James nervous—his deliberate stoking of habitual English racism in the current political climate in order to drum up a crowd. If he fought well, he would soon be the most famous prizefighter in London. Either that or a dead man.

The benches, packed tight with squirming bodies, were already the site of several disputes about space and spillage. Navigating with his elbows, James found a suggestion of standing room behind a cluster of serious-sounding men who looked like experienced boxers themselves. The unheated room stank of sweat, but it was also warm, a rarity during this wintry autumn. James bought two overpriced tankards of ale and handed one to Mary, who smiled briefly up at him. It was much too loud for conversation, so he scanned the crowd as he swigged the beer, plotting a couple of possible swift exits should the crowd turn too bloodthirsty for even Mary's curiosity to endure.

After some time, there came an earsplitting blast from a cracked cornet, and the big doorman announced, "Last call for bets! All bets to be made now!" A final flurry of activity—a handful of boys ran about, ferrying money from bettor to bookie—and then that infernal horn again.

"Gentlemen, workingmen, citizens of London!" announced a new man in a greasy top hat. "Tonight you are privileged to witness a truly unique spectacle: a boxing match unlike any other! Our foreign pugilist, the Chinaman Ching, makes an outrageous claim. He believes that Chinese hands and fists are superior to English ones! He claims that he can best any English challenger in an unarmed fight! Tonight, we shall put that to the test!" The man held out his hands for silence against the cheers and howls. "There will be three matches this evening, all against the same Chinaman. He asks a prize of only one pound for each victory, and promises to pay the same to any who beat him. The fighters will be unarmed, of course; we are Englishmen. But to allow the savage Chinaman a fair chance, to meet him halfway in his foreign ways, and to avoid what would otherwise be an execution—we will allow him to use not just fists, but feet!"

The crowd erupted into roars, half approving, half outraged.

"Men of London, the hour is come. We have our judges! We have our mighty, beef-fed English prize-fighters! Let us now see . . . the Chinaman!"

At this, there began a deep, feral sort of baying that seemed, literally, to shake the room. James felt the noise as much as he heard it, and the beer tankard vibrated in his palm. He noticed Mary craning her neck, her view blocked by a bobbing sea of heads and shoulders. He was just regretting that there was no step on which she could perch when she swiftly tipped out her drink, upended the tankard, and stood on it for a better sight line. He hid a smile. He was a fool to worry about her so incessantly, a greater fool to accompany her here. He seemed doomed to foolishness where she was concerned.

It was difficult to see where Mr. Ching might be coming from, for the room was so tightly packed that it was nearly impossible to budge. Finally, however, James spotted a ripple of movement beginning at the far corner of the room: men turning, their wide-open mouths contorting in a nightmare display of dental neglect. Slowly, unhurriedly even, a black head bobbed through the crowd, picking its way toward the center of the room—with resistance, James noted. Mr. Ching stood a little below average height, and he was being prodded and shoved and goaded by the feverish crowd.

At long last, he arrived in the relative safety of the ring, and James released a breath of relief he'd not known he was holding. Mr. Ching was not thin, precisely, but lacked the squat, heavy musculature one expected of a pugilist. He looked steadily downward, ignoring the hundred or so men screaming filth at him. He was dressed in ordinary worker's fustian. James felt oddly disappointed; he'd expected the loose, silken Chinese costume of the illustration.

"Mr. Ching!" boomed the impresario.

The Chinese man raised his chin. In that moment, James felt Mary tense beside him. He couldn't see her face—she stood slightly farther forward than he—but it was obvious from the curve of her neck, the tension in her shoulders, that she was struggling with strong emotion. He suppressed the impulse to stroke her back, pull her close. Instead, he forced himself to look at Mr. Ching.

The prizefighter's face was a clean-shaven oval, with prominent cheekbones and slightly wide-set eyes. He wore his hair cut severely short, like a sailor. His expression was difficult to read: calm, certainly, and somewhat disdainful as well. Or perhaps it was an excellent mask, and inside he was quaking.

"Lordy, he's a runt," said one of the men in front of

them. "If I'd of known he was only the size of a dog's fart, I'd of fought him myself, for an extra pound."

"You're better saving yourself for tomorrow night's fight," his friend advised him. "I seen some Chinamen fight once. He may be little, but he'll have some sneaky tricks up his sleeve."

James hoped they were right.

The room was a cesspit of aggression—verbal, physical, emotional—all of it directed at Ching. He gave no sign of awareness, merely gazed into the middle distance, acknowledging no one. Only when the announcer bawled did he seem to hear, turning toward the man with mild-mannered politesse.

"Mr. Ching, you claim to have great skill as a fighter! Is that so?"

A small, formal nod.

"And you are here tonight to challenge this great nation of England?"

Another nod.

"You have agreed to fight three matches, one after the other! Is that correct?"

Nod.

"And you swear to fight unarmed?"

Nod.

"Mr. Ching, I must ask you this: ARE YOU MAD?" roared the announcer, throwing his arms open for the audience to reply, too.

The faintest of smiles, followed by a shake of the head.

"Blimey, if he ain't mad, he's a fool," muttered someone behind James.

"Very well, then!" crowed the announcer. "Let us make history!" He gestured toward a corner of the room again. "Mr. Ching, meet your first challenger: the pride of Dagenham, a heavyweight fighter from the age of fifteen, a man who'd sooner knock out his father as shake his hand, Mr. Jem Hoskins!"

The crowd bellowed and hooted its approval, parting to make a path for the tall, fair-haired young man who stalked toward the ring. He had a thick neck, a face that had clearly suffered many beatings in the past, and an ugly scowl. He, too, wore the everyday clothes of a laborer, but on him they seemed part of his skin, his natural covering. He made Ching's very similar shirt and trousers look like a fancy-dress costume.

As he came into the ring, Jem Hoskins stripped off his shirt and raised both fists high, acknowledging the crowd's support. Then, slowly, he turned to take stock of his opponent: once up, once down, and then he spat (a high, arcing globule that landed on a couple of spectators) to show what he thought of the Chinese man. The audience roared its approval of this piece of theater, threatening to surge into the ring to give Hoskins a hand in beating this upstart foreigner to a pulp.

The announcer stepped forward. His voice was

unexpectedly hushed, and the crowd quieted to hear him. "Here are the rules, then: No biting. No stopping. And we'll know when we have a winner."

As the men about him erupted into paroxysms of joyous aggression, James surveyed the room. All these happy, hate-filled men. He'd heard more racial vitriol in the last quarter hour than he had in the rest of his life, and that included his brief sojourn among the Anglo-Indians in Calcutta. Had England changed? Was this heightened racism new, a result of the current bloodshed in China? Or had it always lurked behind otherwise unremarkable facades?

His reflections were interrupted by movement in the ring: an advance from Hoskins to the center, bare fists raised, at the ready. Ching merely stood where he was, hands by his side, seeming to regard Hoskins as an object of only minor interest. This lack of response seemed to enrage the young boxer. He smacked his hands together and swore, foully, colorfully, of course racially, at Ching. After a few more seconds of inaction, he lost his temper and charged at Ching, who reached out a casual arm and neatly flipped Hoskins onto his back.

The room fell silent. James heard Hoskins gasp as he struggled for wind. Ching looked down at him, expressionless and perfectly still, and James realized that Ching had yet to move his feet. As Hoskins clambered shakily to standing, the men in front of him murmured encouragement and curses, and one said, "He must of slipped, that's all," in a tone that sounded utterly unconvinced.

Hoskins's approach was warier this time. He circled Ching tentatively, fists poised, searching for an entry point. When he was firmly to Ching's left, his right arm flashed out in a low jab, and half a moment later Hoskins landed on his back again. The crowd moaned. By the time Hoskins lay sprawled on the sawdust a third time, the audience was restive. There were muttered complaints ("I paid good money to see proper fighting, not some gull falling on his arse!") and the odd cry of "Cheat!," but it was significant that the abuse was evenly directed toward both fighters, not just Ching.

Finally, Hoskins threw his arms out, an open appeal. As though this was the invitation he'd been awaiting, Ching finally consented to move. And when he did, it was a revelation. This slight man didn't care enough for English fighting even to remove his shirt, but he moved like a dancer, or an acrobat, or a snake. Ching circled Hoskins, gliding around him with sinuous steps as though performing an incantation. Finally, with Hoskins—and the audience—reduced to passive confusion, he launched an extraordinary series of blows using both hands and feet, raining down upon the larger man with such speed, it seemed that he had eight limbs instead of four.

A dozen heartbeats later, Hoskins lay sprawled on the sawdust, motionless.

A hoarse cry rang through the pub, echoing James's own alarm. Surely Hoskins was not . . . But even as horror swelled, he saw the boxer twitch, then open puzzled eyes. He had been unconscious for only a moment. It was enough, however. He hauled himself clumsily to sitting, signaled to the announcer, and muttered something.

The man's eyes glittered, and he nodded. "Gentlemen of London, we are making history indeed. In the first match of the evening, Jem Hoskins concedes defeat." Jem Hoskins, the pride of Dagenham, had been in the ring for less than five minutes. He had failed to land a punch.

There followed an interval during which betting resumed, feverish and panicked. What to do? Might Hoskins have thrown the match? Or ought they to trust the evidence of their eyes and bet—heavily—on Ching? The bookies looked tense, recalculating their odds by the moment and swatting away their errand boys' attentions.

Even those who weren't gambling—that trio in front of James and Mary, for example—were perplexed. Those men were now having an animated conversation about what they had just seen, trying to work out what Ching had done and how. For a few minutes, at least, technical admiration outweighed rabid nationalism.

The second contender was Robert "the Master" Bates, a heavyweight with a known history of boxing victories at the Cambrian Stores, and thus a much worthier challenger than Jem Hoskins. Once his name was announced, the atmosphere tipped again toward the buoyantly bloodthirsty. One of the boxers near James nodded comfortably. "Aye, he's a proper fighter, I reckon. Got some speed, long arms, and heavy fists at the end of them. It'll take more than a bit of prancing about to beat him, anyway."

The man was correct. The boxer who entered the ring to resounding cheers of "Bate-sy! Bate-sy!" was very tall and heavily muscular, with knuckles dangling to mid-thigh. The effect was distinctly simian. This resemblance was underscored by his dark hair, cut straight in a fringe across his forehead, and a scowl of concentration. He didn't bother to show off for the crowd; Robert Bates was here to collect his prize money.

Yet once the match began, Bates struggled to land a blow. He swung mightily, of course. But Ching dodged and ducked, slipping around the larger man's fists with a fluid ease that left James mute with admiration. Mr. Ching was more than a fighter; he was an artist. He was also, unexpectedly, a master showman. He'd designed the first match to show off the speed and strength of his blows. This second was intended to reveal his uncanny ability to read an opponent, to anticipate not merely strategy but individual movements.

Minutes elapsed, during which Bates grew visibly tired. It was hard work, swinging to knock a man out yet making only the air whistle. He panted, he spat, he cursed. The dour discipline that had been his initial trademark gave way to eagerness, desperation, and, finally, frustration. Ching, in comparison, seemed to grow lighter and quicker as the match unfolded, and he began to add small acrobatic flourishes to his evasions. As Bates launched a flurry of what should have been short, sharp punches to the head, Ching skipped lightly away and performed a back handspring that landed him at the edge of the boxing ring.

Bates could bear no more. With a roar of fury—the words were unintelligible; the sentiment perfectly clear—he charged, putting his considerable weight and speed into a punch that couldn't fail to knock a man out. If it connected. At the last possible moment, Ching twisted to one side, and Bates's fist drove full-force into the six-inch wooden post behind Ching's head.

The crunch of bone against wood was gruesome to hear, but Bates's scream of agony was much worse. James forced himself to look: Bates's fist was a mangled pulp, resembling nothing so much as a bundle of butcher's scraps awaiting the dogs.

There was perfect silence for ten seconds.

Somebody was noisily sick.

Finally, the announcer reentered the ring, looking rather queasy himself. He bent, had a word with Bates, sent an errand boy shooting off for a surgeon. The outcome of the match hardly needed confirmation, but for the sake of the bookmakers, he said soberly, "Mr. Bates concedes this match to Mr. Ching."

The silence grew monstrous after Bates was led from the ring, with all attention riveted upon Ching. He stood calmly, breathing deeply from his exertions, apparently oblivious to all about him. However, they knew better now. Mary climbed down from her tankard. She glanced up at James, read the question in his eyes, and nodded.

They began to pick their way toward the door, through a crowd that was eerily subdued. The proprietor, who despaired of seeing his bar sales drop off, made an announcement. "As a mark of respect for Mr. Bates, we will have a short interval to drink to his quick recovery." His words struck the wrong note—there would be no such thing as a "quick recovery" for Bates, and every person in the room knew it—but the act of speech itself was a much-needed release valve. Men began to murmur and look around them as though waking from a deep sleep.

James couldn't get outside fast enough. Assuming that Robert Bates didn't die from infection and blood poisoning, he would certainly never fight again. He might never work again, either. Although prizefighters deliberately risked their bodies for money and glory, this seemed too severe a punishment for what amounted to losing one's temper in the ring. As for Ching's extraordinary skill, the way he'd choreographed both fights—for those things, he had James's reluctant admiration. Yet James was, at core, thoroughly English. He'd been taught to value fair play and good sportsmanship. While Ching had technically observed the rules, it still seemed unsporting to toy with hopelessly unequal opponents, to shame them so extravagantly. Perhaps that was the way they did things in China: all glory to the strongest and to hell with the others. But James couldn't help thinking it was an attitude that would land a man in keen difficulty in London.

This evening's escapade had been an error. It would be well if they never heard of Mr. Ching again.

Four

M ary kept close behind James, focusing on his broad shoulders as he carved a path for them through the jammed room. They nearly fell out of the door into the welcome cold, drawing deep breaths of the thick, almost liquid air. By common consent, they did not pause but turned northward and began to walk, side by side. She wished she could take James's arm. That was impossible while in boys' clothing, so she shoved her hands deep into her trouser pockets instead. It wasn't until they were well clear of Leicester Square that she spoke, and then the words tumbled from her mouth. "Do you think Mr. Ching will be blamed for Robert Bates's injury?"

"Legally, it would be impossible to prove. He literally didn't lay a finger upon Bates."

"I didn't mean legally. I was thinking of mob logic. Or the lack thereof."

"Yes. It was foolish of Ching utterly to humiliate both

his opponents. He could have offered them softer, more marginal losses."

"Isn't bloodthirsty spectacle the whole idea? The more savage, the better?"

"You're asking me as a spokesman for all males? I haven't the faintest idea. For some, I suppose." James paused. "I think Ching will find that he's created a large number of enemies. Bates, especially, will have friends who will take his destruction personally. It's one thing to lose a fight, another thing entirely to lose a hand and possibly the ability to support oneself."

"You think they may attempt revenge? Gang up on Ching?"

"It's not unheard of."

She was silent for a moment, her head spinning. "Then we need to warn him."

James spun to look at her. "What did you say?"

She stopped and met his gaze. "Mr. Ching. He's a foreigner. He doesn't know the rules, the history. If you think it's likely that he'll be attacked, then he deserves to know."

He looked baffled. "Mary, he's a prizefighter. Risks like these are inherent in his sort of work."

"You seem to see a difference between the risks run by Ching and the risks run by Bates. They both chose to fight, and they were both in control of their actions in the ring. Do you concede that much?"

He nodded.

"Yet you pity Bates, although he was the person who

smashed his own hand. But you're content to leave Ching to his fate, even if that fate is injury or death at the hands of an avenging mob."

"I suppose I see Ching as the more skilled, experienced fighter. I don't worry about his ability to manage a few men."

"Even an armed gang, with the element of surprise?"

James frowned. "Mary, let me ask you: Why do you feel so protective of Ching? Is it because he's somehow aligned with your father in your mind?"

She fell silent. How could she possibly explain the connection—the positive, subcutaneous recognition—she'd felt, the moment she'd first seen Ching? It was utterly irrational. And yet it persisted. She'd left the pub because she was sickened by the brutality. Yet she was sorry to have turned her back on Ching. Above all, she knew that she needed to see him again. She turned and began to walk. "I suppose I have a great deal of sympathy for outsiders," she said slowly.

"Yes. But this seems to go beyond that."

How could she answer him? She could picture the utter skepticism in his eyes if she told him what she felt.

They walked a hundred yards in silence. Then he asked, "Are you glad you went?"

"I hated the violence." She paused. "But I had to see it. To understand what my father could do, what he wanted to teach me."

"He probably used it for self-defense," said James

rather awkwardly. It felt highly inappropriate, speculating about Mary's dead father's character. "He would have wanted you to know how to protect yourself."

"Are you so certain?"

He was silent.

"I know almost nothing about my father. Your charitable interpretation is possible, but so are myriad others."

They walked some more. As they crossed Oxford Street, the crowds thinned substantially and she kept a little farther from James, as befitted a young man and a boy walking together.

"There's something else worrying you."

He knew her so well. She'd felt his inquiring, assessing gaze upon her at various points through the evening, trying to divine her thoughts. "Yes." She thought about the many ways she'd rehearsed her approach to the subject: delicate, oblique, nonchalant. All seemed either dishonest or cowardly, so in the end, she chose bald fact. "This morning, I had a caller who came, indirectly, from Scotland Yard." It was the best she could do to explain Anne Treleaven and the Agency without lies or betrayal. "I'm told that Henry Thorold is dying in jail, and that Angelica Thorold is traveling from Austria in the hope of seeing him before his death."

James's face was careful, neutral. "Is she likely to make it in time?"

"She's meant to arrive in London quite soon, I believe."

"Why did your caller tell you all this?"

Mary took a deep breath. "It's possible that Mrs. Thorold might also return. If Thorold is dying, she, too, might want to see him again."

"A final good-bye? Why on earth, when she hates him so?"

"It could be an attempt to attach full responsibility for her crimes to a dead man," said Mary, "enabling her free return to England."

Still that bland expression, giving nothing away. "Your caller's intention was to warn you of possible danger?"

"In part. We ought to be wary. You, especially."

"I suppose it's good of them to warn us. You."

Here it was: the point of no return. "I've also been asked to keep watch outside Newgate Prison, to see if I can recognize her if she attempts to visit Thorold there." She hurried on. "It's a rational request: I've lived in her home and seen her on a daily basis, and thus have a better-than-average chance of success." A minute passed, during which a carriage jogged past them; there was a distant burst of laughter, and the wind whistled menacingly. But no response from James, unless she counted the sudden, extreme stillness beside her. "James?"

After a long moment, he looked at her. Even in the semidarkness, she could see the turmoil in his eyes. "What did you say to this person?" His voice was tense. Toneless. Held low and small by the force of his will.

Mary swallowed. "I said I would have to talk to you, as my business partner. I will communicate our decision tomorrow."

He drew a deep breath. "Thank you for waiting."

"How could I not?" Again, silence from James. She stumbled on, hating how defensive she sounded. "We can't allow Mrs. Thorold to reestablish herself in England. I need to do my part." Yet more silence. "James, say something. You may be angry, or have suspicions about the accuracy of this information, but even so: speak to me."

In one swift movement, he turned and pulled her into a bruising hug, the pedestrians of Russell Square be damned. His voice was muffled in her hair as he said in a strangled voice, "I'm not angry."

"No?"

"No. I'm terrified."

Mary almost gasped. James, fearful? She pulled back slightly, fighting against his clasp. "I've been thinking what to do. Your brother is back from holiday soon, isn't he? He could take over some of your site duties until we know more—"

"Good God, Mary, I'm not frightened for myself. But the thought of you out there, alone, being spotted by Mrs. Thorold, or deciding to pursue her: that's what absolutely petrifies me." He shook his head. "I'll be fine. She'll have more important things to do than come and find me."

"I disagree! She tried to kill you. If she's brought to trial, you'll be the most important witness against her.

She has every reason to try again to murder you. And this time, she won't leave the burning building until she knows she's succeeded."

James's jaw shifted subtly into what Mary thought of as his "stubborn angle." "For all she knows, I'm dead. She's too arrogant to think she might have failed the first time."

"And too careless to check? All she'd have to do is consult a builder's directory, or write a letter to your offices, or just stroll through Great George Street and ask any small boy who's idling about!"

"So what are you proposing? That I go into hiding and leave you to track her down on your own?"

"Of course not. But you must acknowledge the danger you're in. And we need to create a plan to protect you."

"Don't you mean 'protect us'? Mary, there are two things keeping you safe. The first is that she doesn't seem to realize you were involved in the original case; for all she knows, you were simply Angelica's paid companion."

"Which is precisely why I'm a good choice to watch for her."

James shook his head. "No: the second reason is that she has no idea of our connection. As soon as she realizes that we are close, you're in as much danger as I am."

Mary opened her lips to refute this, then froze. He was right. Damn it all, he was right. She released her tight clutch on his shoulders. James, too, straightened and let

47

her go. They both breathed as though they'd been running.

"What do you propose?" she said eventually.

"The only thing possible: we must sever all contact until Mrs. Thorold is arrested."

"She might never be. We might never even confirm that she's in the country."

"For a period of time, then."

Mary shook her head. "I don't like it, James. If our courtship escapes her notice — which is unlikely, given how formal and public we've been — there's the small matter of Quinn and Easton."

"That's why we must begin immediately. She's not yet in England, I assume; your contact at the Met won't have been slow to alert you. As detectives, we've never advertised in the papers, thank God. I'll take down the nameplate in Great George Street. Apart from that, it's all word of mouth and rumor, which will blow away in the breeze."

"What if she has an associate who's already been observing you? Your daily routines lead directly to me."

"If she had an associate who knew where to find me, I'd already be dead." His voice was even, unemphatic, but the words made Mary shiver.

"Unless she wanted to confront you herself —"

"Revenge being a dish best served cold, et cetera? Is she theatrically inclined?"

Mary made an impatient gesture. "Well, she did try to incinerate you in a decrepit charity home, rather than simply shoot you or slit your throat." As James opened his mouth to reply, she cut him off. "But this sort of speculation isn't useful. Neither is parting ways. We're much better off working together against Mrs. Thorold."

James frowned. "Why are you so intent on throwing yourself into danger's way?"

She sighed. "Why are you so certain you can bear all the risk for both of us?"

They glared at each other for another long moment, tension rising. Then, finally, James seemed to deflate. "There's no clear path, is there?"

"There seldom is."

But he was scarcely listening. "This is precisely what I feared when we began working together: that you would become enmeshed in something truly life-threatening and I would be powerless to help." He shook his head. "No. It's worse than my nightmare, because I'm actually the cause of your peril. My God, can you imagine if we'd already published banns, or were married?"

Mary's stomach turned over. James was going in a direction she'd failed to envision. "I'm in danger anyway," she said rapidly. "And we accept a certain level of risk in our daily work as detectives."

"That's far removed from the vendetta of a ruthless murderess. Look at me, Mary." She did so, and the agony in his eyes made her tremble. "Do you really think you'd bear the same level of risk whether we're together or apart?"

"No. I was resisting your point of view, mainly because I was afraid you'd already made your decision."

He smiled. "Inherently, reflexively rebellious. It's a miracle you lived to adulthood."

"It's the reason I survived." She arched an eyebrow at him. "So, what's your excuse for being inherently, reflexively authoritative?"

"I'm always right?" He laughed as she swatted at him. "Go on; do you have a better plan?"

"In fact, I have. We suspend any work for Quinn and Easton. I continue with my assignment; you with your usual responsibilities. We take no foolish risks, but neither do we anticipate disaster. And we wait."

"It's still too dangerous to see each other."

"I think you are right about that, in the short term. But the next fortnight will reveal to us a great deal."

He frowned for a moment. "You're correct, of course," he said. It was one of the things she loved most about him: a true humility that undercut his arrogance. It was what enabled two such strong-willed people to find agreement.

"Perhaps in a week's time we could communicate. What do you think of a 'chance' meeting in a public place—Mudie's, perhaps?" she said. "It's bedlam on a Saturday afternoon."

"Four o'clock at the lending library? Sounds very cloak-and-dagger."

"I could do without the dagger."

"Indeed." They began to walk again, across the diagonal of the garden square. As they reached its edge, James spoke again. "Mary, we're going to be all right, aren't we?"

"Of course we are," she said quickly. Too quickly. She drew a steadying breath and tried again. "We're merely being cautious and planning for the worst possible case." She hoped she sounded more certain than she felt.

"The day this is over—the very instant we're safe—I'm going to marry you."

A rush of heat surged through Mary, made her tremble. She couldn't find words, clever or otherwise, to reply.

"What? Speechless? I should like this moment to be officially documented, please. On the thirteenth of October, A.D. 1860, Miss Quinn had no ready retort to a speech made by Mr. Easton."

She half laughed. "James, do shut up."

"Perhaps if offered sufficient inducement."

She glanced around swiftly and discovered a minor miracle: they were, just for a minute, utterly alone in the foggy dark. She clasped his head and pulled him down for a long, luxurious kiss. It was their first proper kiss in many months, and—fear intruded—possibly their last. She pushed that thought from her mind and focused only on the warmth of his lips, his subtle scent, his hand stroking the length of her spine. When they eventually broke apart, she whispered, "How was that?"

His breathing was ragged. "An excellent beginning."

"The breeches aren't a distraction?"

His small puff of laughter tickled her neck, her ear. "I doubt an earthquake could distract me at this point."

"Really? Mmm. Let's try it again."

Five

Sunday, 14 October, morning

Gordon Square, Bloomsbury

Mary was wearing a white muslin frock and carrying a frilly silk parasol: absurd choices, considering they were standing on a stony beach in northern Scotland under a flaying winter rain. She seemed impervious to the weather, however, and was using her parasol to strike the pebbles, one at a time. "One of these is hollow," she cried to him, scarcely audible over the shrieking wind. "When we find it, we'll have it." "Have what?" he roared back. She looked incredulous. "The answer, of course." Her tapping became louder and louder, eventually resolving itself into a series of impatient double raps on a wooden door. James struggled awake into a foggy gray morning not much warmer than the Scottish beach, and realized he was in bed and very much alone.

"Enter," he said, around a yawn.

The door opened silently, but it wasn't Mrs. Vine with his morning coffee. It was George, struggling to balance a tray with a coffeepot, a pair of cups and saucers, and a plate of sugared biscuits. He was wrapped haphazardly in a heavily embroidered velvet dressing gown, and most of his hair was plastered to one side of his head. Still, he looked fully awake, and that was sufficiently unusual to make James sit upright.

"Whatever's happened, George?" The elder Easton was normally a slugabed who languished in his house slippers long after James had breakfasted and left for the office.

"Can't a man deliver his brother's coffee tray now and again?" asked George. "Strikes me as a thoughtful and affectionate thing to do."

"In this house, it only serves to make the brother extremely suspicious." James rescued the tilting tray from George's hands and placed it on his bedside table, then shrugged on his own dressing gown. It was of sober navy-blue wool, in stark contrast to George's dandyish taste. "Here, I'll pour. Did you lose the teaspoons en route?"

George looked annoyed. "I wondered what that noise was."

"Pull up a chair." James poured two cups of steaming coffee, adding large amounts of cream and sugar to the first and passing it to George. "Here you go." He sat on the edge of his bed, took two sips of scalding coffee, and replaced the cup gently in its saucer. He was as ready as he would ever be. "Now, what's this all about? It certainly doesn't feel like good news."

George took a tentative sip and screwed up his face. "I can't taste the sugar at all. Good Lord, I can't believe you drink this stuff black, Jamie."

James tried not to flinch at the use of his childhood nickname. "Stir it with your finger."

"It's bitter! Are you sure you put enough in?"

James half laughed, half groaned. "George, if you don't shut up about the substandard coffee, I'll use my chamber pot to give it a good swirl around. You might like it better, then."

"There's no need to be disgusting. Are you feeling unwell?"

James considered. "Banging headache. I don't think I'll go to church today." He felt perfectly healthy in body. But he wasn't going to risk St. Pancras today, in case Mary was there. Even sharing a parish church was too great a link between them now.

George looked at him carefully. "I thought you seemed off. Grim and terse."

"Well, it's nice you could distinguish between that and my usual behavior."

George failed to smile. "What's wrong, Jamie? Is the headache anything to do with, er, your . . . female friend?"

James became genuinely irritable. "She has a name, George. I'd appreciate your learning to use it."

"Miss Quinn, then." Despite his best efforts, George looked as though the name left a nasty taste in his mouth. "It's something to do with her, and that infernal detective agency she made you set up, isn't it? I knew that was a disastrous idea, but would you listen to me? Oh, no—"

"George!" James leaned forward and pounded the side table, making the biscuits leap and skitter across the tray. "Just because you've a poor opinion of her doesn't mean she's the source of all trouble. And don't give me that look. I know what you're thinking."

"Do you? I'd be surprised. . . ."

James was sick of acrimony. Besides, George was dangerously close to the mark. It *was* to do with Mary, but not in the way that George suspected. "My ill temper has nothing to do with Miss Quinn," he repeated, with a truth that was more emotional than factual. "Now, will you please tell me your news?" He raised his coffee cup to his lips, then set it down again. The early argument had curdled his stomach.

For answer, George pulled a letter from his dressing-gown pocket and placed it triumphantly before James. It was addressed to the Messieurs Easton and had a City postmark. "Came yesterday evening," said George, in tones of great satisfaction. "But you'd gone out. . . ."

James refrained from rolling his eyes, and unfolded the letter. As he read, his eyes widened and he glanced up at his brother's smirking face.

"Keep reading," said George. "It gets better."

James forced himself to read each word slowly—the letter writer prided himself on a dashing and near-illegible penmanship—but there was no controlling it:

56

that instant, prickling excitement of a new and ambitious project. The sort of request to which he couldn't possibly say no. Even if he were so inclined. When he'd finished the letter, he sat staring at it for several moments, his mind already racing ahead to design, materials, time to completion, possible difficulties.

It was George who brought him back to the present with a smug, "Awake now?"

"Fully conscious, yes." This would be one of the largest and most important jobs Easton Engineering had ever been offered: the reconstruction of a series of underground vaults at the Bank of England. Utterly confidential. Highest security. And, naturally, deeply urgent. And yet . . . deep within him, there was an alarm bell ringing.

"Come on, you donkey! This is just the sort of thing you need. That bridge project is boring you silly, I can tell, and that's why you're still lolling in bed this morning." George squinted at James, leaning in close to inspect the patient. "Tell me you're not instantly bucked up by this job: logistical nightmare of new excavation, two stories underground. Vaults full of French gold to be juggled about London in the middle of the night. It sounds damn near impossible, and must be done in as little time as possible. That sounds exactly like you, Jamie." He paused, then added, "Not to mention that there's no competition. You're the man they want."

James nodded, chewing his lip. That sentence, stipulating his specific involvement, made him nervous. "I wonder what they mean by that? I mean, why not you? If it comes to that, why not one of the larger engineering firms? Brunel has far more experience than we do."

"Perfectly obvious," scoffed George. "There was that business at St. Stephen's Tower, which brought you into contact with that chappy, the first commissioner of works. He liked you enough to give you the palace job, and he's probably married to the sister of a director of the Bank of England. Then you did a bang-up job at Buckingham Palace. The bigwigs have been gossiping, and young James Easton is the man." He drained his cup and poured himself another, sugaring it even more lavishly than usual. "I ought to be miffed, really. Nose out of joint, and all that. After all, how could they pass over the elder brother in favor of the younger? Positively unchristian, that."

James's mouth twitched. "If we lived in the Old Testament, I suppose. But take heart, esteemed elder brother. Perhaps it's only that your dashing sartorial style would be wasted two stories below ground level."

George smiled. "Say what you will, but do say that you're chuffed about this job, Jamie. I couldn't devise a better one, given all the money and power of the queen."

James felt a rush of warmth for his brother. George was frequently all bluster and blunder, and he was preparing to marry a young lady who thought him wiser than Solomon, a state of affairs that could only be disastrous for his ego. But he had a disconcerting ability to sift through confusion for the core of the question, and a genuinely kind heart. James had always loved and admired those things in him.

"It's a hell of a prospect," added George. "And then to have it handed to you on the proverbial silver platter!"

James nodded and sipped his rapidly cooling coffee. What to do? How could he possibly explain to George that the proposition simply felt . . . off? Wrong? Too convenient and tailor-made?

"Well?" demanded George. "Don't just sit there drinking coffee and looking grim! Say something!" James silently passed George the plate of biscuits. George adored sugared biscuits, and nearly always became distracted by their presence. This time, however, he waved away the plate. "You're stalling," he barked. "What the devil is wrong with you, man?"

James felt his cheeks grow warm. Usually, he found it easy—perhaps too easy—to produce clever, biting, yet safely evasive replies to inelegant questions. This time, however, he merely shrugged and mumbled, "I wondered if we were already fully committed. We've several projects under way—"

"Don't be ridiculous!" roared George, his face turning the color of beetroot. "Are you doing this simply to torment me?" He rose to his full height, slopping coffee down the front of his dressing gown as he ticked off items on his fingers. "You're on-site for only one building project, a perfectly straightforward repair-and-rebuild that anyone could handle. You've a few bids in the works, but I daresay half of them will come to naught and the others can be reshuffled. And then there's this *golden* opportunity, with invitation, acceptance, a handsome fee, and astonishing future prospects all in one! What is wrong with you, James Easton?"

James shrugged weakly. "Nothing."

"Then?" thundered George. He made as though to tear his thinning hair, but then thought better of it. "Oh, good Lord, you'll be the death of me," he muttered, sinking back into the bedroom chair. "What's the matter, Jamie? What are you hiding that makes it impossible for you to leap at the best opportunity our business and our family will ever receive?" He passed a weary hand over his eyes. A second later, he parted his fingers to fix James with a single beady eye. "Still nothing to do with your blessed Miss Quinn?"

James closed his eyes. He didn't think he could bear it, this invisible contest of loyalties between the woman he loved and the brother who'd raised him. He could protect neither, defend neither, do justice to neither. He sighed and uttered the words he knew he'd come to regret. "I was merely surprised, George. Of course I'll accept the job."

Monday, 15 October, early morning

Newgate Prison, London

She'd not planned to come on a hanging day. It was the crowds that tipped her off, well before she was in view of the prison. The crowds, and the festival atmosphere. Men and women thronged the streets, shrieked and bayed, trod upon children and animals. Others hawked pickled whelks and fried potatoes, boiled puddings and spiced wine, for nothing whetted the appetite like a public execution. There was a sprinkling of gentlemen in the crowd; there always was. But most of this raucous sea of humanity was cheaply dressed, and Mary was glad she'd done the same. If anything, her coarse cotton dress and simple bonnet were slightly too plain. Evidently, many Londoners looked upon a hanging as akin to a play: one dressed up to be so divertingly entertained.

For one long, cowardly moment, Mary considered turning tail. She could start again tomorrow. Tuesday morning would be relatively quiet and offer a clearer view of the grim stone walls that haunted her dreams. Yet wouldn't that be an admission of defeat, fleeing the sight she'd come to see? Undoubtedly. Mary set her jaw. What surer way to rout a nightmare than to confront it at its hellish worst? Besides, she was so tightly wedged in the crowd that retreat would be difficult. Bodies pressed ever closer. They were slowly losing their individuality, becoming part of a river of flesh that flowed toward the gallows on Newgate Street.

Mary edged closer to the jail, guarding her ribs with her elbows and her purse with her fist. The roaring crowd flowed fast, and she was around the corner before she had quite realized it. The grimy stone walls loomed high, but not as high as in her nightmares. The windows were grim, but mere windows, not the malevolent eyes she remembered. Perhaps the prison itself lost some of its fearful power when the real nightmare was to be played out before her: the public execution of a human being.

She knew, of course, that many of the people hanged were violent murderers like Maria Thorold. Yet Mary couldn't think of the loop of thick rope without feeling it about her own neck; couldn't imagine the trapdoor without feeling it swing open beneath her feet. She rubbed her throat to banish the sensation of coarse hemp against her skin, and the tattooed sailor breathing down her collar grinned at her familiarly. "What's a pretty girl like you got to worry about, hey? Got something to confess?"

She shook her head. It was beyond her powers to banter about this subject.

The wooden platform was directly before her now, with its sturdy gibbet. The hangman, a macabre figure all in black, was testing the mechanism, fitting a weighted dummy into the noose. A moment's fiddling, and then he pulled a lever. The dummy dropped; a sarcastic cheer rose from the crowd.

She was going to be sick. This was a ghastly error. She turned around and began to push fiercely through the crowd, heedless of the indignant cries of the people in her wake. There was no escape from the wall of bodies pressing ever closer, always toward the gallows. With desperate strength, Mary shoved her way through, swallowing the burning bile at the back of her throat, sorting people to her left and right as she sought a way out.

There, she saw her salvation: the open door of a pub. She stumbled through it into a cool, cavernous room. It was startlingly quiet—not silent, in truth, but seemingly so after the hubbub in the street just outside. She drew a long, unsteady breath, and then another. Took a few shaky steps toward the bar before her trembling knees forced her to drop onto a bench at the first unoccupied table.

"Miss? You all right?" The voice was gentle but persistent. It might have been speaking for some time, but Mary only became aware of it when a large, plump hand rested firmly on her arm.

"Yes." Mary lifted her head swiftly and flinched with regret as the room tilted and spun around her. She swallowed hard. "I'm fine, thank you."

"This y'first? The first time is always the hardest," the voice confided. "When we took on this place, I was near to fainting at the very idea, but now, why, I hardly notice when they build up the gallows." Mary forced herself to focus on the speaker, a broad, rosy-cheeked woman wearing a frilled cap. The landlady, of course. "And Mr. Calcraft, why, he's a regular in here. Likes a stiff whiskey after the fact, and I can't blame him."

Calcraft was the executioner. A notorious figure, he was both feared and cheered as a celebrity. Even children knew of his penchant for the "short drop," which often failed to break a prisoner's neck. Indeed, "playing Calcraft" was many a street urchin's idea of amusement: lads would simulate an execution, and while one playing the dead man pretended to choke and strangle, another would swing from his legs to amuse his mates, just as Calcraft often did with his real victims. Mary's own near execution should have inured her to gallows humor, but she always looked away when she spotted a game of Calcraft in an alley.

"Sure you're all right? You don't look half pale."

Mary nodded firmly. "Fine, thank you." Then she remembered where she was. "I'd thank you for a brandy, though."

The woman nodded and returned presently with a small glass of amber liquid. "Drink first and pay me later, my dear. Lord knows you need it."

Mary sipped gratefully, the sweet fire burning away the taste of fear and filling her with warmth. "It's a good brandy, Mrs. . . . ?"

"Bridges. That's the finest French brandy, that, and a bargain at tuppence a glass."

Now that she was returning to herself, Mary glanced around the pub. It was smaller than she'd first thought: not a major tavern at all, but an old-fashioned drinking den. While far from full—all the action was in the streets at the moment, awaiting Calcraft's entertainment—there were a few obvious regulars who continued to sip their drinks, oblivious to the excitement of a public hanging.

"How long have you managed this pub, Mrs. Bridges?"

"Oh, Bridges and I took over the Hangman only a year ago. We had a little pub in Essex before then, but our daughter's living nearby, so we thought to move nearer to her."

"And business is good?" Mary noted the gleaming glass and polished brasses, the gaslights that hissed bravely against the dark-paneled walls. How odd to find such a homey, comforting landlady so near to the place of death.

"Too busy," said Mrs. Bridges with pride. "Why, I'm rushed off my feet, most of the time. It's quiet now, of course, but just you wait: an hour after that trapdoor drops, it'll be merry mayhem in here. I swear, nothing gives a Londoner a thirst like a good hanging."

Mary repressed a shudder. Why was she here, making polite conversation with this woman? Then again, where else ought she to be? The realization shriveled her sense of righteous horror. She was here for one reason only: to see if she could, indeed, help bring Mrs. Thorold to justice.

She, Mary Quinn, had survived the death of her parents, a childhood on the streets, a career as pickpocket and housebreaker. She had escaped the very gallows she now quailed before, with the help of the Agency. She had benefited from an education at Miss Scrimshaw's Academy for Girls, and been trained as a secret agent by the Agency. She had chosen a life of action, utility, and independence. Why was she now so scandalized and easily bruised by experience? If this was how life as a lady had transformed her, she needed to change back. And quickly. She drained her brandy and fished out her purse. "Thank you," she said, paying Mrs. Bridges. "That's just what I needed."

But the landlady was looking at the coin, then at Mary. "Tell you what," she said, after a moment's pause. "Keep your money and give us a hand with the washing up, instead."

Mary nearly laughed until she realized the woman was in earnest. "Do you always find your barmaids off the street?" she asked.

"You're a decent sort, I can tell. And we could do with a girl to help us out," said Mrs. Bridges. "Someone neat, what minds her p's and q's, and you're not hard on the eyes, which always helps." She gave Mary a swift once-over. "Eight shillings a week, with your room and board. Start tomorrow."

Mary half smiled. "You're kind, Mrs. Bridges, but I've my own work to get on with."

"What d'you do, then?"

"I sell gingerbread," said Mary, surprising herself. Even as she uttered the words, however, she realized how ideal such a cover would be. She could wander the length and breadth of Newgate, mingling freely with the crowds. She could come and go as she pleased. Gingerbread was lightweight, too: she needed nothing more than a covered basket and a few pennyworth of spiced dough from a bakeshop.

The landlady sighed with regret. "That's cold, hard work, in the streets. You'd be better off here, in the pub."

Mary begged to differ. Pub work would keep her tethered to one spot. And with the offer of room and board, she'd find herself working eighteen-hour days. Nevertheless, she said politely, "If I change my mind, I'll come and find you."

"Come and find me anyway, dearie," said Mrs. Bridges, getting up and starting to polish the pumps again. "We all need a sit-down and a gossip now and again."

Mary smiled and made her way back into Newgate, fortified both by brandy and a sense of purpose. The street scene was as squalid and raucous as ever, the high wooden gibbet still a scar against the low gray sky. This was her London: brutal, coarse, dangerous. It was a part of her history. It had molded her character. But she would not allow it to shape her destiny.

Six

Late morning, the same day

Threadneedle Street, the City of London

J ames Easton had a fairly good imagination. Even so, the best description he could find for the underground vaults of the Bank of England was "unimaginable." The rows upon rows of gold bars stored within, stacked like so many cakes of soap on simple metal shelves, gave the place a surreal, childish quality. One wanted to laugh and scratch off the gold paint to show that they were, in fact, ordinary and unprecious lead. Even so, how much would such a vast quantity of lead be worth? Transfixed by the sheer scale of things, James automatically began a calculation, but abandoned it a moment later.

"How do you intend to manage your assets during the period of construction?" he asked the party of five men, members of the court of directors of the Bank of England, who were showing him around.

"Eh?" said an older man named Bentley who seemed, unofficially, in charge of the committee. "How d'you mean?"

"Will you move the gold to a separate storage facility while the work is under way?"

"Yes," said Mr. Bentley with a fussy nod. He spoke with his upper lip perpetually curled, so that his "yes" sounded like "yis." "Yes, unfortunate and risky as the task will indubitably be, that is essential. We simply haven't enough extra space to redistribute the gold." He coughed and glanced doubtfully at James over his pince-nez. "Not to mention the security risk of having workmen down here on a daily basis, with the gold close by."

James wasn't offended. His laborers were all carefully vetted, but there was no need to expose them to temptation. Different men had different breaking points. "I must advise you that the removal and storage of such precious cargo is new to me. While I am willing to undertake the work, you may wish to organize that yourselves."

Mr. Bentley looked vaguely surprised. "Your point is noted. We shall, er . . . hem. We shall have to discuss that among ourselves."

"Very well. Let us treat the two matters—the clearing of the vaults and the repair work—as entirely separate tasks for now. It will be difficult to know just how much time we'll need to complete the work until the vaults are completely emptied. We may discover further rot or areas of structural instability that are presently concealed."

The directors frowned as one. "Oh."

"I shall need a copy of the original plans for the storage

vaults, as well as details of any alterations that have been carried out."

The youngest of the gentlemen, who was still James's senior by two decades or so, presented him with a card. "I shall have those delivered, by secure guard, to your office this afternoon. Please communicate directly with me should you require anything further along those lines."

James thanked him. "As we're contemplating such a significant expansion, you will perhaps also consider if you'd like to include gas lighting in the new and rebuilt vaults. We shall have to address the question of air exchange, which means it's quite straightforward to lay a gas line at the same time." There was a brief pause in the group's mutterings and throat clearings, during which James's keen ears picked up a faint but distinct rustling noise. Naturally. "It sounds as though I must also mention the rather impolite matter of vermin. Is there currently an infestation of any sort at the Bank?"

Blank expressions. Confusion. Then, gradually, the dawn of understanding. Affront. Horror. Denial. Here? At such an august institution?

James smiled and held up his hands to quell their sputtering. "Forgive me, gentlemen. I shall investigate the matter if and when we find it necessary." He made a mental note to engage a rat catcher.

Mr. Bentley stepped forward from the group, eyeing him warily. "Quite. Er. Hem. Is there anything else you wish to see in the vaults, Mr. Easton?" The man's long nose twitched, and James found it difficult not to stare at the mole that decorated its tip.

James knew a dismissal when he heard one. He was roughly one-third this man's age, an upstart child in the eyes of the court of directors. He wondered again who'd chosen him for this task. Certainly not one of these fellows. He permitted himself to be escorted from the building, confirmed that the necessary plans and renderings would be delivered to his offices as promised, and stood for a while in the late-afternoon drizzle of Threadneedle Street, contemplating the Bank's unwelcoming facade.

As George had gloated, it was a perfect job: logistically complex, technically demanding, and handsomely paid. Already, James was itching to begin. It was the sort of project that could become entirely absorbing, that would force him to stretch and learn daily. In fact, it was too perfect. Beneath his thrumming anticipation, James remained conscious of a steady, cold trickle of suspicion: Was he being set up?

He shivered, and the hairs rose on the back of his neck. This Bank job had been too straightforwardly laid at his feet. To begin with, what sort of financial institution failed to force its suppliers to compete for business? He knew that the first commissioner of works, whom he'd favorably impressed during that business at St. Stephen's Tower, had a great deal of influence within government. However, the Bank of England was probably outside his jurisdiction. George had suggested that the first commissioner might be the brother-in-law of the Bank's governor or some such, but was it sufficient to believe in such a high degree of coincidence?

Then again, coincidence seemed as likely in life as it did onstage. It had ensured that on three previous occasions, against all probability and logic, he'd met up with Mary Quinn and worked with her on jobs that redefined the irregular. He saw, each day, how small coincidences had immense consequences. It was well within the realm of the possible.

He simply had to persuade himself that such was the case this time.

Tuesday, 16 October, 7 p.m.

Along the border of Soho and Bloomsbury

He didn't hear it coming.

One moment, James was walking home from his offices in Great George Street, enjoying the brief respite from rain and thinking about what Mary might be doing. The next moment, the ground rose up to meet him. His hands failed to break his fall, and he slammed, with crushing force, into the foul, pebbly soil of a narrow alleyway. He kept his head up and thus managed to avoid smashing his face, but the impact was such that all he could do for several long seconds was try to breathe. What had happened? What was wrong with his arms? Why could he not move?

"Where's your wallet?" snarled a voice in his ear.

Light dawned. "Breast pocket," he said, and was relieved to find his tongue and teeth still intact.

His right shoulder was pinned to the ground—he guessed it was the thief's knee—and an unknown hand fumbled to extract the billfold from his suit. James moved his legs experimentally, and the voice hissed, "Keep still, or I'll slit your throat." The threat was accompanied by the flash of a long metal blade.

The same clumsy hand began to pat down his coat pockets. James's arms were still pinioned behind him, and he wondered what the thief would do next. Few thieves killed their marks; it only slowed their escape. And this one had the advantage of coming from behind so that James couldn't identify him. However, logic might not be a street thief's forte. How could James possibly presume that his life was worth anything at all to the man kneeling on his back? He could only wait. This ordeal would end, one way or another, in a minute or two.

In fact, it was quicker than that. An instant later, he heard the clatter of a wooden rattle. The thief stiffened, cursed, and the weight on James's back suddenly lifted. There was a scrabbling sound, and footsteps skittered away down the alley. A moment later, heavier, slightly slower footsteps approached, slipping and crunching their way toward him. "Sir! Can you speak, sir?"

He groaned and tried to roll over.

"Don't move, sir! Keep still until I can see what damage that dastard has done."

James ignored this advice and rolled onto his side, then heaved himself to a seated position. "It's all right, Constable. Mainly scrapes and bruises, I suspect."

The police constable frowned anxiously. "Well, I'm glad to hear it, sir. That was a nasty great knife he was carrying."

"All's well that ends well; isn't that so?" James tried to stand and groaned. "I think this overcoat, however, is done for."

The constable offered him a hand up. As James stood, the faint jingling of his pockets made them both pause. "You were quick, Constable. I still have my keys and coins and pocket watch." This last would be cracked or broken from the impact, but James was glad to have it, nevertheless. It had been his father's. He glanced around the alleyway. "But I don't see my drawings."

"Drawings, sir?"

"A roll of architectural plans. In a cardboard tube."

The constable searched the alley, quickly and carefully. "Not here, sir. You certain you had them, until that cove tackled you?"

"Under my arm."

The constable pursed his lips. "It's a funny thing to take, that. I've never known a thief to take papers and leave a watch."

"He may have lost his wits when he heard your rattle." Or perhaps he'd wanted the drawings all along.

"I don't suppose you saw his face at all, sir?"

"Afraid not. I shouldn't think there's much use in filing a report, Constable. All I know is that it was a man with a knife."

The constable was reluctant to let him go, but short of arresting the victim, there was nothing he could do. "Shall I find you a cab, sir?"

James looked down ruefully. "I doubt a hansom would have me in this condition. I'll be all right walking."

He was only ten minutes from home, but it took him longer than usual to get there. His ribs ached, he limped slightly, and he was unable to shake the ghostly pressure of the thief's knee in his back. More than all that, however, he was distracted. Actually, he wasn't: he was furious. It wasn't the loss of the actual drawings that troubled him most. They were of an older project, already completed, copies of which he'd wanted for his home office. The originals were safe in Great George Street, and one of his draftsmen could make a new set. It was a matter of what else the incident suggested.

Between the return of Maria Thorold and his new commission at the Bank of England, it would be hopelessly optimistic to think the robbery random or coincidental. No, it was connected. The difficulty was that he couldn't know how. Had the thief aimed to snatch highly confidential plans of the most secure building in London? Or was the theft of the drawings merely a blind? Perhaps the assault was intended as a warning to James, to frighten him away from the Bank's offer. Or, just possibly, the thief

75

had been interrupted before he used his knife to send Mary a message written in blood.

James shook himself, mentally and physically. He was running away with himself here. There was still no clear public evidence of any connection between him and Mary. He had to believe that, if he wasn't to shake with fear every moment of every day. It was easier said than done, though, and he was still brooding when he stepped into the warm, bright hall of his home in Gordon Square.

"There you are, Jamie!" called a beloved but presently most unwelcome voice. George strode through the hall to greet him. As he approached, however, his expression changed from impatient welcome to indignant perplexity. "What on earth happened to you? You're not injured, are you? Oh, heavens, you need a doctor! Mrs. Vine!" He bellowed these last words, and their housekeeper popped into view half a moment later.

Normal speech was trampled in their joint uproar. "Please!" James shouted after a minute's doomed effort. "I'm fine. I should like a wash, and then a peaceful dinner, if you please. I'll tell you what happened afterward," he added.

"I say," said a new voice from the first floor. "I do hope I'm not intruding. Ought I to come back another time?"

James stared up the flight of stairs. "Oh, it's you, Alleyn," he said after a moment. "Pay no attention to us. George likes a good bellow when I get home from the office."

"Well, I couldn't help but overhear his call for a physician. I'm at your service, as ever," said Rufus Alleyn in his unruffled way.

"You forgot, didn't you?" muttered George. "Alleyn's invited to dinner, and so are the Ringleys."

James suppressed a sigh. The Ringleys — George's fiancée, her parents, and her two younger sisters — were far from his favorite people. They were pleasant, well-meaning, and deadly dull. After ten minutes in their company, James was always tempted to climb out the drawing-room window. "Sorry, George, I did forget. Give me a minute to tidy up, and I'll join you in the drawing room."

"He's your friend," persisted George under his breath. "I can see your forgetting about the Ringleys, but I thought you liked Rufus Alleyn."

James flushed. Was he so very transparent in his preferences? "The Ringleys are excellent people," he said. "I like them for your sake, George."

Some of George's obvious hurt faded, and he patted James's shoulder gently. "Take your time," he said. "I ordered dinner for eight. And Jamie . . ."

James turned to look at him.

"You would tell me if you were injured, wouldn't you?"

James swallowed. "Of course I would, George." He began to climb the stairs, making an effort not to limp. *I just can't tell you why.*

* * *

An hour later, James sat in the dining room, a glass of wine in hand, wishing he were anywhere but here. It was a good house with comfortable furniture and cheerful company. Rufus Alleyn was a genuinely interesting chap, a physician who chose to work among the poor of London's East End. The Ringleys were exerting themselves to talk of subjects other than hat trimmings and the weather. And Mrs. Vine's dinner menu was both delicious and bountiful. Yet the persistent ache in his ribs was a nagging reminder of the dangers just outside. James kept glancing at the clock on the mantel, wondering how rapidly he could shoo them all out of the house.

George had taken charge of the seating and placed James between the two eligible Ringley girls. Of course, thought James: Alleyn was invited to balance out the number of gentlemen, as well as the conversation. The Misses Ringley were agreeable girls, comfortable, lace-trimmed bundles of dimples and ringlets, distinguishable only by their ribbons: Miss Polly's dress was trimmed in pink; Miss Harriet's in yellow. They were flatteringly, almost alarmingly, riveted by everything he said. James felt quite certain that if he observed that the night was dark, both would turn their fascinated gazes upon him and breathe, "Oh, how very true!" If only they felt free to speak their minds, he thought, this evening would be more enjoyable.

But enjoyable or not, it was a risk that made him feel stupid and culpable. He ought to have remembered the dinner party and insisted that George cancel it. He had been so miserably absorbed in his own difficulties—Mary, the Bank of England, the assault—that he'd not paused to consider the danger to which he was now exposing their guests. If Mrs. Thorold was indeed on his trail, she might try to avenge herself by hurting those dear to him. George, the Ringleys, and Rufus Alleyn were all part of his observable orbit this evening. He could only pray that they went unscathed, no thanks to him and his appalling selfishness.

Miss Polly Ringley broke his train of thought by angling her body toward him—close enough that he was suddenly, intensely aware of the rose perfume rising from her wine-warmed skin—and murmured, "Have you been to any interesting concerts or lectures in recent days, Mr. Easton?"

"Why, yes," he replied after a brief hesitation. "This past weekend, I went to Leicester Square to see a Chinese pugilist."

She was already smiling with expectation, but his words caused her to blink and pause. "I beg your pardon; did you say 'pugilist'?"

"I did." To his left, he heard Miss Harriet squeak with anxiety. "It was most instructive. I'd no idea it was possible to spar so effectively with both hands and feet."

The Misses Ringley might have been lost for words, but Rufus Alleyn, sitting on Miss Polly's other side, immediately leaned forward. "I say, did you? I was called out on Saturday night to patch up a fellow who was unlucky enough to have challenged the Chinaman. Quite a job, it was. His right hand was so terribly smashed up that I was forced to—"

Miss Polly looked dismayed. "Mr. Alleyn, I fear that my sister is of a delicate disposition. . . ."

"I do beg your pardon, Miss Polly," said Rufus smoothly. "I'm afraid I allowed my professional enthusiasm to carry me away. I won't go into the unsavory details, but it was a long ordeal for my patient. Vicious little rat, that Chinese must have been. Or perhaps 'rat' is too small an animal. 'Terrier,' maybe?"

James couldn't suppress his irritation. "Why not simply 'man' or 'fighter'?"

Rufus looked blank. "Well, they're a smaller race. . . ."

"They are still people. Certainly, they are more like us than they are like animals."

"If you like," said Rufus, clearly trying to humor James's sudden ill temper. "I didn't mean anything by it, dear fellow."

James ground his teeth together. "I know." He looked around the table at all the merry pink-and-white faces and thought briefly, bleakly, of Mary. She'd changed him more than he'd ever dreamed possible. He was no longer entirely at home with his peers, thanks to her. If he lost her now, what on earth would become of him?

Seven

Wednesday, 17 October

Newgate Street, London

On her third day as a strolling vendor, Mary found herself feeling oddly at home in Newgate Street. All evidence of Monday's hangings had been cleared away, and only the looming wall of the jail reminded passersby of the suffering within. Any shadow it cast over the street was mostly literal. The people of Newgate Street carried on their daily lives much like those in any other road. There were the traders: butchers and bakers and candle-stick makers, and laborers of all descriptions who trudged through on their way to work. There were women aplenty, too: market traders like Mary, sleepy-looking prostitutes at noon, the occasional apple-cheeked countrywoman, all agog at what the capital had to offer. And at each end of the street, there was a coffee stall where one could buy a mug of coffee and two very thin slices of bread and butter for a penny.

There were, of course, others: a one-legged beggar, rank and ragged, sucking comfort from a filthy bottle; an angry, chattering woman who stalked the street, lurching and screeching at anyone who looked in her direction; and the usual contingent of idling errand boys playing with whatever refuse approached the shape of a football.

And then there were the characters who embraced Newgate Street precisely because of the jail and the nearby Old Bailey. There was a gaunt man with long wisps of gray hair who paraded daily before the prison, crying at frequent intervals, "Repent ye and be saved!" There were the bookmakers, who materialized on hanging days to offer odds on everything to do with the execution: whether death would be instantaneous, how long the condemned might strangle before finally suffocating, what method Calcraft might use to speed his (or, occasionally, her) death, and even whether Calcraft might speak or sneeze as he performed his job. There was more variation of the food and drink vendors depending on the weather and, of course, whether there was a crowd gathered for an execution. At those times, there was a distinctly festive feel in the air, and the food reflected it: hot mulled wine, roasted nuts, and lardy cakes, rather than the daily fare of boiled puddings and jacket potatoes. After Monday, Mary had exchanged her gingerbread for apples, to reflect the altered atmosphere.

One of the regulars who caught Mary's eye was a slightly threadbare but respectable-looking lady who stood by the prison gates handing out tracts. Each morning, she arrived a little after ten o'clock with her basket of improving literature and spent her days meekly offering it to all who passed through the prison doors. She seemed inured to angry rebuffs, cold shoulders, and the general chaotic rudeness of humanity.

Unusual, thought Mary. A shabby-genteel widow — the lady wore mourning clothes — was an unlikely candidate for this particular type of religious obsession. Oh, she might earnestly desire the salvation of all souls. But to stand outside a jail, day by day, in highly variable weather? It seemed distinctly strange. Add to that the woman's serenity in the face of screamed insults and obscene gestures, and Mary thought it possible that the widow was seeking something else entirely.

Could it really be this straightforward? The woman was tall, neither slender nor fat, and much of her head and face was conveniently concealed by a deep bonnet. She just might be Mrs. Thorold. But truly, she might be almost any woman in London. What Mary required was a closer look.

Unfortunately, that was nearly impossible. A clear view of the widow's face would require her to expose her own, and Mrs. Thorold was not the sort of person one underestimated twice. As James had learned, she preferred murder to the benefit of the doubt. Furthermore, the widow hadn't yet attempted to enter the building, so far as Mary could see. If she did, that might justify dramatic action. But for now, discretion remained the better part of valor.

She was taking another turn of the street, keeping half

an eye on the tract widow, when she saw him. He was walking in her direction with swift, long strides, his head slightly lowered. His face was a good deal more battered than the last time she'd seen it: a swollen, yellow-purple eyelid and a short, wide scab across the opposite eyebrow were the most obvious injuries, but it was unmistakably Mr. Ching. She halted and stared.

His chin lifted slightly, and he met her eyes. He did not speak, merely held her gaze as he approached. He had nearly passed her when the words tumbled from her lips, entirely unplanned. "Who on earth could have beaten you in a fight?"

The merest suggestion of a smile. "You think I lost?" His steps slowed, but he did not stop.

Mary cast a last glance at the tract widow, who remained serenely in position, and turned to walk with Mr. Ching. "I suppose that's a sloppy assumption. But I saw you fight on Saturday. Neither of the first two challengers landed a blow."

"The last fight was against three."

Mary's eyes widened. "Three men at the same time?" He nodded.

"But you won the fight?"

Another nod.

Mary scrabbled for a reasonable way to introduce herself, frame her questions. She couldn't find anything remotely conventional, so instead she simply repeated herself. "I was there."

"You said."

"Dressed as a boy."

"Is that a common English pastime?"

She almost smiled, but his question was quite serious. "No. It is . . . inappropriate for women to attend prize-fights. I came because my father used to practice your kind of fighting."

He scanned her face again, carefully this time. "You are not Chinese . . ."

"Half," she said defensively. "My father was a Lascar."

"And he taught you?"

"He was going to. When I was older."

He nodded. They walked on in silence for a minute, studying each other from the corners of their eyes. Mary watched for a flicker of impatience, a sign that he wished to be left alone, but he seemed remarkably accepting of her intrusion.

"What do you call your sort of fighting?" she asked.

"*Chu jiao.* As you saw, it is faster than English boxing. Uses all parts of the body, not only the hands."

He must have learned it from childhood, to fight so well, she thought. "Did you know you could beat the three men in the last match?"

He shrugged. "Some men, yes. Some no."

She nearly laughed with shock at such fatalism. It was difficult to imagine being so indifferent to one's safety . . . *Except,* a quiet inner voice reminded her, *you were once the same way. Before you cared whether you lived or died.* She

85

looked intently at Ching, trying to glimpse signs of the same desperation within this familiar stranger. His face was handsome, beneath the injuries. And young. She realized with a jolt that he was not much older than she.

"Your father is still alive?"

That question would never cease to hurt. She tried not to wince, but her voice was unsteady. "No." She rushed on, to cover her emotions. "You learned to fight from your father? *Chu jiao?*" She thought she'd managed a passable mimicry, but he smiled.

"Not 'choo jow'; *chu jiao*," he corrected her, in just her father's tone of gentle chastisement.

She caught her breath, her carefully repressed stock of memories threatening to tumble free. "I must go. Good day, Mr. Ching."

His chuckle stopped her midstride. "You are indeed more English than Chinese." He grinned, trying not to laugh again, but failing.

"I never pretended otherwise," she snapped. The tears were still there, just beneath the surface, and her eyes stung.

"I took my stage name from the Qing dynasty," he explained, still too amused for her liking. "I did not expect the English to know better. But you . . . your father did not teach you?"

She didn't bother to answer the question. "What's your real name, then?" she demanded as she turned to leave. Not that she cared, but if she knew his name, at least she'd not make the mistake of seeking him out in future.

The look he gave her was deeply patronizing. "Lang Guowei. But English people have trouble with it, so I use the name Jim Lang."

Mary stood perfectly still. She felt distinctly queasy. As a coincidence, this was simply too monstrous. It was like a stage play, when two long-lost friends blundered across a deserted heath in the middle of the night only to run smack into each other. She'd always been scornful of such theatrical contrivances, and here she was, living one.

She shook her head to clear it. Sentimental nonsense. And she could prove it. "Lang is a common enough name," she said, striving for indifference. "My family name was Lang."

Sudden interest lit his eyes. "Your father's name? What were his other names?"

She turned away. "You will probably think I pronounce them incorrectly."

"It doesn't matter," he said quickly. He was anxious now, turned fully toward her, leaning in slightly, searching her face for an answer. "Please."

She swallowed. It was difficult to produce a sound, but eventually she said in a hoarse voice, "Lang Jin Hai."

After what seemed an eternity, he asked quietly, "The same Lang Jin Hai who was in the newspapers?"

Mary was startled. "You can read English?"

He shrugged. "Some."

"Yes. The same man who was accused of murder, and who died in prison." She managed to say this in a tolerably even tone, and counted that as a victory.

Lang's expression was peculiar. "And you are his daughter? Truly, his own daughter by blood?"

She nodded.

He exhaled and made a strange, helpless gesture with his hands. "Then you are—we are—cousins. Lang Jin Hai was my uncle. My mother's twin brother."

Mary stared at Lang Guowei for a full minute. This was precisely the sort of coincidence she'd scorned. Precisely the sort of revelation she'd longed for all her life. Her desire for a tidy fairy tale must be so transparent, so overwhelming, that she was falling into the trap of a confidence man. She'd been a fool, disclosing her father's name. It was a notorious name, linked to a sensational tangle of events.

Her father's killing of a young aristocrat in an East End opium den had been the scandal of the year. Then, inevitably, the gruesome event had been misreported, exaggerated, embellished, and exploited to a degree that shocked even Mary's healthy cynicism. The first theatrical retelling of the tale, *The Bloody Knife, or the Opium-Mad Lascar*, was about as subtle as its title. It had debuted in the West End within a month of Lang Jin Hai's death. To Mary's chagrin, this "yellow fever," as the penny dreadfuls called it, showed no sign of abating. Any half-wit with the faintest interest in news, Lascars, high society, crime, scandal, or Chinese people would know the name Lang Jin Hai.

Mary shook her head. "I must go," she said. "Good day."

"Wait!" called Lang.

Mary walked away quickly, breathing a prayer of thanks that the tract widow was still in her place outside the prison. It was enough to be a sentimental fool; compounding that with irresponsibility and incompetence would be a true disgrace.

"Wait!" A strong hand touched her just above the elbow, but she shook it off. Lang caught her again, and this time spun her about to face him. "Where are you going?"

"Don't touch me."

"Then don't walk away from me."

"I am free to go."

He glared at her. "And I am free to follow you."

She stopped and scowled back. "I'm not going to give you anything."

"What are you talking about? I haven't asked for anything!" He looked at her as though she were mad. "Did you forget that you spoke to me first? You told me about your father. You told me his name."

"Yes, and I regret that. Please forget our conversation."

He made a sudden, chopping gesture with his hand, and she leaped back. Instantly, he was still. "I wasn't going to hurt you," he said quietly. "I only fight in the ring. Please. I must talk to you."

She shook her head. "It was a mistake. I should never have spoken to you."

"It wasn't a mistake," he said, his voice thick with emotion. "It was fate."

Mary stared at him. How skilled an actor did one have to be to manufacture that sort of intensity?

"I came to England to find my uncle," said Lang in a low voice. "I arrived to find his name in the newspapers. But you are the only person I've met who has claimed him as family."

"I could be lying," said Mary softly.

"People lie for glory, or advantage, or money. Not for disgrace." He paused. Then, with quiet insistence, he repeated, "If Lang Jin Hai was your father, we are cousins."

Mary had no idea what to say or how to proceed. She didn't even know what she felt, apart from fearful incredulity. The only mercy was that, judging from Lang's expression, he shared that emotion.

"Well, Cousin," he finally said. "Did you even know I existed?"

Mary shook her head. "My father never spoke of his family. Did you know of mine?"

Lang nodded slowly. "Yes. It was one of our family tales: my mother's twin brother, who sailed to foreign lands and settled there. We received a letter from him once, describing a foreign wife and a daughter. There was a photograph, even." He stopped and studied Mary's features. "You are like your father, I think."

She shook her head. "Don't say that. That is what a liar would say in order to buy my faith. And you are only telling me things that I have already told you."

"Then look at me, instead," he said. "My hairline. My mouth. The line of my jaw."

Mary stared at him, and her heart began to pound. Her father's features had faded in her memory, but she had seen that hairline, that mouth, that jawline much more recently. They were Lang's, and they were also her own.

"I thought you looked familiar when I first saw you." She didn't know whether she could trust this stranger, what his character was like. All the same, she heard herself saying, "That is why I spoke to you."

He nodded. "Fate."

Mary scrambled for some sense of narrative. "You said you came here in search of him?"

He shivered. "It is a long tale. I need a hot cup of tea. Chinese tea."

Mary noticed that his lips were blue with cold: not surprising, given that he was coatless. What had he done with his prize purse, if he couldn't afford a third-hand coat? "There is no possibility of Chinese tea near here," she said firmly. "Only public houses. If they will serve us."

"You mean, if they will serve me? I think you must pass quite well, even in this city."

She ignored his shadowy question. "This one should be all right," she said, steering him into Mrs. Bridges's cozy pub. She took charge inside, installing Lang at a table beside the picture window, where she could keep an eye on the tract widow and the prison gates. At the bar, she ordered two large brandies and dared Mrs. Bridges, with her eyes, to comment on the foreigner she'd dragged in. Mrs. Bridges sucked in her cheeks but said nothing, although her eyes rested for a little longer on Mary's features than they might normally have done. Mary squared her jaw. Mrs. Bridges could draw whatever conclusions she pleased; Mary was sick of skulking and flinching and apologizing for her blood.

She waited until Lang had drunk his brandy and the cold, pinched look receded from his features. At that point, the pounding of her heart was so violent as to be intolerable, and it was difficult even to frame a coherent question. "Will you tell me what you know of my father?" she asked at last.

He hesitated, and she thought she might scream with frustration. He said, cautiously, "This is all from my mother. There might be errors."

She nodded. "Please. Just tell me."

"My mother and your father were twins, as I have said. Your father, Jin Hai, was the elder, the dutiful one;

my mother's name was Jin Ye, and she was rebellious from the start. They were close, much closer than most brothers and sisters. They were always so, according to my mother, even from infancy." He looked at her curiously. "How much do you know about the Chinese?"

"Almost nothing," she confessed.

"Most Chinese treat their sons and daughters very differently. Sons inherit, and are expected to take care of their parents in old age. Daughters are always outsiders, because they will eventually marry and become part of their husbands' families. The Lang family—our family—is different, because we are part Hakka. The Hakka value all children equally. We do not bind our girls' feet. Our grandparents were poor, but they sent both children, even their daughter, to school for a few years."

Mary nodded. A shiver had rippled through her body when Lang uttered the words "our family"—a phrase she had never expected to hear with reference to herself. She swelled with pride at Lang's description of the Hakka.

"Our grandparents are farmers. At least, they were. But there was a series of bad crops and, in our parents' fourteenth year, an enormous fire on the property. They lost their home and also their land. Suddenly they were destitute.

"Jin Hai was tall and strong for his age. One day, he secretly went down to the harbor and signed up as a sailor on a merchant vessel. His family was distraught, especially Jin Ye. Yet Jin Hai's solution proved successful:

he earned good wages on commercial voyages and was able to send money back to his family, even after settling in England with an Irish wife and starting a family."

Mary wasn't surprised to hear this: it was exactly her father's character as she remembered him. Duty and family had been his idols. As a child, when she'd asked about his parents, he'd simply said, "They are half a world away." Mary pushed her untouched brandy toward Lang. "Do you know what happened to my father when we were children?" she asked quickly, before her throat could close around the question. She had to know. She was terrified of knowing.

Lang twirled the glass in silence, apparently absorbed in the ripples and tremors of the amber liquid. His hands were thin and strong—deceptively attractive, thought Mary, considering the pain they routinely caused. At last he spoke. "I know some of the story. A very small part."

"I need to know that much, at least."

"My mother was left at home when your father went to sea, and she was lonely. Angry, too, because of her family's poverty. After the fire, her parents lived as tenant farmers, working furiously in order to make their landlords rich, and they only had enough to survive because of your father's help. My mother was not just rebellious, but also very idealistic. When she was eighteen, she fell in with a cult." Lang's fingers tightened on the glass, and his breathing deepened. "It is a strange cult, and a powerful one. Its leader is a madman called Hong Xiuquan, and he claims to be the younger brother of Jesus Christ." He glanced at her swiftly. "It is a very foolish claim, don't you think? But Hong promises more than a better afterlife; instead, he preaches of a Heavenly Kingdom on earth, in which every citizen is safe and prosperous, there are no rich and no poor, and the corrupt are punished.

"My mother was ready for such a message. Hong and his followers took up arms to combat coastal pirates and highway bandits. They performed much of the work that should have been done by the authorities. So the people of Fujian were safer, more prosperous, and profoundly grateful to Hong's cult. My mother wanted justice for citizens. And my mother admired a man who understood the value of strong, intelligent women. Hong allows both men and women to lead in his Heavenly Army."

Mary felt an unexpected pulse of sympathy for her aunt. It was just the kind of promise that would have secured her loyalty, too. "It all sounds quite reasonable, so far. Apart from the relationship to Jesus Christ."

Lang looked queasy. "So far, yes. After some years—by your reckoning, the year 1846—Hong promoted my mother. She became the first female colonel in the Heavenly Army. This led to a terrible quarrel with her husband, who eventually abandoned her. And me." His voice turned hoarse on that last syllable, but he hurried on. "My mother had no regrets. She changed my name—gave me her own family name, and a new given name. 'Guowei' means 'May the country be saved,' and she believed that she and I, as members of Hong's Heavenly Army, would be part of that salvation." He exhaled slowly and lifted his chin, fixing his unseeing gaze on the streetscape through the window. "I now come to a part of the history that I do not fully understand. About a year later—1847, when I was twelve years old—your father appeared."

Mary had been waiting for it, preparing herself for a revelation, but the announcement still jolted her. It was the matter-of-fact way in which Lang spoke, as though her father was a real person, and not an infamous criminal or an idealized abstraction. She reminded herself to breathe.

Lang sipped the brandy. "My mother had not written to him. Perhaps my grandparents had somehow managed to contact him. Or perhaps, as her twin brother, he sensed that something was very wrong. I have heard that twins are sometimes connected by an invisible cord, and I would certainly believe it of our parents." His voice softened. "It was a wonderful time, when I first met your father. My mother was ecstatic: she wept for joy when they were reunited. And she had told me so many stories of their childhood that I already idolized him." He paused. "He was a good man, your father. Intelligent and kindhearted, the best of brothers."

Mary felt suddenly resentful. It was enough to hear her father's story from a stranger's lips; she didn't like Lang flaunting his superior knowledge of her own father's character. "What did he think of the Heavenly Army?" she asked.

Lang shook his head. "He was farsighted, your father, perhaps because he had been away for some years. He saw trouble and corruption within Hong's army, and he pleaded with my mother to return home. She was furious: she thought he was envious of her success, and selfish in asking her to respect her family's wishes rather than the common good. They had many long conversations every night after I went to bed. Your father believed that Hong's cult would lead to civil war, to great suffering for all who followed him. My mother argued that while there were many faults within Hong's system, they had both God and justice on their side, and that right would prevail. Your father stayed for the full month of his shore leave, but he failed to change my mother's mind." Lang's focus dropped to the scarred table.

Neutral as his expression remained, Mary felt prickles rising along her spine. They were finally reaching the critical part of Lang's tale, at least so far as it concerned her.

Lang cleared his throat. "At the end of his leave, my uncle offered to take me to England with him. I know this because I stayed awake, listening to them talk. He offered to train me as a sailor, and said there was much I could learn outside Hong's cult." He swallowed. "My mother was incensed. Not only had her brother failed to appreciate her talent and hard work, and the divinely inspired visions of Hong Xiuquan; not only had he tried to persuade her from her moral obligations in favor of the lesser ideal of family; he now threatened to take her only child with him. She denounced her twin brother as a traitor to her heavenly family."

Mary stared at him for a long moment. "What happened?" she whispered.

Lang's expression was blank, his voice flat and clear and hard. "Your father was savagely beaten before my eyes. All our eyes. He was then driven to the nearest harbor and thrown, unconscious, onto the first cargo ship leaving Fujian. That was the last time I saw him, and I never heard anything else. Until recently."

"Why didn't they kill him?" asked Mary. "If they thought him a traitor, they should have executed him."

"At the last moment, my mother begged for clemency."

Mary stared at him. "But she denounced him . . ."

"And almost immediately regretted her words. She found, in the end, that she couldn't choose between Hong and her brother."

"And they listened to her?" Mary still found it astounding, the concept of a woman commanding male soldiers in combat.

Lang nodded. "It cost her dearly, of course. She was demoted to foot soldier because she was so closely allied with a traitor. But Hong was wise enough to keep her loyalty. She was too intelligent and committed to the movement to discard entirely."

Mary nodded. She could surmise the rest: severe injuries leading to opium addiction, a high possibility of capture and enslavement by pirates, and an eventual return of the broken man to London. Upon learning of the death of his wife and the disappearance of his only child, his heartbreak and disgrace would have been complete.

She sat, dry-eyed, in a Newgate pub, across the table from her newfound cousin. She was, for the first time in her life, in possession of the facts of her father's last voyage—of one partial version of the story, at least. It was a most peculiar thing to hear. The tale was simultaneously so much more and so much less than she'd tried to imagine. Of course, her father had attempted to save his beloved sister; of course, his heart had broken when she'd turned on him. And he'd returned to England, to the family he had not meant to abandon, only to find that it had evaporated as well.

Mary thought once again of the cigar box containing her father's papers, which had burned in the fire at the Lascars' Refuge. Would having that box help her now? Would it reveal any more than Lang had told her? Assuming his tale was accurate, that is. He'd been a child of twelve and subject to a boy's misunderstandings, the misting of memory by time. Yet he was here now, apparently on the strength of that story.

"What do you expect from me?" she demanded.

Her sharp tone didn't seem to surprise Lang. "You were the one who wanted something from me."

"A story."

"More than a story. History."

"And if I want nothing more to do with you?"

"Then I remain as I was an hour ago." He seemed to mean it, too. He sat perfectly still, those clean, deadly hands wrapped loosely around the brandy glass.

"You knew he was dead some months ago. Why didn't you give up then?"

"Leave the country, you mean? I suppose I hoped it was a case of mistaken identity. That your father was still alive and could set me straight. Foolishness."

She took a deep breath. "And now that you know he is dead and disgraced?"

He lifted his gaze to hers, truly looking at her for the first time since he'd begun his tale. She suppressed a gasp: from this angle, his undamaged eye was just like her father's. "That depends upon you," he said. "Cousin."

Eight

The same day, early afternoon

Newgate Street, London

E ach day, after the dinner hour, a sleepy lull descended upon the streets of London. Laborers trickled back to their tasks, sluggish with bread and beer; market traders had done the best of their day's business; the homeward rush of workers seemed impossibly far in the future. Mary usually took this opportunity to review her morning's work. Today, especially, she would have welcomed a quarter hour to think about her fateful morning—an unlikely chance meeting, the discovery of a long-lost cousin, the sudden revelations surrounding her father's disappearance. Lang was gone now; she knew not where. They had agreed, vaguely, to meet again, but they each had much—almost too much—upon which to reflect.

Just now, however, there would be no pause: the tract widow had suddenly decamped. One moment, the lady was there as usual, seeking to save the world. A minute later, she had lowered her veil, swept her array of reading materials into her dainty basket, and started at an uncompromising pace down the street, deeper into the City.

Mary blinked and pushed all thoughts of Lang from her mind. Progress at last. She gave the widow a lead of about a hundred yards—it was easy enough to keep her in sight during this relatively quiet time of day—and then set off in pursuit. However, she had scarcely taken a dozen steps when a large black carriage drew up beside her. Mary looked up with a frown—most coachmen were no respecters of pedestrians—and was startled to see a lady's gloved hand, wearing a signet ring, in the window. The ring was engraved with a lightly stylized capital A, a symbol that was as plain as it was familiar to Mary. Could it be? She glanced at the driver, who nodded once, a small movement.

Mary sighed and stopped while the carriage halted by the roadside. An instant later, the coachman was at Mary's elbow, unfolding the steps and offering her an arm for stability. Mary couldn't resist: she looked this person—another agent?—in the eye, but didn't recognize her. At least she presumed it was a woman incognito. How many agents had remained loyal to Anne Treleaven and the Agency? She wondered if she'd ever find the courage to ask.

The carriage door had scarcely closed behind her when the woman on the bench spoke. "Thank you for stopping," she said in a quiet voice.

Mary didn't sit. "Miss Treleaven, I'm just this moment on the trail of a woman who could be Mrs. Thorold. I still have time to catch up with her, if I get down now."

"The lady in mourning, carrying a basket? That wasn't Mrs. Thorold."

Mary stared, astonished. "How can you be certain?"

Anne's smile was slightly twisted. "It was Felicity Frame." She paused to let Mary digest the news. "Remember, Felicity and I knew each other intimately for over a decade." Anne's use of the past tense did not escape Mary, and she wondered again about the painful split between her two former managers. "She is one of the few people I would recognize anywhere in the world, regardless of disguise. I'd say the same is true of me, in her eyes."

"In that case," said Mary, deeply embarrassed, "I am sorry to have wasted so much time and opportunity monitoring her."

Anne shrugged. "It was a reasonable theory. And I suspect Felicity was also watching you, hoping that you would lead her to Mrs. Thorold."

The carriage lurched suddenly, turning around, and Mary sat down with an involuntary thump. "Where are we going now?" she asked.

"To a coaching inn near the Crystal Palace."

The Crystal Palace! Mary thought of that strange edifice of steel and glass, sprawling over the prim suburban villas of south London like a vision of the future.

"You will wonder why," said Anne with characteristic understatement. "But I fear that I must begin by asking you a question. For another favor, in fact."

Now that Mary was seated and listening, she realized that Anne's facade of calm was precisely that. Beneath the surface, Anne Treleaven was abuzz with excitement. Anne was generally the epitome of cool professionalism, and this departure made Mary's stomach lurch, not entirely unpleasantly. "Yes?"

"Angelica Thorold has arrived in London," said Anne. "She is alone." She paused, and Mary found that she needed the moment. It was extremely difficult to imagine Angelica Thorold, a spoiled only daughter, undertaking such an arduous journey unaccompanied. Although her sheltered and luxurious life had ended with her father's imprisonment and her mother's flight from justice, Angelica was still a young lady born and bred. And young ladies did not travel alone.

"I received word that she arrived this morning on the overnight coach from Dover," explained Anne. "She's been traveling nonstop for nearly a fortnight now in order to reach her father in time. But something has gone wrong—it seems she hasn't a place to stay."

Mary absorbed that. "Do you know what her original arrangement was?" Angelica Thorold was pampered, but she possessed a keen practical intelligence: she would never embark on a grueling, seven-hundred-mile journey without considering the basics.

Anne shook her head. "I've not been able to get close enough. We've had agents posted at the major coaching inns in London, watching the Dover and Folkstone coaches. She was only spotted a few hours ago as she disembarked, at which point I was notified."

"Do you think she knows she's being watched?"

Anne hesitated. "It depends. At this point, we must operate using two simultaneous theories: The first is that she is in league with her mother. In that case, she would presume that Scotland Yard is searching for them, and that all possible precautions are necessary. Alternatively, she may be what she appears: a grieving daughter come to see her dying father, in which case she will merely be exhausted and angry and feeling lost."

Mary thought about that. "And there was no one to meet her?"

"No. She has twice sent messages through an errand boy to a house in Ashburn Place, not far from here, but no reply was given."

"What else has she done?"

"Waited. Wept a little. She asked about a room at the inn, and when the landlord found her question funny—he made rather an off-color joke about it—she grew very angry."

Mary smiled. That rang true; Angelica had always been hot-tempered and imperious. Whatever her reason for arriving in London, the past fortnight must have been among the most exhausting and humbling of her life. "What would you like me to do?" asked Mary. The carriage tilted slightly around a corner, and part of Anne's answer slid into Mary's lap: a large, tidy bundle of women's clothing.

Anne looked vaguely apologetic. "I expect you've already guessed. I'd like you to feign a chance meeting at the inn and renew your acquaintance. Ideally, you'll arrange for her to stay at the Academy, where we can keep a very close eye on her, but the overall aim is for you to gain her trust. I need hardly add that she's our best chance of getting to her mother." Anne paused, the slightest hint of uncertainty entering her expression. "Do you wish to hear more at this point?" The classic Agency challenge, yet Mary was already deeply implicated in the project.

Instead of answering the question, Mary asked, "Do you know whether she's definitely in touch with her mother?"

Anne shook her head. "I'm afraid not. And I need hardly warn you that it's a sensitive subject, best approached obliquely."

"Of course." A pause. Mary sifted through the heap of fabric at her side: good-quality woolens and muslins, well-worn, neatly mended. Naturally, Anne had thought of this. Mary's street seller's dress was cheap and showy — to a lady's eyes, at any rate. Even prostrate with grief and exhaustion, Angelica Thorold was unlikely to miss such a clanging error. "Have you thought of a cover story? It seems I'm to appear as a governess or lady's companion of some sort."

Anne nodded. "I'll explain it as you change. That is, should you accept the assignment."

Mary answered the question with her actions. As the carriage jostled along the cobblestones, she quickly shed her coarse frock and began the laborious process of putting on a lady's dress. Climbing into a crinoline, even a narrow one, inside a small carriage was awkward and required some fierce wrestling with the hoop, but she managed it without kicking the door open. A heavy flannel petticoat came next. Anne would need to adjust this afterward, as there was no space for Mary to ensure that it sat evenly on the metal cage. And finally, the dress. This one wasn't too bad: it had buttons in front, for women who did not have maids to dress them, and a narrower skirt than those currently in vogue.

It was impossible to go through this rigmarole without recalling the first time she'd changed in a carriage: at James Easton's behest, only days after they'd met. It was startling to remember how little she'd liked him then. Fortunately, his arrogance had been tempered by sound judgment and a grudging respect for her intellect. That combination had enabled them to collaborate, and eventually to become friends.

Mary shook herself free of reminiscence. Standing as best she could in the swaying carriage, she asked Anne, "Do I look the part?" She had to admit that the dress fitted extremely well: it was a reminder of how acute Anne's judgment usually was, even in small matters.

Anne busied herself with the skirt hems, arranging layers of fabric so that they draped evenly over the crinoline. "Of course you do. As you know, it's more about the way one carries oneself than the details of the costume."

Mary nodded. "You're the one who taught me that." *You and Felicity Frame,* she thought.

Anne cleared her throat. "The simplest explanation for being at the inn is that you are meeting someone from your employer's household: a new housemaid, perhaps. You should choose someone who populates the household as you imagine it. She'll be coming in from Maidstone, and thus she would have been on the same coach on which Angelica traveled."

Mary nodded. "And if Angelica asks where I'm currently living, what shall I say? If she agrees to stay at the Academy, I don't want to tell her I'm nearby."

"I see your point. Well, what about Knightsbridge? We've a useful contact in Victoria Road who could help us maintain the fiction, if it comes to that."

Twin sensations of excitement and anxiety wormed their way into Mary's stomach. Anne's use of "if it comes to that" suggested a prolonged involvement with Angelica Thorold, and thus with this case. Prolonged usually led to complicated, and complicated always led to dangerous. Yet this was just the work she loved best: active, unpredictable, fully absorbing.

The carriage slowed. Mary drew the window curtain aside an inch. They were very near the inn, and the roadway was dense with animals, coaches, carts, carriages, people, and confusion. The inn was called, appropriately enough, the Coach and Horses. It was a two-story building that seemed to sprawl in all directions, squatting as it did on the corner of a busy junction. Two long-distance coaches were being loaded on the street outside, with all the attendant bustle and shouting and commotion that seemed inevitably to attend a journey.

Mary scanned the crowd for anything significant. The scene felt like something Anne and Felicity might have devised for her during her training as a test of observational skills. Travelers milled anxiously, supervising the loading of their baggage: neat valises, heavy corded trunks, even a vast, irregular bundle that reminded Mary for all the world of half a cow wrapped in burlap. As always, coachmen and travelers had their familiars: half-grown boys ducking and darting about the wheels, intent either on earning a penny or stealing anything unguarded; travelers' friends and families, watching the preparations with misgiving in their eyes; and the usual assortment of bystanders a busy street produced, all with advice to give, things to sell, opinions to declare.

Anne's voice was as cool and quiet as ever. "I know this is highly irregular, Mary. I must also caution you to consider yourself in the company of a dangerous person.

Mothers and daughters are so often cut from the same cloth. Bearing that in mind, are you ready to begin?"

The question was purely a formality. Mary was the only person for the task; there was no possibility that Angelica Thorold would follow a stranger out of the pub toward a promise of safe lodging. "I'm ready, Miss Treleaven."

To her surprise, relief softened Anne's tightly drawn features. A pause. Then, very quietly, "Thank you, Mary. I appreciate this."

Mary nodded, sudden tears stinging the backs of her eyes. Anne Treleaven was normally so clipped, so perfectly emotionless, that even this modest admission came as a revelation. "Well, then," she said, trying for a lighthearted tone, "wish me luck?"

"Of course," said Anne, with the smallest of smiles. "Although I doubt you'll need it."

Outside the Coach and Horses, the scene was hectic; inside was pure chaos compressed within timbered walls. Mary paused on the threshold, struck by the vivid differences between the types of public houses she'd recently visited. She was beginning to appreciate what a clean, orderly ship Mrs. Bridges ran, and just how difficult that must be. In fairness, the Coach and Horses was roughly four times the size of the Hangman, and bursting with coaching passengers and all who served them. Still, every person in there was striving, with varying degrees of success, for attention. Coachmen hollered at the ostlers, who barked at the stable boys. Cooks bawled at their skivvies. They dodged, whining, around the barmen, who, in turn, roared at them for getting in the way. Somewhere in the middle of the mayhem, a tiny baby yowled: a round, dark hole of a mouth that seemed to emit no sound, so great was the din.

Mary covered her ears and stood quietly in a corner. Gradually, as she watched, some sense of order emerged. The dining room, it seemed, was overfull; many of the customers slumped along benches in the main taproom were waiting for, and grousing about, a table and a meal. The walls were lined with a cornucopia of travelers' trunks and cases awaiting collection or dispatch. These threatened to trip up any who passed, and loud complaints and curses contributed to the din.

She couldn't see a person who fit her memory of Angelica Thorold: elegant, blond, haughty. Mary wondered if there was a separate dining room for ladies, and if that's where Angelica might be. But just as she was about to explore the inn further, her eye lingered on a woman curled defensively into herself in a corner of the room. She looked vaguely familiar: Could it be? This woman was very thin, her hair mousy and straight, her expression one of sheer pinched misery. Then the wide blue eyes flashed a glance at the ceiling—a look of frustration and despair—and Mary smiled. It was Angelica Thorold.

Mary began to work her way through the room,

stepping over and around people and things with an air of mild confusion. As she drew closer to Angelica, she began to ask people: "I beg your pardon, but has the Dover coach arrived?" "Do you know when the Dover coach is expected?" "I'm looking for a passenger from the Dover coach, a young woman." Most people hadn't a clue; others were too absorbed in their own weariness and misery to reply.

At last, Mary reached Angelica. "Excuse me, miss," she said, raising her voice slightly to be heard even at this proximity, "I'm looking for a young woman who was meant to be on the Dover coach."

Angelica's eyes flashed with hope, and she sat up straight. "I was on that coach! Are you from the Milnes'?"

Mary wondered when, or if, Angelica would recognize her. "I'm here on behalf of the Newlands, to meet a Sally Tranter." A moment, and then a frown. "Could you possibly have mistaken the name? Are you Miss Tranter?"

Angelica shook her head. "I almost wish I were, for the time I've been waiting here. Look, the Dover coach arrived absolutely hours ago. Your Miss Tranter's probably made her own way to . . ." Her sharp eyes raked Mary from boot tips to hat, assessing the value of her ensemble. "To whatever you said the family's name was." Her gaze arrived at Mary's face and sharpened, perceptibly. "Oh, my good Lord: I know you. It's Miss Quinn!"

Mary allowed recognition to dawn on her face. "My goodness—Miss Thorold! I do beg your pardon. I'd have known you immediately, only I was preoccupied —"

"No, no," said Angelica, rising hastily and shaking Mary's hand. "I've changed a great deal. Not quite the spoiled debutante you once knew." She touched her light-brown hair, slipping from its arrangement. "Not to mention the rigors of travel. And living as a music student."

This couldn't have gone more smoothly. "So you did go to study music in Germany? Or was it Vienna? How marvelously exciting!" Mary huffed with exasperation as a long, thin parcel, badly carried, nearly knocked the hat from her head. "It's bedlam in here. Let's go somewhere quieter. Haven't they got a ladies' parlor? I'll bet this Miss Tranter's neatly tucked up there, wondering where the blazes everyone's gone."

"The ladies' parlor is closed," said Angelica with a sigh. "Fire damage, they told me. Listen, Miss Quinn, I couldn't be more pleased to see you. You're the only practical, intelligent person I know in town. After you find your Miss Tranter, I don't suppose you could spare a moment for my own predicament?"

Mary blinked. This was entirely too easy: Why was Angelica throwing herself into her clutches? What did she truly want? "But of course. I don't suppose you remember a young woman who traveled with you? She'd have been inside the coach, not on top."

Angelica shook her head decisively. "No young woman. Two elderly sisters, and me. All the rest were men."

"In which case, I'll have to come back tomorrow.

113

Coaches are *so* unreliable, are they not?" Mary looped her arm confidently through Angelica's. "Let's find a corner where we can hear ourselves think, and you can tell me about your difficulty."

Inside the inn was impossible. They ended up standing just outside the building like, as Angelica put it with a nervous giggle, "a pair of common tarts."

Mary laughed openly. "You've changed, Miss Thorold. And if I may be so impudent, I like you a great deal better."

Angelica made a noise that could only be described as a snort. "That's not such an extravagant claim, Miss Quinn. You could scarcely have liked me less two years ago." She paused. "In my own defense, I worked quite hard at being unlikable."

"You were extremely unhappy," suggested Mary quietly.

Angelica nodded, and her blue eyes clouded. "Grieving as I am now, I am infinitely happier." She blinked, and offered Mary a small smile. "But I am speaking in riddles. My situation, baldly put, is this: My father is dying, in jail. I've come from Vienna to see him, and I don't know if he's still alive.

"I wrote to a friend before my departure asking if I might stay at her family's home. We had been close friends, in a schoolgirlish way, and although my family's reputation is destroyed, I had hoped she might agree. After all, it's not as though she needs to see me;

114

she only comes to town for the season. I've now been sitting in this appalling excuse for an inn for more than four hours. I've sent as many messages to my friend's house in Knightsbridge, and all have come back unanswered. I know that they keep a full staff at the house even when they're in the country. They used to, anyway. But given my father's current residence, and my mother's mysterious disappearance, it's almost certain that I'm considered beyond the pale.

"I suppose a reputation such as mine is quite capable of denting hers. And I'm sure I'd have done precisely the same thing a few years ago. Hindsight is so very acute, don't you find, Miss Quinn?" Angelica sighed and rubbed her eyes wearily. "In any case, I've been traveling nonstop for a fortnight and I'm about to faint from exhaustion and I'm asking you, oh wise and resourceful Mary Quinn, if you could possibly advise me on what to do next. I'm afraid I'm not giving you much choice," she concluded with a brittle chuckle. "If you don't say something reassuring, I think I might just burst into hysterics!"

If this was a performance, thought Mary, Angelica Thorold ought to star in the West End. If it was genuine, Angelica would soon be completely shattered. Once her mother was arrested, she would suffer a second cataclysm of humiliation and tragedy, a human sacrifice for the greater good.

"Let me think," said Mary slowly. "I haven't friends capable of putting you up."

"I don't expect that," said Angelica quickly, her old pride asserting itself. "I suppose I meant . . ." She gestured helplessly. "A cheap but respectable lodging house? Does such a thing exist? To be perfectly, humiliatingly frank, I'm not the heiress I once was. I earn my living teaching music, and I simply haven't the money for the sort of hotel in which a lady could stay alone."

It was all so absurdly, improbably easy that Mary had to pretend to flounder. After dithering for a minute or two, she finally said, "You've given me an idea. I attended a boarding school for several years, Miss Scrimshaw's Academy for Girls. It's a good-size place, plenty of bedrooms, and one doesn't get more respectable than a girls' boarding school, really. I'm still quite friendly with its head teachers. Head teacher, that is," she corrected herself. "I shall ask them if there's a bedroom you could have for a few days." She paused. "Or shall you be staying longer?"

Angelica shook her head. "It would be terribly kind of them to let me stay just for a night or two. I'm sure I can organize something for myself, with a little time. It's only—I'm just—it's so . . ." And she abruptly burst into tears.

Mary found herself in the absurd position of comforting Angelica Thorold. "There, there," she said awkwardly, patting her shoulder. "You must be half dead with exhaustion. I don't know how you managed two full weeks packed into a jouncing, swaying public coach with a circusful of strangers. Did you stop for even a single day to rest?"

"I couldn't," she replied in choked tones. "My father . . ."

Miracle of miracles, Mary located a clean handkerchief that somebody—Anne—had tucked into the reticule she was carrying. "Here," she said, dabbing Angelica's face gently. "You've arrived now. You're in London. I'm sure there will be a spare bed for you at the Academy."

Weary as she was, Angelica soon stopped crying, blew her nose, and took a few deep breaths. "I do beg your pardon," she said, her voice still shaky and waterlogged. "I'm making such a colossal exhibition of myself, and so much inconvenience for you, too. I suppose your employers will be wondering where you are." There was a faint ring of hope to that last statement, as though she was hoping Mary would deny it.

"I can stay a few minutes longer, to organize your things, but you're right: I shall have to go." Mary felt no real regret in saying this. Angelica was so entirely convincing in the role of distraught daughter that Mary needed two minutes alone, to remind herself of the other gruesome possibilities Angelica represented. "Here's what we'll do. I'm going to write a note of introduction and find you a cab. While I'm doing that, you collect your belongings, and then you're off. The school is in St. John's Wood."

"But I need to see my father as soon as possible."

"You look ready to faint. Once you're at the school

you can have a meal and a bath, and then see about your father. The headmistress will assist you, I'm sure. And I'm permitted to go out occasionally. I'll call at the school in a few days to see how you are."

Angelica nodded obediently, took two steps back into the inn, then turned back. "What if there's no space at the school?" she asked, eyes filled with panic.

Mary shook her head. "Let's not borrow trouble," she said. "Besides, I have a strong feeling about this. They won't turn you away."

Nine

The same afternoon

The offices of Easton Engineering, Great George Street

B eg your pardon, Mr. Easton, but you have a caller."
James frowned and looked up from his nest of
papers. "I'm not expecting anybody."

"Lady here to see you," said his chief clerk. "On urgent
and personal business."

Mary. The thought bubbled up before he could control
it. *No,* he admonished himself. Mary was known to all his
staff, so this was not Mary herself, but a messenger. Fear
clawed at his guts. "What name did she give?"

"None, I'm afraid, sir."

"Half a minute," he said. "Then show her in, please."
He gathered up all the Bank-related plans and sketches,
notes and calculations, and rolled them into a tube. He
wasn't so nonchalant as to leave them in open view, but
neither was he inclined to refile them. He had only just
cleared his desk when a tall woman stepped through the
door into his private office.

She was dressed in plain black silk, her face concealed

by a light veil. James wondered, for one bizarre moment, whether it might be Mrs. Thorold, come to settle the score. He stepped forward to greet her. "James Easton, at your service, ma'am."

"Thank you for agreeing to see a perfect stranger," she said, her voice rich and low and unfamiliar. "I know you must be busy."

"Not too busy to be intrigued by your mention of urgent business." He drew out a chair, and she sank into it gracefully. "Mrs. . . . ."

"Frame. Felicity Frame." She lifted her veil and fixed him with a level, green-eyed gaze, waiting until he, too, was seated. "We have a mutual friend in Miss Quinn."

He would not be tricked that easily. "Miss Quinn?" he repeated in a faintly puzzled tone.

"Your associate, of course, in the firm of Quinn and Easton. The senior partner, one might presume." She leaned forward, planting one elbow on his desk in a gesture of confident intimacy. "I was surprised to find the nameplate missing, but I believe you are still in business?"

James swallowed hard. "That depends upon who asks."

"Someone who wishes you both well," she said. The words were accompanied by a small smile that did not seem particularly reassuring. "I see that my name is unknown to you; that is a credit to Miss Quinn's discretion. But I assure you, I have known her since her girlhood, and I am well aware of her distinct talent for discreet observation and detection."

James's thoughts were racing. Was this Mary's connection from Scotland Yard? But what role could a middle-aged woman play there? "How may I assist you today, Mrs. Frame?" he asked quietly.

She pursed her lips in thought, and James realized with surprise that she was very beautiful. "I'm here to talk to you about Mary's current assignment. At the risk of boring you with information you already know—but how else can I demonstrate that I, too, have knowledge worth sharing?—this is the third day of her watch over Newgate Prison."

James held perfectly still.

"I do not believe there has been any sign of Mrs. Thorold in the area, although Mary had some unconfirmed suspicions about me. Not entirely surprising," she added, "given my constant attendance at the jail over the past few days." She paused. When he remained silent, she gave the merest suggestion of a shrug and resumed speaking. "I am inclined to believe that the surveillance of Newgate Street is a waste of time. I doubt that Mrs. Thorold would take such a large risk to clear her name. It would be simpler for her to establish a new identity and proceed unimpeded by her husband's history of disgrace." She looked at James. "I can see the question in your eyes. This might all be interesting, but what has it got to do with you and Mary?"

James half smiled despite himself. "I can neither confirm nor deny anything, Mrs. Frame."

"Such wise circumspection."

"Pray continue your . . . narrative."

"I am here today because I believe you are now the person best placed to watch for the reappearance of Mrs. Thorold."

"Oh?"

"Have you already accepted the commission for the proposed alterations to the vaults of the Bank of England?"

James raised an eyebrow. "I beg your pardon?"

"There's no need to play the fool with me," she said amiably. "I know you attended a confidential meeting with the court of directors of the Bank of England. I also know that, despite the relatively small stature of your family firm, and your rather startling youth, you personally were offered the contract. You weren't even made to compete for the job. It would be rather difficult—impossible, even—to decline such an opportunity, don't you think?"

"If all that were true, it certainly would," agreed James.

Felicity's smile was quite feline. "Oh, I do appreciate your discretion. Let me explain: Mrs. Thorold holds an account at Coutts Bank under the name of Fisher. Yesterday, a woman attempted to make a large withdrawal from the Fisher account. Because the account was flagged for watch, the bank attempted to delay her while calling Scotland Yard. The woman became suspicious in her turn and left the bank empty-handed before the police could arrive."

James was intrigued. "Did nobody at the bank try to stop her?"

"The woman injured two guards and escaped down a

side street. There was a brief chase, but they very quickly lost her trail."

"So there is no possibility she will attempt to access that account again."

"Precisely. But the very attempt suggests that Mrs. Thorold is in need of funds. She is not the sort of criminal to stoop to common burglary: she operates on a more grandiose scale. I now believe that she will attempt a large-scale theft. Your project offers a spectacular opportunity."

"Surely the project is *too* spectacular?" argued James. "The Bank of England is one of the most secure buildings in the country."

"Not while it is under construction, with its hoard of gold roaming the countryside."

"Even if it is necessary to move gold from its vaults for the period of construction—and it might not be so—the gold will be heavily guarded. Such a theft would require extensive planning, a large team of criminals working together, and an informant on the inside, at the very least. Not to mention a means of transporting such a large amount of gold and melting it down. If I were Mrs. Thorold, I would look to jewels or cash—something easily smuggled on my person."

"None of the challenges you cite are insurmountable obstacles," returned Felicity. "Mrs. Thorold has worked with a gang before. She has the intelligence and audacity to plot such a scheme. And the potential payout is precisely the sort of thing that would attract a woman of her ilk. If the job were successful, it would be her last. She could vanish once again and never return to England."

James thought about this. "Let us suppose you are correct," he said slowly. "If Mrs. Thorold lost access to the Fisher account yesterday, she must only be starting to plan a new theft."

"She may have been plotting something all along, and this recent failure has given the scheme a new urgency."

"Either way, she would want to act swiftly, within the next couple of months, at most. How on earth could she have heard about the Bank's need to expand its vaults?" He knew he was committing himself, but he continued nevertheless. "This is extremely recent information. I met with the Bank only yesterday."

"The directors would have been discussing it for some time. There's that inside contact. . . ."

"A rather lofty inside contact."

"Is it so impossible?" demanded Felicity.

"It is certainly far-fetched. Fantastical, even."

"So were her previous crimes: She organized an international pirate crew that attacked her husband's merchant vessels. She must also have extensive black-market contacts, since she was able to dispose of valuable Eastern artifacts on a regular basis. And she is ruthless. Although I need hardly remind you of that."

"No," agreed James, an involuntary shiver traveling the length of his spine. Mrs. Thorold had been responsible for the deaths of dozens, perhaps hundreds, of Lascar sailors in her piracy schemes. She had murdered with her own hands an elderly Chinese man and a child of ten. She had then tried to kill James in an arson attempt that failed only because the building was too damp to burn.

Felicity broke the silence. "Are you still so skeptical of my theory?"

"It remains a theory," said James. "If we accept the possibility that she has been planning this theft for some time, do you think she was instrumental in the choice of Easton Engineering?"

"Quite possibly," said Felicity. She sounded entirely unconcerned. "It carries with it a certain sense of poetic justice."

James frowned. "What evidence have you that any part of this theory is likely? What other potential thefts or crimes have you considered? Or, perhaps, where else need you search?"

"This is where my indiscretion ends," said Felicity. "I can assure you that I am diligently casting a broad net, but I shall not attempt to prove it to you. Think of the matter this way instead: If I am grasping at straws and proposing wildly unlikely schemes, you are safer than you know. The expansion of the vaults will go ahead, Mrs. Thorold will never turn up, and you'll be handsomely rewarded for a straightforward contract." She leaned forward and fixed James with a look. "But would foresight change your course of action? If you knew me to be correct, would you then decline the contract?"

"So you are merely informing me of a theoretical possibility? I appreciate your concern, Mrs. Frame, and shall certainly be alert to the potential reappearance of Mrs. Thorold. Should I recognize her, I shall report the matter to Scotland Yard immediately." James paused, gazing steadily across the desk. "Or is there something else you require of me?"

A small smile. "You are not slow, Mr. Easton. I should like you to report any sightings—whether suspected or certain—to me, as well."

It was what he'd expected to hear, and yet he was nonplussed. "Just like that?"

"Would you believe any explanation I offered?"

"Try me."

"Yours is not the only detective agency in London with an active female partner, Mr. Easton." Felicity paused. "Surprised?"

"Not nearly as surprised as I might have been before I met Miss Quinn."

She nodded. "I have been connected to the Thorold case since its inception over two years ago. It would be immensely satisfying for my organization now to bring this case to a conclusion. To that end, I should like to offer you a retainer for any services you may be able to provide."

James frowned. "You sound as though you're in competition with Scotland Yard."

"Hardly; we act as independent assistants to the Metropolitan Police. Many hands make light work, and all that."

"And you were empowered by the police to act in the first Thorold case?"

"Certainly."

"What a fascinating insight into the work of the Yard." James glanced out the window behind him, then back to Felicity. "What is your relationship to Miss Quinn?"

"That is a question you must ask Miss Quinn yourself," said Felicity. "Mysterious as that sounds, I assure you that she and I remain on good terms."

Then why have I never heard of you? wondered James. The woman's story was coherent enough, if rather farfetched. She was intelligent, confident, and charismatic, which made her seem all the more dangerous in his eyes. But there was a problem somewhere. . . . "I notice that you allowed Miss Quinn to observe you outside Newgate Prison," he said slowly, "but did not reveal yourself to her. Wouldn't that have been useful, if you are looking for many hands to lighten your work?"

"And now you come to the heart of the matter," said Felicity sweetly. "Miss Quinn is a talented observer, and her services were swiftly requested by another party connected to this case. Had I been able to meet with her quickly enough, I should have invited you both to join with my efforts. Unfortunately, I could not, and as a result am asking you alone instead."

James blinked. "How many independent agencies are working on this case, apart from the police?"

"Two."

"And you do not collaborate? Whyever not?"

"That would require a long explanation, and we do not have time. I am well aware of how curious my request may sound, Mr. Easton. But in the end, I am not asking you for much: only to continue with your usual work and to inform me if and when you encounter Mrs. Thorold."

"I dislike hasty decisions," he replied. "And in this case, I must first consult with Miss Quinn. I am not at liberty to accept your offer at this moment, even if I were so inclined."

Felicity tilted her head. "Are you and Miss Quinn so very scrupulously united on all fronts?"

He bristled at her tone. "We are equal partners in the firm."

"I take it, then, that Miss Quinn would never receive a third party into her confidence without first speaking to you?"

James narrowed his eyes. "What are you insinuating, Mrs. Frame?"

"You ought to know, Mr. Easton, if your precious partnership is so pure and sturdy." She examined the backs of her black gloves for a long second, before fixing him again with that green gaze. "I speak, of course, of Miss Quinn's sudden intimacy with the young Chinese man."

James swallowed hard.

"But you knew all about that," she said in velvety tones. "Did you not?"

James remained silent. He composed his expression

to be calm and indifferent. Judging from the gleam in Felicity's eyes, it was imperfectly so.

She rose elegantly, withdrew a calling card from her reticule, and placed it neatly on his desk. "You may contact me at this address at any time of day or night."

James stood mechanically, half a moment too late for perfect politesse.

"Good day, Mr. Easton. I look forward to hearing from you."

Thursday, 18 October

Burton Crescent, Bloomsbury

When Mary's bell rang at two minutes before eight in the morning, it was hours too early for a social call. Not that she would expect her cousin Lang to know that. Mary, at least, was still dizzied by their unexpected reunion and needed time to adjust to the news. As a result, she descended the stairs with some trepidation. When she opened the door, she blinked in mild surprise to find not Lang but Anne Treleaven on her doorstep.

Anne sat down in the drawing room, kept her hat and gloves on, and came straight to the point. "Mr. Thorold died at midnight; Angelica received word from the jail first thing this morning. She is there now. Mrs. Thorold now has no reason to enter Newgate, and you may discontinue your assignment."

Mary nodded, her thoughts leaping irresistibly to James. She couldn't wait to tell him. Surely she could do so before Saturday, in some discreet way? Two and a half days seemed an interminable wait.

But Anne was still speaking. "It remains possible that Mrs. Thorold is in town and simply didn't get to her husband in time. I have taken the precaution of having Angelica followed until her return to Vienna in case her mother decides, for some reason, to make contact. However, I am here to ask if you would accompany Angelica about town for these few days, help her with making arrangements, and generally smooth her way. She needs a friend, and you are the obvious choice."

"A friend? Or a confidante?"

A hint of a smile. "The two roles go together, do they not? Your thinking is clear, Mary: Angelica is nearly alone in the world. After an event such as this, she is likely to talk of her family and her mother, and we need more information—much more—if we are to locate Mrs. Thorold. I propose having you stay at the Academy, sharing a bedroom with Angelica. That is easy to explain: we are genuinely short of space, and the room has two beds. Any clues you are able to glean would be most gratefully received."

So she would be on duty, day and night. "Have you any idea where Mrs. Thorold might be right now?"

Anne shook her head, her lips compressed in a clear sign of frustration. "No, and that is why simply shadowing Angelica is no longer sufficient. The timing is ominous: if something is going to occur, it will be soon."

Mary thought a moment. "How is Angelica taking the news?"

"Rather well. I must say, she's grown up enormously since I last saw her."

"She would be the first to acknowledge that there was much growing up to be done."

"Quite. Now, I know I've burst in rather abruptly with this proposal, Mary, but I imagine you rather expected it. I must ask you now: Are you willing to accept this assignment, knowing that your personal risk is constantly heightened in Angelica's presence, and knowing also that the situation may bring you into direct contact with Mrs. Thorold? I need hardly advise you that it is considerably more dangerous than keeping watch from afar."

No, there was no need to tell her that. "I accept, on one condition."

Anne was visibly surprised. "What is that?"

"The moment you receive definitive information about Mrs. Thorold's location, you must inform James Easton. Directly, please. Not via Scotland Yard."

Anne nodded briskly. "Certainly. Have you any further questions at this point?"

Mary rose. "Yes, but I imagine you will answer them in the carriage. I am to come with you immediately, am I not?"

Anne smiled. "If you please. And do pack a small trunk. You'll be staying a few nights."

Ten

Mary had her doubts about the extremely convenient timing of her reappearance in Acacia Road. However, Angelica Thorold appeared to accept Mary's explanation at face value: her employers had accused her of stealing a necklace and dismissed her without a character. It was a perfectly ordinary story, the sort of thing that happened dozens of times a day, all over London.

"What will you do now?" asked Angelica sympathetically. They were sitting down over buttered rolls, cold ham, and boiled eggs: a late breakfast for Angelica, who had just returned from Newgate.

Mary shrugged. "Look for a new place, I suppose. I'm luckier than most in being able to stay here in the meantime."

"Of course," said Angelica, but there was a small frown between her eyebrows as she toyed with her food. "However, there's not a great deal to look forward to, is there? Another wealthy family, who may or may not treat you well? Who may accuse you of worse, or have unreasonable expectations? And you can't be well paid. Shall you ever be able to save enough money to support yourself, if you cannot find work for a spell? Or once you are too old to work? And what of your life? What do *you* want to do?"

Mary was divided between amusement and alarm. Was Angelica on her way to becoming a full-fledged member of the Academy, or was this merely a polite way of expressing her suspicions? "It's all very well to ask those questions," she said with quiet dignity. "You have a music scholarship in Vienna and the chance to win fame and fortune through art. You are blessed with talent, money, and education, Angelica, and I am glad of it for your sake.

"But my life will be entirely different. The life that I lead now, poor and restricted though it seems to you, is far more worth living than the one fate allotted me. I shall do my best with it, because it's what I was granted, and because I know it is more than I deserve." Mary had begun this defense as part of her role, but she meant what she said. Although the specific details were a sham, the sentiment was entirely truthful.

Angelica flushed crimson. "I beg your pardon," she said quietly. "I was thoughtless."

Mary squeezed her hand. "We are all thoughtless at times. And here I am scolding you, when I ought to ask how you are faring."

Angelica sighed. "I feel . . . insensible. Numb. Even when I saw his body this morning, I could not persuade myself that my father was truly gone. It's as though I'm waiting for somebody to confirm it." She made a helpless gesture. "Perhaps I'd believe the news if I heard it from my mother. She was often ill, and thought herself frail, but she was the real head of our household. Perhaps I can't believe that my father would do something so bold as to die without her consent."

Was this permission to ask after Mrs. Thorold? It seemed too open, too sudden an invitation. Best to let it pass and try again later, when she had a clearer idea of Angelica's frame of mind. They sat in silence for a few minutes. Then Mary asked, "Is there anything I can help you to organize, since I'm here? Goodness knows, I've time to spare."

Angelica thought for a moment. "The funeral's tomorrow."

Mary couldn't contain her surprise. "So quickly? And you've arranged everything?" Burial plots in London were rare and difficult to come by. Perhaps Mr. Thorold would be buried in a rural graveyard. It wasn't as though Angelica would be able to visit him frequently.

"Oh, heavens, it wasn't me. Miss Treleaven's been endlessly helpful; she's so extremely kind and knowledgeable, isn't she? She knew just the person to contact, and it so happened that a family had booked a funeral and then canceled it. I don't know what kind of people do that, do you? Perhaps they were only hoping the person was dead, and are now very disappointed?" Angelica gave a tiny giggle. "In any case, we got the lot—carriage, horses, casket, and six feet of ground—at a price Miss Treleaven says is a fraction of what it ordinarily costs." She giggled again. "Papa would be ever so pleased; he loved a good bargain."

Mary had heard stranger things. "It's very soon," she said, nudging their talk back on track.

"What? Oh, yes." Angelica paused, then found the thread of the conversation. "I haven't any mourning clothes. I suppose I ought to get some crape." She met Mary's eyes defiantly. "Oughtn't I?" Crape fabric was fragile and impossible to launder, and anything Angelica bought would be ruined on her journey back to Vienna. Still, it was impossible to imagine doing without it.

Mary held her gaze. "You're the mourner."

"Did you wear mourning for your parents?"

Mary swallowed. "I was a child. I made myself a black armband from a ribbon I found." "Found" on a lady's hat, that is.

"A child? Oh, Mary." Angelica's eyes welled with tears.

Mary shook her head. "Don't cry for me, please." She paused. "Pretend you're wearing crape! One good cry and it'll be ruined."

Angelica laughed and wiped her eyes. "You're impossible. And you've helped me to an utterly radical decision:

I shall wear black, but not crape." She pushed aside her half-eaten roll and drank the last of her tea. "You're a dangerous person to have about, Mary Quinn. My mother would have your head, if she knew even half of what you've inspired me to."

Mary was inclined to agree.

On the omnibus ride to Regent Street, both women remained quiet. Mary looked at Angelica's narrow face, carefully stripped of expression, and wondered what she was thinking. Was she preoccupied by thoughts of her father's last days? Was she considering how to contact her mother, or reviewing the plans they might already have in place? Angelica might even be contemplating immediate action, a reminder that Mary had always to be on her guard with Angelica, especially beyond the safety of the Academy. Or perhaps Angelica was merely consumed by the enormity of the crime she was about to commit against polite society's requirements for mourning wear.

At Jay's General Mourning Warehouse, an emporium that combined the hush of a church with the confusion of a bazaar, Angelica completed her shopping transactions: a black woolen dress, ready-made but for the hemming and a few seams in the bodice; a plain black shawl; a black bonnet, minimally trimmed; black gloves in stout leather. All to be delivered that evening, in time for tomorrow's burial. Angelica was remote, expert, price conscious, her long years of peacocking once more an advantage.

When they stumbled out of the shop just a half hour later, shivering in the chilly damp, Angelica said, "I did it. I was afraid I'd not be able to go through with it, but I did."

"*Were* you afraid? You looked fearfully resolved to me. And the sales clerk didn't even try to tempt you with extras, he was so overawed by your authority."

"He tried to argue with me on the gloves. He said they were unladylike."

"What did you tell him?"

Angelica grinned. "I told him I wasn't a lady."

They walked in silence through the hubbub of Oxford Street for a few minutes, until Mary asked, "What else have you to do? Any other duties or commissions?"

"Nothing in the world, although I rather wish I did. A spate of busyness would do me no end of good right now."

Back to London, back to the enforced idleness of the lady. And ladies always needed diversions. Diversions or cakes. "Do you need to sit down for a spell? There's a decent coffee room nearby."

Angelica made an impatient gesture. "Oh, God, not more sitting and sipping. I've had enough of that for a lifetime!"

"A good long ramble?"

"Better, but my boots won't take it. . . ." Unexpectedly, Angelica's eyes gleamed. "I've got it: the museum."

Mary suppressed a jolt of surprise. Was she reading

too much into Angelica's visit to the British Museum, that vast treasure-house of the nation? Hers could be a perfectly innocent visit, the sort that hundreds of people paid each day. Or it might be a statement of intent, a coded message that Mary didn't yet know how to interpret. After a morning in Angelica's company, she was no more confident about Angelica's real motives than she had been last week.

Angelica knew the way to Great Russell Street, a detail that Mary found noteworthy. The museum had recently been rebuilt at enormous expense, and the two women were silent as they entered the courtyard and contemplated its elegant facade. On holidays, the building swarmed with bodies: courting sweethearts, scowling pedants, packs of mewling children. Today, however, it was relatively quiet—which is to say only half full—and they made their way into the imposing entrance hall without difficulty.

"I didn't know you were fond of museums," said Mary.

"Oh, it's the only part of my character that's not hopelessly superficial," replied Angelica. "My father used to take me, as a child. I was absolutely fascinated by the natural specimens. I once frightened him terribly by disappearing. After a frantic search, he and some museum employees found me beneath a hippopotamus, contemplating its, er, underbelly."

The cloakroom attendant who took their umbrellas

gave them a disapproving look, which made them both smile. "The natural history exhibits are closed today, due to illness," he said.

"The exhibits are ill?" asked Mary with mock innocence.

Angelica couldn't quite stifle a giggle.

"Illness on the part of the museum staff," snapped the cloakroom attendant.

"Did you tell your mother about the hippo incident?" asked Mary after they'd moved away. It was slightly awkward, but the most natural way of introducing the subject of Mrs. Thorold.

"Not at the time," said Angelica. "But of course, it was too good a story to be kept forever, so my father told it once I passed the age for wandering off. I'm afraid I don't remember the event myself; only his fondness for the tale." Her eyes glinted with moisture as she uttered this last sentence, and she dabbed them fiercely with a handkerchief. "Perhaps it's just as well we can't pay homage to the hippopotami; I couldn't bear the disappointment if it turned out they weren't twelve feet tall."

This was the tone of their visit: lighthearted yet nostalgic, sentimental but disciplined. They wandered the vast halls in companionable silence. Angelica volunteered an occasional remark, but she remained, for the most part, in a contemplative mood.

Mary counseled herself to patience. While it was impossibly tempting to question Angelica on the subject of her mother, that was the fastest route to mistrustful silence. It was enough that Mary was conveniently idle and available just at the time Angelica most wanted companionship. The rest would come. She believed that. But still, the question buzzed about her mind, taunting, distracting: Would it come in time?

It might not have come at all except that they wandered, perhaps by chance, into a room crammed with artifacts from the East. There were curved swords and thick, round shields; sculpted breastplates and silver-tipped helmets; sheet-gold drinking cups and fanciful talismans. And in a glass-topped case at the center of the room lay an extraordinary amulet: a polished circle featuring the shape of a bird in flight, worked in gold and rubies and emeralds. It gleamed in the prosaic London daylight like an ember amid ashes.

Both Mary and Angelica fell silent at the sight of it. They drifted closer to the jeweled disc, gazes fixed and unblinking, until the frames of their crinolines brushed the base of the wooden case. It was a heart-stopping piece, a physical token of arrogance, power, and unimaginable wealth.

Mary swallowed hard and glanced at Angelica, whose face was creased with something that looked very much like pain. Mary's instant thought was of Mr. Thorold, imprisoned for smuggling these sorts of treasures. She bit her lip and remained silent, staring at the piece, scanning their surroundings. This was the critical moment, and they were alone in this narrow chamber.

One room over, a group of museumgoers was being condescended to by a man in a rusty-black frock coat. There was a young couple paying more attention to each other than to the exhibits. A shabby clerk with an untrimmed beard. A middle-aged bluestocking wearing pince-nez. But near them, nobody. She needed to exercise patience. Keep silent. Pray that they weren't interrupted.

After a long minute Angelica spoke, her voice scratchy. "Mary . . . do you think he did it?"

Too many thoughts clamored for voice. *Yes, of course. Who else? Do you know something that Scotland Yard doesn't?* Eventually, Mary said very quietly, "I don't know. I suppose I assumed the police had the right man." *What about the right woman? What else was there to know about Angelica's mother?*

Angelica nodded. "Everybody does." She glanced swiftly, accusingly, at Mary. "Including my mother, for why else would she live in isolation in rural France? She was born in Chelsea. She's a Londoner, through and through. She would never leave this place, even if her own life was at risk. Do you remember how she flatly refused to leave town during the Great Stink? You must remember; you were there. My father was beside himself with anxiety; he had already let a house in Kent, or wherever it was, and my mother wouldn't hear of leaving! And that was it: my father knew she couldn't be budged.

"But the day after my father's arrest, she vanished. I came back to the house—the house in Cheyne Walk, I mean—before leaving for Germany. She had disowned me—again, you were there—but I thought she had spoken in anger. I thought perhaps we could be reconciled before I left the country. But she was . . . gone. Servants dismissed. Everything abandoned. I couldn't even get in to retrieve my things.

"I thought about breaking a window. After all, it was my house. But there was a constable on the corner watching me—I suppose my behavior did look suspicious—and I didn't want to explain anything. . . . Anyway. It's all in the past. But all this to say, even my mother must believe in his guilt. If she thought him innocent, she would stay here and damn the social consequences."

Mary nodded. This was the most obvious interpretation if one knew nothing about Mrs. Thorold's piracy. Yet it seemed incredible that Angelica should be ignorant of the fact that there was an arrest warrant out for her mother. "Did she . . . did Scotland Yard never contact you?"

Angelica shrugged. "They interviewed me before I went to Germany. But how I could have known the first thing about my father's business? The firm was Thorold and Son, not Thorold and Daughter. I was too busy being polished and finished and finding a suitable husband." There was no mistaking the bitterness in her tone. Yet . . .

"What about your mother? Did the police mention that she might be involved?"

Angelica snorted. "I told them what I thought of that asinine theory. My mother was far too fragile, not to mention too self-absorbed, to assist my father in his business. And why would she work against him? She had a comfortable life, a large house, and nothing to do each day except ride out in the carriage and consult her physicians. Undermining the company would have destroyed her own comfort and security. Only a fool would consider it."

A fool or an embittered, hate-warped criminal, thought Mary. "And they believed you?"

"They had to. I was the person best placed to know, and by then, Mama had already vanished."

"Some would call that suspicious behavior on her part. Why not stay and prove one's innocence?"

"Questions like that are why you'll never truly be a lady," muttered Angelica, although she didn't seem to intend it as an insult. "My mother was far too well-bred to submit to questions from the police." She uttered the word "police" in much the same tone she might have used for "vermin."

"But leaving the country so precipitously . . . Doesn't that look like an admission of guilt?" persisted Mary.

Angelica flushed and paused. "It would be, if she were accused of anything that was actually within her powers. But the charges against her are so outrageous, so absolutely, utterly fantastic, that I can scarcely believe they've been made. They seem more like a monster of my imagination than anything in real life."

Mary was quiet. Denial was endlessly powerful, and there was no point in antagonizing Angelica further. After a minute, she asked, "Do you think she might come back once the scandal is forgotten and the charges dropped? It's been more than two years. . . ."

Angelica sighed. "She might. Truly, I had hoped she might come back before Papa died. You know, to see him one last time. Impossible, of course."

Mary watched her face for a moment before asking, "Do you *want* to see her?"

A fast-moving cloud of misery scudded across Angelica's expression. "Yes and no." She paused and traced a pattern in the dust of the glass jewel case. "I still have nightmares about the last time I saw her, you know. The shouting, the recriminations, that vicious look in her eyes . . ." After a few moments, she sighed and said, "Nevertheless, something changes when one is nearly alone in the world. With my father gone, I've begun to long for my mother in a way I never did when they were both alive. There's something about her being my last remaining relation. . . . I don't know if you'll understand the feeling, being an orphan."

Mary's mouth was dry but she managed to whisper, "I can imagine."

Angelica glanced at her skeptically. "Can you indeed? I won't say it's worse than being an orphan, but at the moment, she's more of a phantom than a relation."

Mary drew a deep breath. "I don't suppose you're in contact with her at all?"

Angelica made an equivocal gesture. "Occasionally I write to her at a poste restante address in rural France. It's very unreliable, the foreign post, and unbelievably sluggish. But we have managed to exchange letters, now and again."

The tingling sensation in Mary's body was almost unbearable. A link! An undeniable, traceable connection between mother and daughter! She managed to say in a tolerably normal voice, "Did she know you were coming to London? Because of your father's illness?"

Angelica shook her head. "I wrote to her, of course, to let her know, but I didn't stay to receive a reply." She sighed. "That's the most frustrating part: she hadn't any close friends or family, and all the others must be as dead to her as my so-called friends are to me now. Even if she were here now, in town, we'd never find each other unless we actually collided in the street."

Mary thought about that. There was no reason for Angelica to tell her all this. If she were secretly in cahoots with her mother's criminal activities, it would be much simpler and safer for her to deny everything: no contact whatsoever since that fateful spring of 1858. "What about an advertisement in the newspaper? Didn't she read the *Times*? You can get that abroad. . . ."

"What a memory you have, Mary Quinn. She did."

Angelica straightened, as though braced by the idea of action. "I suppose if I advertised and received an immediate reply, I could delay my departure by a day or two. Or if she's still in France, I could detour to see her on my journey back to Vienna. Yes. It's only a very remote chance, but I shall place an advertisement in tomorrow's paper. I daresay your excellent Miss Treleaven would give me permission to use the Academy's address."

Mary controlled the dangerous impulse to smile. The image of Mrs. Thorold walking boldly into the lion's den was tempting indeed. "I daresay."

Angelica drooped suddenly, remembering. "Is it worthwhile, do you think? It's more of a fool's errand than anything else."

"I suppose it depends. Might it help soothe this yearning to see her? To know that you've done everything possible to contact her?"

Angelica rubbed her temples. "If nothing else, it might allow me to sleep. I can't take many more of these broken nights." The two women turned away from the jewelry display and began to retrace their steps through the museum, past the pompous guide, who was just leading his group toward the amulet.

"Three more days in town," mused Angelica. "I suppose a great deal could happen in the next three days."

To Mary's ears, her words sounded like nothing less than a prophecy.

Eleven

As they emerged from the museum, Angelica declared her intention of returning to the Academy for a nap; she had scarcely slept for more than a fortnight. She insisted that she would go alone and asked Mary, instead of accompanying her, to deliver the text of her advertisement to the offices of the *Times*. Mary hesitated. She had a strong sense of being manipulated. Was this simply part of a larger plan for Angelica and her mother to meet up privately? Yet Angelica was insistent; good manners and the need for discretion meant that Mary could only agree. She consoled herself with the knowledge that Angelica was still being shadowed by another member of the Agency, and left her on the front steps of the museum without a backward glance.

The *Times* office was located in Blackfriars, not the sort of area that Angelica would have been brought up to know, but familiar enough to Mary. She chose to walk.

It was a distance of only about two miles, and the after-noon promised to be relatively dry.

Printing House Yard was unsigned, and Mary found it only by threading her way in and out of each narrow street and unpromising alley in the area. She had expected to nav-igate by the roar and rattle of a printing press, the dashing of reporters and errand boys, and a steady stream of insid-ers feeding precious information to the paper's editors. Instead, she eventually stumbled into a sleepy-looking courtyard with a couple of scruffy, ailing trees behind a high iron fence and a sign that read, simply, THE TIMES.

Once inside, she understood the reason for the quiet: this was the lull in the news cycle, the one period dur-ing which the building was permitted to drowse. In a few hours, the Yard would teem with journalists, editors would arrive to bring shape and order to information, and the small, ink-stained boys known as printer's dev-ils would gamble their lungs and their fingers to ensure that the printing presses kept turning. The roar of the presses would rattle the gates until four or five in the morning.

Now, however, she edged past a shriveled-looking man peeling an equally shriveled orange, who directed her toward the Advertisements Office with a lackadaisical tilt of the head. This office stood separate from the main building. Even before Mary opened the door, she heard the hum and clatter of activity within.

The room was populated by men for whom tidiness,

let alone fashion, had never been a concern: faded, ill-fitting frock coats, torn and ink-stained shirtsleeves, and squashed, greasy hats were the order of the day here. They hunched over desks, clustered around tables, lounged dangerously in open windows. The room was lit with a bizarre combination of candles, gaslight, and oil lamps, each light source adding its own characteristic odor to the overwhelming smell of stale sweat, old cooking, anxiety, and, curiously, wet dog, that filled the room with a near-visible fug.

Mary entered, presented herself at the desk nearest the door, and coughed discreetly. The desk's occupant, a freckle-faced young man with extremely grubby shirt cuffs, blinked up at her, blushed, and leaped up, promptly knocking over his chair. "Beg your pardon, miss," he said, scrabbling to right the furniture. "Er, are you here to see somebody?"

"The clerk in charge of personal advertisements, if you please."

"Right you are. You want Jimmy Hobbs, I reckon. Just a moment, miss." He turned his head thirty degrees and bellowed in a honking sort of tenor, "Hobbs!" When no answer came, he tried again. "Hobbs, I say!"

"What?" came the eventual, surly reply.

"Customer!"

At length, Jimmy Hobbs deigned to appear, scowling at Mary through a pair of spectacles cloudy with finger-prints. "What's your business, miss?"

149

Mary unfolded Angelica's carefully worded note. "I'd like to place this advertisement in tomorrow's paper, if you please."

Jimmy Hobbs squinted at the copperplate script, pretending that it was difficult to decipher. "To Mrs. H. M. T., late of Cheyne Walk, Chelsea, now resident in France. A member of your family dearly wishes to see you and requests your confidential reply to Miss Scrimshaw's Academy for Girls, Acacia Road, St. John's Wood, London." His gaze flicked up to Mary. "Just one day? Chances of her seeing it are slim to none, miss."

"The next three days, then."

He remained dissatisfied. "An ad like that, you ought to run it for a week, at least. Supposing she's poorly for a few days and doesn't get the paper for a spell? Wasted money, that. And there's a saving of ten percent if it runs over a week."

"Three days, please," repeated Mary.

Jimmy Hobbs sighed at the stupidity of the world and said, "Right. That's thirty-five words at ha'penny a word, for three days, makes four shillings, fourpence ha'penny, if you please. Cash only."

A few moments later, Mary was out the door with a lighter purse and a head full of unanswered questions. Ought she to have continued to advertise on Angelica's behalf? Any contact from Mrs. Thorold might be useful, even if Angelica was safely back in Vienna by the time she replied. Or was this a fool's errand, with Mrs. Thorold either unreachable in rural France or too clever to respond to such a transparent ruse? The geographic scope of this assignment was quite new to Mary, and she wondered if she would have cause to travel abroad as part of her search. And if requested to do so by the Agency, how might she respond?

Her thoughts reverted immediately to James. This was the fifth day of their self-imposed separation; the first time since their engagement and the founding of Quinn and Easton that they had been out of contact for more than a day or so. Despite her hectic days and sound-asleep nights, James's absence was more profound than even she had anticipated. She was continually addressing mental remarks to him, inventing sly quips for his plea-sure, and eagerly consulting his opinion — only to remem-ber that not only was he absent, but he would continue to be for some time. Life without James was flatter, duller, oddly hollow. It was a realization that alarmed her: How had she grown so dependent upon a single person? Her only consolation was that she, with all her flaws, seemed equally necessary to his happiness. So this was modern love. Or another of its iterations, at least.

She awoke from her reverie to find herself striding southward down the Commercial Road. Thoughts of Mrs. Thorold must have directed her, in an unconscious way, toward the river. Thanks to the wintry chill, she couldn't smell it from here. She could, however, hear its constant life: the horns and bells of ships and barges; the clamor of voices calling orders, immediately augmented by others protesting, countermanding, and grumbling about the same. Instead of going directly down to the docks, however, Mary turned her steps toward one of the small side streets off Butcher Row. Lang had given her his address, and now that she was relatively near, she could not deny herself the satisfaction of passing by his lodgings. She had no expectation that he would be at home. She merely wanted a little more detail with which to furnish her mental image of her cousin.

The road was narrow and crammed with ramshackle buildings in the way of east London streets, and populated by a diverse mixture of steadily moving men, women, children, beasts of burden, and languid beggars. What set it apart from other streets in the vicinity was the sudden preponderance of Chinese faces. This was not unusual, especially in Limehouse, but its reality startled Mary nonetheless. Her London, these days, was almost entirely Caucasian, and it was always a jolt to arrive in a place where the people looked like the other half of her.

Toward the middle of the street, she saw a thick knot of dark-haired children intent upon some spectacle. Mary drifted closer and was not entirely surprised to see a slim young man walking upon his hands, much to the urchins' delight. "Like so," he said without a hint of breathlessness. "Careful, slow, balance. You must control the movement." With the precision of a lever, his legs folded downward and his boots touched the muddy road. "If you rush, you will fall." He straightened up and grinned at his young audience, and then at Mary, standing a few yards behind them. "Now you practice," he said to the children, and came toward her. "Cousin," he said, with another gleaming smile. "It is good to see you."

Mary beamed back. "I didn't know you were an acrobat as well."

Lang brushed off his hands, and Mary noticed for the first time the wooden blocks he had been holding to keep his hands from being caked in mud. "I do not perform for money."

"Only for children?"

"It keeps them from trouble. And it is good to learn care and control with the body."

Mary gave him a questioning look.

"Control the body, control the mind."

She'd never thought of it in quite that way.

"Where are you going?"

"Nowhere in particular. For now, at least."

"May I come with you?"

"Yes. I'd like that."

Neither of them were dawdlers, and they set off at a pleasant clip westward along Cable Street. This was a deliberate choice for Mary, who wanted to steer him away from George Villas, the site of the newly rebuilt Lascars' Refuge. One day, she would show Lang the place where her father had come to deposit his secrets for safekeeping before his journey back to Fujian province. The manager of the home, a frail and dignified Chinese man named Chen, had diligently preserved the cigar box of secrets for more than a decade—in fact, until just two years ago, when Mrs. Thorold had murdered him and attempted to burn down the home. Mary had been a day too late to reclaim her father's cigar box from the wreckage, and she still tasted bitterness when she thought of its loss.

"Did you live in this area as a child?" asked Lang.

Mary nodded. "The Chinese in London tend to stay together. As you did," she added. It was only logical: in a foreign and hostile country, the bonds of language and experience took the place of family.

"Then you left."

Mary wondered how much of her history to offer. Her instinct was always to remain silent on the subject, but Lang deserved at least the outline. "Not long after my father disappeared, my mother died. I was still a child. I lived on the street, stealing food, picking pockets. I later turned to housebreaking." She paused, still unwilling, or perhaps unable, to reveal the agony of prison, her criminal trial, the sentence of death that now seemed like a particularly grotesque nightmare. "Sometime after that, I was taken to a boarding school in northwest London. St. John's Wood. The women who run it took me in and educated me."

"You were extremely fortunate."

"Yes."

It was clear that Lang wished to ask more. Instead,

after a short pause, he said, "Do you still know the house where you lived with your father and mother?"

Of course she did. She'd gone back to it for months after her mother's death, standing quietly on the street corner, imagining herself coming home after a day's play or school. Her mother would be in the garden, her quick needle flashing through silk, or perhaps weeding the vegetable bed. Her father, newly returned from a sea voyage, would be waiting to tell her a story, another installment in the adventures of a gang of wandering Chinese demigods. Mary caught Lang's eye and managed to speak around the lump in her throat. "This way," she said. They reversed their steps, walking eastward again, deeper into Limehouse. It was perhaps a quarter hour's walk, and they made the strange pilgrimage in silence.

They picked their way through twisting streets that squeezed ever narrower, their boots squelching deep in a claggy mire no crossing sweeper had ever attempted to clear. The tang of the river was pungent, its noises sharp. Mary wondered if this was at all wise. She'd not been back since she lived at the Academy. Her dramatic rescue and strange rebirth had opened such a different world to her. She'd had difficulty imagining that the old one still stood.

But they rounded yet another corner and there it was, shrunken and shabbier than she had remembered. The houses huddled close together, heads bowed, shoulders hunched. The whole street seemed tinged with grief, although it was impossible to think that the Lang family's specific disaster mattered more than others. Perhaps it was only the daily tragedy of poverty without hope that Mary saw today. "It was the third house from the left," she said. The small plot of garden at the front was overgrown and strewn with rubbish; the window was boarded up.

Lang was still and silent for a minute, and then he nodded to Mary. "Thank you."

She wondered just what he had seen.

Mary and Lang walked in silence for some time. She wondered if Lang might prefer to be elsewhere, but decided that such anxiety was needless: if he wanted to leave her company, he would. Their journey took them westward again. They wound through east London until, quite suddenly, mud and slime became cobblestones and squat wooden tenements gave way to large stone buildings. They were in the City.

Lang's usual expression was of calm indifference, but now he appeared guarded. He kept his chin tilted down. He hunched slightly, compressing his frame. His gaze flicked about rapidly, as though suspicious of every person whose path they crossed. It was true that they drew an unusual amount of attention, but at least part of that was due to their sartorial contrast: Lang was again dressed like a laborer, in fustian, while she wore the garb of a shabby-genteel lady.

Mary glanced at him sideways. "Would you rather walk elsewhere?"

He shook his head. "I am still unused to seeing so many *gweilo*."

Mary smiled. "You're walking with a half-*gweilo*."

"*Gweimei*," he corrected automatically. "The term for a young woman. And still, I do not understand how you can live among them. Do you not miss your people?"

Mary's mouth twisted. "I'm neither Chinese nor Irish. Certainly not English. In any case, I don't have a people."

He thought about that. "The Chinese, as a whole, disapprove of racial mixture. Are the English so different?"

"No," said Mary. "They have that in common with the Chinese."

"Then I understand your bitterness."

"There is no need to pity me. My parents were remarkable people. They must have been, because they saw beyond racial prejudice and loved each other. I am evidence of that."

Lang accepted the reproof with a small nod.

"And perhaps if you spent more time among the English, you might grow accustomed to their faces. They are, after all, no better and no worse than the Chinese."

"They seem to be very often drunken and violent."

"And how else do you earn your living?"

A faint smile hovered on Lang's lips. "True. And that

brings me to a question I have been meaning to ask you, Cousin. Are you willing to come and see me fight again, this Saturday night?"

"Certainly. But why?"

"Have you noticed that whatever the question, the answer is usually 'money'?" he asked. "I have a manager whose tasks are to book a boxing ring, to negotiate my payment, to advertise the matches, and to ensure that I am paid what is owed. I suspect that he is cheating me: maybe on purpose, or maybe because he is neglectful and lazy. I need to know if this is true."

"And how could I confirm all those things?"

"I would ask you to start by counting the number of men who come to see the match. I am paid according to their numbers, so that is one simple way to judge if my manager is being honest."

That was interesting; Mary hadn't realized that prize-fighters also received a share of the admission charge. "Do you also set the door fee?"

"No; the pub decides how much to charge and pays me a portion."

"So you want to compare my head count with your manager's."

"Yes. To start with."

It was a small, simple favor. He was the only cousin she'd ever known. How could she possibly refuse? "I am happy to help you as best I can," she said. "But, Cousin, my time is not my own right now. If I am able to come on

Saturday, I will certainly be there. If I am not, it is because I have already made a promise to somebody else that cannot be delayed or neglected. I will do everything I can to help at your next match, in that case."

Lang nodded. "Thank you. That is good of you."

"We ought to meet before the match so you can point out your manager to me. I will also watch him discreetly to see if he does anything unusual."

Lang held her gaze for a moment, intrigued. "You sound confident and experienced at this sort of thing."

"I am."

"Very well, then. Let us meet at seven o'clock at Leicester Square."

"If I am not there by ten minutes past the hour, it is because I have been detained by this prior commitment, in which case you must not expect me at all that night."

Lang nodded, and they walked on. After a few minutes' silence, he pointed to an imposing building, balanced on Grecian columns and adorned with frescoes: a proud island in a sea of chaotic traffic. "Is that a church, or perhaps a palace?"

Mary smiled. "A little of both. It is the Royal Exchange, a center for trade and commerce." They stopped by unspoken consent, the better to admire the secular cathedral. It was most impressive: the sort of architecture that demanded confidence in its institution—or perhaps hoped to inspire the sort of unquestioning awe its occupants desired of the world. They watched streams of top-hatted gentlemen flow in and out of the building, alone or in pairs. Mary wondered what sorts of schemes and ventures were being nurtured in their private thoughts, their confidential conversations. And she could not help but ask herself who might gain and who would suffer from the consequences thereof.

She was deep in her dark musings when another pair caught her notice, at the very corner of her eye. They emerged from the building behind them, a wide mass of stone that turned blind eyes to the city: the Bank of England, she realized, an institution that had no need to advertise its presence. Against that bland facade, her attention was snagged because one of the couple was a woman. Or rather, a lady. The gentleman was in his sixties, bearded and top-hatted, a perfect banker in his dull black wool. The lady's age was more difficult to judge. She wore a deep bonnet, its brim tilted down against the wind, but the set of her mouth and jawline suggested middle age. Sober black silks, upright bearing, a confident step. They were an unremarkable pair, and yet Mary's attention was arrested.

She watched as the gentleman handed his companion up the steps of a waiting hackney cab. A moment before the driver closed the carriage door, the lady glanced up and addressed a final sentence to the banker. For just a fraction of a moment, her face was visible, and what Mary saw made her catch her breath. The gentleman bowed and remained on the curb, watching the four-wheeler pull aggressively into the main stream of traffic. Swerving and hollering greeted this sharp maneuver, but a moment later the carriage was away, flowing with the steady westward current of the other vehicles.

In that ever-shifting landscape, the only perfectly still figure was of Mary herself, gaping slightly after the cab—or, rather, where it had been. A moment later, she came unfrozen. "I must go," she said to Lang, already suiting movement to words. There was an insupportable delay in dodging through traffic to the other side of the road so that she could follow the cab.

Lang had watched Mary's transformation with keen interest. "Shall I come with you?" She was already walking, and he with her. The question seemed purely a courtesy.

"You can't," she said, and it was true. A Chinese man made far too memorable a shadow. But there was no need for apology between them. They were close enough to each other's true selves now, the prizefighter and the spy, the foreigner and the misfit.

"I'll go, then," said Lang, turning his steps. He sounded entirely agreeable. "Until Saturday."

"Until then."

In the treacly, late-afternoon flow of traffic, it was easy to keep the hackney in sight. It sat high in the snarl of vehicles; there was no possibility of its slipping rapidly away down a side street. Mary's main concern was to remain unnoticed, and this too was straightforward enough as a pedestrian clad in dark colors. She tacked back and forth in a leisurely fashion, lengthened and shortened the distance between herself and the cab, all without losing sight of the vehicle. It was a slow walk by her usual standards, but about an hour later they drew up to the curb of a building that made her bite her lip: the British Museum.

Mary thought instantly of Angelica and their visit earlier in the day. Angelica had suggested it; had even led her there with a sense of confidence. How could such a return be explained by mere coincidence? Yet if it had been by design, what was Angelica's intention? Was it an obscure warning of some kind? Or a teasing, arrogant sort of provocation? Nothing made sense.

Mary waited, pulse racing, skin prickling, as the cabman climbed down from his bench. She had been so certain, for the last hour. Had even permitted herself a small taste of triumph at having successfully spotted Mrs. Thorold in all the chancy hurly-burly of London. As the cabman stretched stiff joints and prepared to unfold the steps, Mary had a moment of anxiety: Suppose it wasn't her at all? It might well be another lady of middle years, intending to poke around the museum for half an hour before going home to family, dinner, and conventional obscurity.

No, she told herself. The sighting had been fleeting but definite. A certain gait, a particular angle of the chin:

those were the infinitesimal details that set one hooped-and-draped lady apart from another. Mary knew, in her bones, that the lady in the cab was Maria Thorold. All the same, she held her breath as the cabman opened the door.

A moment.

Then another, and yet a third.

The cabman looked impatient and called something up the steps. After another pause, he climbed up partway, forehead creased, one arm extended in an offer of assistance. As he vanished into the carriage, Mary felt an entirely different sense of certainty: a sickening one that began in the pit of her stomach and made her glance nervously at the faces of those around her. As if that would help.

She waited with queasy conviction until the cabman reappeared on the steps. His expression—perplexity, outrage, suspicion—was all the confirmation she required. It had indeed been Mrs. Thorold in the hackney. And despite Mary's supposedly careful surveillance, she had somehow vanished from a closed carriage in broad daylight.

Mrs. Thorold was back.

Twelve

O ne of the few things that seemed clear to Mary was what to do next. After waiting for the hackney to set off, the driver still scowling and muttering about his lost fare, she turned toward St. John's Wood. It was near the supper hour by the time she arrived, and for once she was glad for the delay in her report to Anne. She changed her mud-spattered dress, washed her face and hands, and joined the school body for the simple meal: a thick vegetable soup, bread and butter, and a wedge of aged cheddar, intensely salty with its undertone of sweet cream. It was good medicine for the frustration and anxiety that dogged her, and she noticed its similar restorative effect upon Angelica's thin, tired face at the far end of the long teachers' table. By the time Mary knocked on Anne's study door, she was able to present a composed report on her day's observations.

Anne, as was her habit, listened in perfect silence.

When Mary had concluded, Anne rose, stirred the fire, and balanced two fresh logs atop the bright embers. "If I understand you correctly," she said, "there are four main points of attention here. The first is that Angelica has, in fact, been in contact with Mrs. Thorold at various points over the past two years. We have only Angelica's description of the tenor of their relationship, but it is worth considering the possibility that they are working in partnership, and may have been for some time.

"The second point is Angelica's interest in the British Museum. Was her decision to take you to the museum purely sentimental? Childhood memories of her father and all that? Or had she an ulterior motive in drawing your attention toward it? If she is indeed working in tandem with her mother, her intention would be to divert attention from their planned crime. While we must continue to consider all possibilities, I think it is reasonable to presume either that her visit to the museum was coincidental or else a deliberate attempt to lead us astray. The destination of this afternoon's hackney carriage intensifies that likelihood.

"The third matter is your definitive—that is not too strong a word?—identification of Mrs. Thorold, however brief. It would be much better to know her approximate location, of course, but you did your best." Mary flinched inwardly at this implied criticism but managed to maintain her external composure. "We must now proceed with the knowledge that she is in town, and active. I hope the police will increase their efforts to locate her as a result of your identification.

"We now come to the fourth point: the Bank of England and Mrs. Thorold's presence there. Are you inclined to consider it another attempt to confuse and distract?"

Mary shook her head. "If I had followed her into the City, then certainly. But I noticed Mrs. Thorold entirely by coincidence, and she was in the company of a gentleman who returned to the Bank after seeing her off. It should be relatively straightforward to confirm his identity, if he works at the Bank. He's in his sixties, with a distinctive mole at the end of his nose."

Anne nodded. "I'll inquire. If he is indeed an employee of the Bank, you have identified Mrs. Thorold's most plausible target."

Mary suppressed a small surge of pride. This was all highly conditional, and might come to naught.

"At this point, Mary, have you any proposals as to your next course of action?"

This was an entirely new question from Anne, and one Mary didn't know quite how to answer. Nevertheless, Anne was looking at her expectantly, so she drew a deep breath. "Much hangs upon the identification of Mrs. Thorold's gentleman companion," she said. "Until that is accomplished, I think I ought to stay near Angelica. She told me of her father's funeral tomorrow. It was not quite an invitation, but I'll try to turn it into one. It's not impossible that Mrs. Thorold might be present there, in some way."

Anne nodded. "Entirely reasonable. If Angelica prefers to be alone, let her go. It will build her trust in you, and I'll ensure that she's shadowed by someone she won't recognize." There was a brief hesitation, then Anne asked, "Mary, when were you last in contact with James Easton?"

Mary started at the mention of his name, then promptly blushed at her utter transparency on this subject. "This past Saturday," she said after a second, with only a slight tremor in her voice. "Five days ago. Why? What do you know?"

Anne looked embarrassed. At least, thought Mary, she didn't look tragic or solicitous—sure portents of truly bad news. "Perhaps the most regrettable consequence of Felicity Frame's departure from the Agency is the rivalry between our firm and her new . . . establishment," Anne said. As she spoke, a faint tide of pink rose from her throat to cheeks to ears. "We find it necessary to track Mrs. Frame's activities, as she does ours. She would have been fully aware of my request to you nearly a week ago."

Mary found herself spellbound, both by Anne's admission and her evident emotional state. *This*, from the most disciplined and formal woman she knew! "You *expected* Mrs. Frame to be watching me outside Newgate?"

Anne didn't quite meet her gaze. "I identified her for you, from inside the carriage."

"But you implied that it was coincidental!"

"I thought long about the omission, but decided you didn't need the additional distraction."

"It distracted me, anyway. I spent unnecessary time and energy watching the widow outside Newgate! Had I known Mrs. Frame might be present, that would have helped me to recognize her."

Anne nodded, her eyes closed in pained apology. "It was an error on my part. One I shall not repeat."

Mary disciplined her anger. "We were talking about Mr. Easton."

"Yes." Anne, too, drew on her deep reserves of sangfroid. "Yesterday, Mrs. Frame paid a visit to Easton Engineering. Clearly, we were not privy to her conversation with Mr. Easton, but it is quite likely that she attempted to recruit him to her cause."

Felicity's "cause:" Anne made it sound underhanded and reprehensible. Yet what had Felicity done, really, apart from welcome men to her new firm? It was no different from Quinn and Easton, only on a larger scale—except, of course, that Felicity's departure had sundered the Agency as all knew it. It had also destroyed the profound intimacy that existed between Felicity and Anne, a bond that Mary had never before thought to question. She wondered which Anne regretted more.

Mary spoke quietly into the loud silence and with more assurance than she felt. "You need not worry about my arrangement with Mr. Easton. We have an understanding, and we will not permit other rivalries or distractions to undermine that. If Mrs. Frame asked for Mr. Easton's help in locating Mrs. Thorold, my only concern is for his continued safety. I believe, otherwise, that he will act with his usual intelligence and discretion." She paused. "In fact, if we still believe that the Bank of England is Mrs. Thorold's target, then Mr. Easton, as an engineer, could offer insight as to how such an audacious robbery might be possible."

Yes. That was entirely logical. Her confidence rose slightly, although not so high as her firm tone suggested. She couldn't abandon the subject, however, without some reassurance. "So far as you know, Mr. Easton is safe? There have been no threats or approaches?"

"He seems to be conducting business as usual."

"Thank you." Earlier, Mary had wondered whether to mention her two appointments on Saturday: with James at Mudie's, and with Lang in Leicester Square. Now, in light of Anne's excessive secrecy, Mary decided that she, too, was entitled to some privacy.

"Mary, I understand your anxiety for Mr. Easton's well-being," said Anne with perceptible hesitation. "Would it ease your mind if we were also to monitor his movements? We should be able to inform you of any irregularities or incidents in his day."

Mary's first impulse was to accept, wholeheartedly and with profound gratitude. As she considered, however, she shrank from the idea. It wasn't purely the trampling of James's privacy that she disliked, or the prospect of Anne knowing every detail of his life. It was the presumption that more knowledge on her part would keep James safe. It was the arrogance of attempting to play God in the life of a man she loved and respected. Perhaps, at core, it was the outrage she would feel at the prospect of his doing the same to her.

She raised her head and said, "Thank you, Miss Treleaven, but no. My duty now is to remain focused upon my assignment, and I trust Mr. Easton to do the same."

And on Saturday they would meet.

Friday, 19 October

Miss Scrimshaw's Academy for Girls
Acacia Road, St. John's Wood

Where is Mrs. Thorold?

Mary lay in her bed early on Friday morning, the words swelling within her until they seemed to press against her skin. She was gritty-eyed, jittery, frustrated: the fraying threads of her investigation, her anxiety on James's behalf, her frustration with Anne's needless secrecy, combined with Angelica's desire to talk late into the night, had made for a short and fractured rest. All the same, it was time to rise. It was the morning of Henry Thorold's secondhand funeral.

Mary sat up and glanced at the narrow bed on which Angelica lay perfectly still, eyes open and unblinking. It was an evocative pose—her hands were clasped across her chest, corpse-like—and Mary froze, reluctant to interrupt her meditations.

"It's all right," said Angelica in a remarkably normal voice. "I'm not going to have hysterics." She continued to study the ceiling—or perhaps her attention was focused on something well above the rooftops.

Mary slid her feet into slippers and huddled into her dressing gown. Bedrooms at the Academy were always cold; only the main rooms had their own fireplaces. "I doubt you've ever had hysterics. Unless, perhaps, it was strategically useful?"

That raised a smile. "You're rather uncanny, Mary Quinn. I shall neither confirm nor deny that." A pause. Then, "I was just thinking about today. I think . . . I know you've offered to accompany me, and I'm grateful—but I think I'd prefer to go by myself."

Mary watched her for a moment. "So long as you're certain."

Angelica nodded and swung her legs out of the bed, pushing her long braid over her shoulder. "I think all that bosh about women being too delicate to attend funerals doesn't really apply in this case. If I'm strong enough to visit my father in jail, I'm certainly capable of burying him."

Mary nodded. "You're much braver than anybody could reasonably expect."

"I don't feel brave. Or reasonable."

"I imagine you feel numb."

Angelica's head snapped up, her eyes wide. "Yes. How did you guess?"

"Numbness is useful. It gets one through difficult times."

"What sort of hard times have you been through, Mary?" Angelica sat up straight. "As an orphan, I expect you're speaking with good authority."

Mary paused. She was unwilling to share much of her own story with Angelica; to reveal just how much she had in common with the former débutante, despite first appearances. "Oh, the usual," she said, filling the basin with a small amount of water from the jug. "I was a perfect Oliver Twist." She washed her face briskly and came up gasping. "Lordy, that water's cold."

Angelica looked at her for a long moment, and Mary could almost see the questions brimming on her lips. In the end, all she said was, "Well, Oliver, we'd best get dressed if we're to have any porridge."

After a communal breakfast, Mary helped Angelica to dress for the funeral. This was hardly necessary: Angelica's new wardrobe was as spare and practical as Mary's own, obviating the need for a lady's maid. But the newly delivered mourning clothes still lay in their box, swathed in sheets of crisp tissue paper, and Angelica was loath to unpack them. The assumption of mourning dress was a confirmation of the fact, a public declaration of private grief.

Once dressed, Angelica surveyed herself solemnly in

the long mirror: a very pale, oval face nearly overwhelmed by layers of black. She opened her lips once or twice, then shut them again. Eventually, she said, "It's time I went."

They walked down to the front door in silence, passing a small cluster of pupils in the corridor, who scattered at the sight of Angelica. A hansom idled at the curb, steps already folded down. Anne Treleaven had organized this yesterday.

As she mounted the last step up to the cab, Angelica turned to Mary. "This doesn't feel possible," she said in a thick voice. "I keep thinking I'll wake in my own bed and discover this was all a dream. My old bed, I mean, in Cheyne Walk."

"Are you quite certain you'd prefer to go alone?" asked Mary.

The cabman's horse stamped and jibbed impatiently, and Angelica hastily sat down. "Yes. That is, I think it's what Papa would prefer."

The cabbie looked from Angelica to Mary. "All right, then, miss?" At her nod, he slammed the door and climbed stiffly into the driver's seat. Mary's last sight of Angelica was hindered by the black veil, but there was no mistaking the hunched shoulders and bowed head.

Angelica Thorold was weeping.

Thirteen

Early afternoon, the same day

Miss Scrimshaw's Academy for Girls
Acacia Road, St. John's Wood

At precisely one o'clock, all pupils and teachers at the Academy filed into the dining room. They seated themselves, noses twitching at the tantalizing aroma of fish pie. As the girls ate, gossiped, teased each other, argued about their morning's lessons, and anticipated the afternoon's, one chair at Mary's table remained conspicuously empty.

It was to be expected, Mary told herself. The funeral would have been deeply distressing. Angelica would need time to be alone afterward. It was quite likely, in fact, that she was already back in their shared bedroom, unable to face the cheerful dinnertime throng. Despite these exceedingly reasonable justifications, however, Mary was uneasy. And after the grace was said and the girls dispatched to Regent's Park for fresh air and exercise, Mary discovered that Angelica was nowhere to be found. Not in their bedroom, not in the school's small but surprisingly private garden, not at the nearby park.

By the time the girls' light supper was served at six o'clock, there was still no genuine cause for panic. Darkness was falling, true. But Angelica was a grown woman, intelligent and well-traveled. A few hours' delay in her return was still within reason, especially given today's emotional freight. All the same, when Mary heard a hesitant knock at the front door, she dashed to answer it and swung the door open wide. She stifled a scream.

It was a cabman, a broad, middle-aged fellow with an anxious face, cradling in his arms the too-still body of a woman. "This here Miss Scrimshaw's?" he asked, tripping slightly over the name.

"Yes. Come in, please." Mary ushered him into the drawing room, lit the lamps, spread a blanket on the longest sofa, and asked him to settle the woman upon it. She commanded the startled girl who answered the drawing-room bell to fetch Anne Treleaven, a doctor, a basin of fresh water, and as many clean towels as possible; also vinegar, honey, and smelling salts.

It had been dark in the room when they'd first entered. Now Mary turned to the sofa and saw, with a jolt, that it was not Angelica Thorold after all. The woman was lying on her side, facing the sofa cushions. Graying chestnut hair spilled from her battered bonnet. She had a handle sticking out of her back, between the shoulder blades.

The sight was so peculiar that Mary bypassed nausea and panic and arrived directly at numb efficiency. She placed the back of her hand against the woman's cool cheek—it was cold out, she reminded herself fiercely—and thought she felt a whisper of breath escape her mouth. "It's all right," Mary said softly, quite certain she was lying. "You're safe now. You're at the Academy." She peered at the knife handle. It protruded a good four inches from the woman's back, just to the right of her spine. Mary knew better than to try to pull it out, but what did one do with stab wounds, precisely?

"Thank you for bringing her," she said to the cabman as she waited for clean water and dressings to arrive. Unless Mary was grievously mistaken, this woman was the agent who had been trailing Angelica Thorold today. "What—what happened?"

The cabman looked sick and confused. "Damned if I know," he said. "Pardon my language, miss, but it ain't every day I finds a dying woman in the street. If it hadn't been for her eyes—she looked at me, you know, just looked straight at me, and I swear, they were my own dead sister's eyes looking at me—I don't know I'd have gone near her, otherwise."

A new voice, low and taut, demanded, "At what time did you find Miss Murchison?"

Mary and the cabbie spun to see Anne Treleaven, who edged past them toward the sofa. Her skin was ashen.

The man gaped at Anne, mouth opening and closing silently.

"It's all right," said Mary before he could take a step backward. "This is Miss Treleaven, our head teacher.

Please tell her everything."

"Less than half an hour ago, ma'am. I brought her here directly, soon as I could tell what she was saying."

Hope rippled through Mary. If this woman had spoken within the last half hour, and spoken clearly enough to give an address, she might still live. They had to believe that.

"You called for a physician, of course?" Anne's voice was recognizable now.

"Yes." Mary bent over the woman again, trying to see just how much blood was seeping from the wound. "Would you be so kind as to shine this light upon the lady?" she asked the cabman, pointing at a small table lamp. He complied, but the beam of yellow light shook. "Did you notice anybody with her? Or running away from her, perhaps?"

"I—I don't know, miss. I was that surprised."

Two maids arrived, bearing hot water and other supplies. Mary placed a cushion beneath Miss Murchison's chest and said, over her shoulder, "Steady with the light, if you please."

"Allow me," said Anne Treleaven. The light bobbed for a moment, then became stable. "Please do sit down, Mr., er . . . ?"

When the man failed to give his name, Mary glanced back at him. She saw his eyelids flutter as he swayed gently backward. Anne turned a moment later, but neither woman was in time to catch him as he crashed to the floor, rattling every lamp, table, and ornament on the ground level. Mary winced.

"Poor fellow," murmured Anne. "He's had little thanks for being a Good Samaritan." She knelt on the carpet and began to slap his cheeks firmly and dispassionately. As Anne roused the squeamish cabman, Mary returned her attention to Miss Murchison and began cutting away her cloak.

A faint groan came from the cab driver. "Oh, lordy, what a nightmare!"

"I must ask you to keep still a few minutes longer, sir," said Anne. "I'm afraid you fainted."

"Eh?" The testy confusion in the man's voice would have been amusing, but for the present emergency. "What's that you say?"

"You fainted, sir," said Anne, raising her voice slightly. "Do keep still in case the dizziness returns."

Silence. Then, "I thought this were all a nightmare."

"I wish it was so, too. But I'm afraid it's very real, and we are extremely grateful that you brought our friend back to us."

"She alive?"

"I—I don't know." Anne's voice was leached of emotion. "Mary?"

"I think so." Mary breathed a prayer that she would be able to distinguish between help and harm. All agents received some basic medical training in case of emergency, but she had never dealt with a wound this severe.

She opened the cloak and began scissoring through Miss Murchison's brown woolen shirtwaist. It sprang open willingly, revealing a bloodstained corset and, just above that, a one-inch slit framing a knife blade. Mary placed a clean towel around the wound and pressed firmly. "She's bleeding fairly slowly, for now. If the physician arrives soon . . ."

A deep sigh: the sound of a large man hauling himself, painfully, to a seated position. "I found her over in Camden Town," he said. "She were leaning against a lamppost, waving, trying to get a cab. I thought she'd been on the gin at first, she were that unsteady on her feet. And why didn't she just find a taxi rank, if it came to that? Anyway, there weren't nobody else stopping, and I'd have driven on, too. Only the look on her face, it weren't the face of a dru—begging pardon, I mean, a lady indisposed. I thought, here's a lady in genuine trouble, and what's she doing in Camden, anyway?"

The room was utterly silent, save for the faint whisper of the lamp. "Go on, please," murmured Anne.

"It weren't until I tried to help her into the cab that I saw that blooming great thing sticking out her back. By the time I got her inside, she didn't have much breath. She asked me to bring her here. I said shouldn't I take her to a hospital, and quick, but she said no, just here. After that, I didn't ask no more questions, ma'am; it were plain that she were in a bad way."

"You did the right thing," said Anne, "and you shall be rewarded for your kindness and clear thinking." She turned to Mary. "Are you able to stay with Ivy until the doctor arrives? There are a few things I must see to."

Mary nodded. Anne would need to mobilize all possible Agency staff to search for both Angelica and Mrs. Thorold. "I shall let you know the moment Miss Murchison says anything," she said. And with a quiet swish of skirts, Anne Treleaven vanished, leaving Mary and the cabman to their awkward vigil.

Mary stared at Ivy Murchison's face, which was drained of color and pinched with pain. Was it a shade paler now? Impossible to be certain. She snipped the corset strings too and, with that loosening, thought she could see the woman's rib cage rising and falling with each breath. She drew comfort from that and refused to allow her imagination to run riot.

The doctor was taking his time. While she waited, she cleaned the wound with vinegar and water and daubed honey around the oozing hole to help prevent infection. She changed the towels and continued to stanch the blood. She endeavored to ignore the ticking of the mantelpiece clock, and tried also not to curse as she wondered how long they might wait for a physician.

When he finally arrived, irritable and impatient, Anne accompanied him into the room. Her face expressed no great confidence in the man, but she kept her lips pressed tightly together. He pulled off his gloves and dropped them on his medical bag; his fingernails were dirty. There was macassar oil on his collar. When Mary described what she had done thus far, his professional *amour propre* was offended. "Far better to leave the doctoring to professionals," he sneered. "A lady's timid poking about invariably makes things worse."

He ordered Miss Murchison moved to a bedroom, where he braced himself against her shoulder and jerked out the blade with considerable grunting effort. Its removal was accompanied by a huge gush of blood, so copious that both Mary and Anne gasped. The bleeding seemed as though it would never end. After far too long, he dropped the last sodden towel on the floor and ordered that the wound be bandaged. Mary was relieved to do it herself, rather than trust those clumsy, grubby hands. From his battered medical bag, he produced a series of pills and powders, to be administered as rapidly as possible. He held out little hope for the patient, given the depth of the wound and the likelihood of infection. The bill reflected his absolute confidence in his judgment.

Mary saw him to the front door, struggling to contain her revulsion, then returned to Miss Murchison's room, where Anne was sitting beside the bed. The physician had left a trail of mud across the braided rug, she noted numbly, and then she felt a flash of anger. Why couldn't he use the boot scraper, like everybody else?

"I'll watch her tonight," murmured Anne. "You should rest."

"Any word of Angelica?"

Anne shook her head. "I have agents out searching

for Mrs. Thorold. If she's with her mother, they will hopefully find them both. If not, she'll return on her own."

Mary thought she understood. The Agency had fewer operatives these days. Some—perhaps many—had thrown their allegiance behind Felicity Frame when she departed. Others, like Mary, might have gone out on their own. For those who remained, Mrs. Thorold's treatment of Ivy Murchison could hardly be misinterpreted: it would have been simple enough to make an agent disappear, to tip her body into the Thames. But in allowing Miss Murchison the chance to find her way home, Mrs. Thorold was sending a clear warning. "You've informed Scotland Yard, of course?" asked Mary. It was a question she'd never have dared to formulate before. It was a measure of just how much things had changed between her and Anne.

Anne's hesitation was scarcely perceptible but managed, nevertheless, to communicate her surprise at being challenged. "Naturally." There was a hint of hauteur in her voice as she wished Mary a good night.

For the first time in hours, Mary felt slightly amused. Even a very small reason to smile came as a relief after this ghastly evening. The smile carried her down to the kitchen—where she scrubbed her hands well and collected a hot-water bottle and a candle—and then up the stairs with weary legs and an aching head, and finally over the threshold of her bedroom.

Straight into the arms of Angelica Thorold.

* * *

Figuratively speaking, of course. Mary squinted into the room, just able to make out a figure the dim light. She was nearly persuaded that she was hallucinating, but no: Angelica was slumped on the chair beside her bed, still bundled into her hat and cloak. Her attention seemed to be fixed on something in the middle distance. Mary eased the hot-water bottle onto her bed and lit the oil lamp.

The additional light seemed to rouse Angelica. She blinked as though waking, then looked vaguely in Mary's direction. "Oh. Hello."

"Hello," replied Mary, for lack of a better greeting. After a moment, she added, "I'm glad to see you safely back."

There was a pause. Then, with visible effort, Angelica said, "I hope I didn't create cause for alarm. There was — That is, I had a great deal to think about. After the funeral."

Mary nodded and sat down carefully, facing Angelica. She took care to move slowly and quietly, half afraid that, like a wild animal, Angelica might suddenly take flight. "It must have been very difficult," she murmured.

"What? Oh. Well, yes, it was. Difficult." Angelica seemed on the verge of saying something else, then abruptly closed her mouth.

"Was everything adequately prepared?" asked Mary after a short interval.

Angelica snorted, although there was little humor

in the sound. "Oh! I'm no judge of funerals. All my life, I've been considered too delicate to attend. Suddenly, I'm not only the chief mourner; I'm the only mourner." She sighed. "They buried my father. That is all I know."

Bitterness and a tendency to melodrama, noted Mary. Was that better or worse than feeling numb? Which rendered Angelica more likely to fall in with her mother's designs? She wondered how to broach the delicate subject of Mrs. Thorold. "Have you eaten at all?" she asked, although she thought she knew the answer.

"I beg your pardon?" Angelica shook her head, stirred once again from her private thoughts. "Oh. No. But I'm not hungry."

Mary nodded. "Impossible to think of food, I know. But allow me to get a pot of tea." She stepped into the corridor, and luck was with her: she met a pupil at the top of the staircase. A nighttime tea tray was one of the privileges of a teacher or guest, and the girl nodded amiably and went to relay the message to the kitchen maid.

As she slipped noiselessly back into the room, Mary saw Angelica sprawled facedown on her bed, shoulders shaking, weeping quietly, violently, into her hands. Mary watched her in uncomfortable silence. This was the most reprehensible part of a morally questionable job: taking advantage of those who truly needed help. But if Angelica said something useful in these moments of abandon, that would, for Mary, justify the betrayal. It was possible, Mary supposed, that this scene of grief was also staged—part of a complicated performance in several acts, meant to elicit trust and sympathy. But it was the less likely scenario. After a few moments, she slid back into the corridor, keeping the door ajar. It was enough to listen.

Even the most devoted daughter had only so much energy for stormy weeping, and after several minutes Angelica's intensity slackened. From the change in tone, Mary thought Angelica was no longer covering her face. Mary pictured her sprawled prone on the bed, face turned to one side, mopping her face with a handkerchief. There was a distinct sort of lull—sniffles and sighs and the odd murmur of "Oh, Papa"—but the storm had passed.

Mary eyed the door. In her experience, this period of calm was the best time in which to gain someone's confidence. This was the moment in which to appear with a clean handkerchief and a sympathetic ear, and carefully unspool a confession from her weary subject. She pushed down her distaste, forcing herself to think of Mrs. Thorold, and prepared to step back into the room. In that moment, she heard Angelica's voice, soft but clear and intelligible. It said, "What shall I do, Papa?" A sniffle. "Shall I meet her?"

The question raised goose bumps across Mary's neck and arms. She held her breath, waiting two, three, ten eternal seconds, then released it softly.

Angelica said, "She didn't come. She could have. She knew it was your funeral, and she didn't come." Another pause, then plaintively, as if to the uncaring world: "What kind of wife does that? What kind of mother?" Another charged silence, then a sigh of disgust. "As if talking to myself could help the matter. I'll end up in an asylum, at this rate."

A faint rattle of china and silver at the end of the corridor distracted Mary from this revealing monologue. She glided silently toward the approaching maid and took the heavy tray from her with a smile. "Thank you, Rachel. I'll take it into the room." Small Rachel, the newest and youngest of the Academy's kitchen staff, flexed her arms in relief and vanished back into the depths of the house.

When Mary entered the bedroom, all calm innocence and steaming tea tray, Angelica was sitting up on the bed, dabbing her swollen eyes with a fresh handkerchief. "That was quick," she said, and blew her nose with an unladylike honk.

"Was it?" Mary lifted the covers and discovered a large plate of buttered toast, a deep bowl of beef broth, and another plate of jam biscuits. Anne Treleaven must have been hovering near the kitchen when the order came in.

Angelica made a quavering attempt at a laugh. "If this is what you fetch for somebody who's not hungry, I can't wait to see your idea of a square meal."

"If you can't manage it, I will," promised Mary. "I have an astounding capacity for buttered toast."

Angelica was already sinking her teeth into a warm triangle. "Who doesn't?" When she had drunk the soup and polished off the toast, Angelica sighed with satisfaction.

"That felt like a proper schoolgirl feast. We used to have them now and again, at my finishing school." Her mouth twisted. "Then we'd help each other lace our corsets extra tightly and go to bed. Can you imagine? A stomach full of cakes and sweets, and shallow breathing all night so the stays didn't dig in so much. Lord, it was agony."

"But you did it again," observed Mary.

"Every chance we got."

In the small lull that followed their laughter, Mary asked, "Do you miss your old life?"

Angelica considered. "I miss its ease," she said slowly. "I never spared a thought for the essentials: eating and staying warm and always having clean clothes to wear. I appreciate those comforts immensely now. But do I miss the balls and parties, the constant calls upon people who bored me silly, the imperative to marry well? Not at all. I'm far happier eking out a life as a music student in a foreign country where I have only friends of my own choosing. No family to worry about. I'll be glad to return to Vienna."

Mary nodded. But before her sympathy for Angelica could root itself too deeply, she introduced the necessary subject. "Speaking of your journey . . . Yesterday, I took that advert to the *Times,* as promised. It's only a very slim chance that she's seen it, I know, but I don't suppose you've heard from your mother yet?"

Angelica flushed quite suddenly, from collar to hairline. "I—I'd quite forgotten about the ad," she whispered.

"Thank you." She swallowed hard, and Mary's unanswered question hung in the air between them. After a couple of false starts, Angelica said, "You're right, of course: it's quite unlikely that she'd notice it, even if she were in England and reading the newspaper." An attempt at a laugh. "I'm not certain why I thought it such a good idea at the time."

"I encouraged you," said Mary. "You'd spoken of a strong desire to see your mother."

"I did, didn't I? Those dreams."

Mary watched her carefully, the shifting undercurrents of her expression. A strong desire to tell. An equally powerful impulse to secrecy. Guilt. Confusion. Anger. Fear. Longing. She thought she understood how Angelica felt. She'd been in a parallel situation herself not so long ago, with the nightmare reappearance of her father, and she'd kept silent. "Well," she said, twirling a teaspoon between her fingers, "if she suddenly appears, I'm sure you'll know what to do."

"D'you think so?"

"Why not?" said Mary. She felt suddenly ruthless. "She's your mother, after all."

Angelica looked distinctly queasy. "Yes," she finally replied. "I suppose she is."

Fourteen

Saturday, 20 October

Gordon Square, Bloomsbury

James awoke suddenly, well before sunrise. He blinked and sat up, wondering at the churning excitement in his stomach. It wasn't unpleasant; it reminded him of Christmas mornings from his childhood, the bone-deep knowledge that lovely things were soon to come. A moment later, his brain caught up with his body. Today was Saturday. Mudie's day. He had an appointment to meet Mary at the lending library. Today would be their first glimpse of each other in a week. His pulse quickened at the very thought of it. Her face. Her voice. The small weight of her hand upon his forearm.

He glanced back at his pillow and tried to imagine her there: Mrs. James Easton. Dark hair spilling over the crisp white linen. The curves of her body beneath a thin nightdress. The scent of her favorite lemon soap enveloping them both. He trembled. Yet even as his imagination took flight, some dark part of his mind transformed the scene: from bed to bier, from white linen to velvet-lined casket. From warm, soft flesh to cold, rigid limbs. His stomach roiled in an entirely different way and he leaped from the bed, so desperate was he to shake off that malignant fancy.

In the bathroom he washed with cool water, eager for a rational reason to shiver, and wondered at the sudden turn his imagination had taken. He considered himself realistic, and was keenly aware of the potential dangers he and Mary faced. Yet he wasn't given to gloom and dark foreboding; he'd always considered such things a waste of time. And now his foolish imagination had cast a pall over what should have been a day of delicious, near-impossible anticipation. He tried not to give it weight, but it troubled him nevertheless.

Fortunately, Saturday was a working day. There was plenty to keep him busy until the appointed hour. A couple of years ago, Easton Engineering had embraced the new Saturday half-holiday movement, closing the offices at one o'clock in the afternoon. It was good for their employees' morale, and thus good for business. For James, Saturday afternoons were typically a time in which to catch up on paperwork. Put that way, it sounded dreary, but James didn't mind. He liked the silent office, the slightly quieter streets. George generally popped in, and they repaired to a chophouse or ordered in meals from the nearby pub and caught up. They began by briefing each other on how their respective building works were coming along, but it was also the most companionable time of their week. Engineering talk trickled into more general conversation, and James seldom felt closer to his brother than during those informal meetings.

Before that, however, there was much to do. He breakfasted swiftly and alone—after that tête-à-tête on Sunday morning, George had returned immediately to his leisurely ways—and set out briskly for the office as the sun was still rising. James loved the city at this time, the way the sun burnished the rooftops and windows, lending it the illusory gleam of a city of gold. On the more frequent days when the sun lurked sullenly behind the clouds, there was still a softness to the light, a sort of hesitancy. At this hour, London was not yet the brash, cacophonous capital of commerce and trade. It was something out of a fairy tale, a shadowy city dense with characters, all awaiting their cue.

By the time he turned onto Great George Street, he felt himself again. He had a new idea about the Bank of England job, but before he could sketch that out, he wanted an update from his chief clerk. Then it was time for a site visit: the bridge project had been delayed yet again, this time by the incorrect supply of urgently needed materials. He needed to supervise this morning's delivery in person.

The main door to the building was slightly ajar—unusual this early in the morning, as James was generally the first to arrive. He frowned briefly, then shrugged it off: Easton Engineering shared tenancy of the building with two other firms. Someone else must have decided to use the early hours to stride ahead with their work. But as he ascended the stairs to his offices on the first floor, his instincts told him otherwise. Something was wrong here. He was visited by a swift, vivid memory of the night he'd been attacked. He rounded the corner and saw, with little surprise, the unoccupied chair outside the door. Where was the night watchman?

Of course, the unguarded office door was unlocked. He examined it quickly. The main bolt had been picked but not broken. Then, as though the intruder had lost patience, the two smaller locks were smashed. He pushed at the door slowly. His first thought was that it would be weighted closed by the inert body of the watchman. When the door swung freely, however, James's thoughts of the missing man evaporated in the face of the utter chaos he saw within: the long room was strewn with papers, all pitched about like hay in a stable.

An involuntary curse escaped his lips, and he clamped them tight. Walking farther into the room, he noted mechanically the extent of the destruction. Tables, desks, and chairs were intact, although somewhat flung about. Filing cabinets dangled open, gutted like fish. Cupboards gaped. Desk drawers drooped and tilted, showing their empty depths. Shelves had been comprehensively cleared with the sweep of an arm. And above all this carnage, the large wall clock ticked on steadily.

James thought he understood: this was no ordinary burglary. Otherwise, they'd have taken the clock, the furniture, the technical instruments. No, the intruders had been after information, and he was quite certain what they wanted. He crossed the length of the office to a door with a maimed doorknob. He swallowed hard and steadied his breathing. Opened the door. Saw what he'd expected, and feared: the heavy steel door of the vault, like all the other doors, slightly ajar. As though the thief had thought to close it, then changed his mind at the last moment. No: *her* mind.

He opened the vault door, to be certain. Empty. Closed it with a groan. He forced himself to walk through the ruins, checking each corner, surveying the full extent of the damage. The least unpleasant aspect of it all was the absence of the night watchman's body. He had braced himself for the worst, but it appeared that the man had taken the opportunity to escape. Or possibly to collude with the thief.

At this notion, a scalding current of anger washed over him. He ran down into the street, shouting for a constable. He bellowed for a good while, loath to leave the office unprotected, although he wasn't certain what further harm could come to it, short of total destruction by flood or fire. After what seemed hours but was probably only ten minutes, a constable came running. It took him a few minutes to grasp the situation, and then he was off again, swinging his rattle to summon all officers within earshot. The street was filling with workers now, a black-clad tide of clerks sweeping into the city, some of them his own employees. James was left to stand sentinel, informing them of the outrage and sending them home for the day. It was a simple task made exhausting now that the initial anesthetic of shock and anger was fading away.

He thought of the hundreds of hours of work ahead, gathering and sorting and refiling the papers. He thought of the need to inform the Bank of England that their security was now compromised. He tried not to think of the consequences to his professional reputation, and to the family business in general. Most of all, he tried not to think of Mary.

Logic dictated that if Mrs. Thorold had been busy here in Great George Street last night, Mary was probably still safe. Yet logic seemed impotent in the face of this hovering, all-encompassing danger: it was one of the very few times in his life that logic had failed him. When he realized that, a black despair gripped him. It seemed that Mrs. Thorold was always several steps ahead, toying with them, leisurely unfolding plans that they were powerless to disrupt. All they could do was react and further entangle themselves in her web. Was that it? James swallowed hard. If this was the case, he might as well give up now. If there was no point in trying, one may as well embrace one's fate and lie down meekly, waiting for Mrs. Thorold to appear.

"Mr. Easton, sir?" It was the original constable.

"Yes."

"If you're ready, we'd like to take you to Scotland Yard, sir, to speak to an inspector."

"Isn't an inspector coming here to view the scene for himself?"

The constable shuffled. "Well, that's the usual way of things, sir, but what with those being plans for the vaults of the Bank of England, sir, and your saying that this might actually be the second attempt to steal them, we've got all our senior staff working on that, from this moment. It'd be a deal easier for us if you didn't mind coming down to the station."

"What about all this lot?" James waved at the half dozen or so policemen tramping about the office.

"Well, they'll keep looking for clues, but the best way to find your thief is to catch the man who's trying to break into the Bank, sir."

There was no denying the logic: it was another way of saying that there is more than one way to skin a cat. A hoary old proverb. And yet it was the most bracing thing James had heard all morning. He felt the dark despair begin to lighten a little, and he straightened his shoulders. "Of course I'll come," he said. "I think I'd better speak to Chief Inspector Hall, if he's available. I met with him a couple years ago on a different matter, and I suspect it might be connected to this one."

* * *

A little before four o'clock, Saturday

Mudie's Circulating Library, New Oxford Street

James winced as somebody jabbed him, hard, in the shin. He turned and glared at an oblivious older gentleman who'd just walked past him, brandishing a very sharp umbrella. Then he sighed. There wasn't a great deal he (or anybody else) could do, wedged as they all were into the circular hall of the lending library. The vast, double-height room teemed with borrowers, their eager voices floating up toward the soaring ceilings to be amplified and multiplied before reverberating endlessly. Clerks darted back and forth, scaling ladders, retrieving ziggurats of books that wobbled precariously yet never seemed to topple. It was the perfect place for a clandestine meeting, or to lose oneself altogether.

James resisted the temptation to check his watch yet again. Just an hour ago, he had been certain that he would have to miss this appointment with Mary. He had tried not to think of how she might interpret such a failure. Yet, quite miraculously, his meeting at the Bank of England had come to a rapid conclusion and he'd run the whole way to Oxford Street, desperate not to be late. In fact, he was ten minutes early. But despite his present leisure and the temptations all around him—three-volume novels, their green fabric spines stamped bravely with gold; delicate leather-bound octavos brimming with verse; proud, burnished volumes of science and politics, testing the limits of knowledge and convention with verve and elegance—he was, for the first time in his life, unable to appreciate their appeal.

The rest of the morning had been disastrous, of course. He'd spent hours with the police, explaining and re-explaining the situation in the aftermath of the burglary. Then had followed a humiliating emergency meeting with Mr. Bentley and the rest of the court of directors of the Bank of England, in which he'd had to confess the theft of their architectural plans from a locked safe within a guarded office. Yet the theft, and the humiliation of his firm in the eyes of the public, were no longer at the forefront of his mind.

"Are you still reading the catalog, sir?"

For a fraction of a moment, James's heart leaped and he turned to the lady standing by his elbow. A heartbeat later, his spirits sank again. She was dark haired, but there the resemblance ended. It was absurd of him to have imagined that shrill voice could have been Mary's. "No. Do take this place," he replied, and relinquished his spot in front of the enormous register. He preferred browsing the bookshelves, anyway.

He made his way through the crowd to one end of the room and selected, at random, a book from the shelves. From this vantage point, he could keep an eye on the door and the bobbing sea of hats and bonnets, while turning the pages in a studious manner. He'd no idea what Mary might be wearing. Would he recognize her as a lady's maid come to fetch the latest sensation novels for her mistress, or playing a well-to-do lady of fashion? Of course he would, he told himself robustly; he'd know the back of her head purely from the way she turned her neck.

Had time ever passed so lethargically? James frowned at the book in his hands and discovered it purported to be the memoirs of a factory worker, a dramatic but dignified account of one laborer's many hardships and injustices. He was familiar with the interests of working men — from a certain distance, at least. As a conscientious employer, he tried to listen to their requests. The Saturday half-holiday had been one of those. He had read the great minds of the age, male and female, on the subjects of poverty and industrialization. He'd even read that extremely sentimental poem by Mrs. Browning about the plight of factory children. But this book was different. The perspective, for one: it was the first time he'd seen, in print, the unmediated voice of a working-class man. He wondered how the man had learned to read and write; how he had come to have his life story printed. Despite his thrumming impatience, James was intrigued, and took the book up to the great counter so that he might borrow it.

At last, the clock's hands assumed the four o'clock position, and James resumed his post by the stacks. His gaze was fixed upon the great double doors, continually swinging as people pressed in, flowed out. Mary's stature made her easier to spot. He could dismiss three-quarters of the crowd from his attention simply for being too tall. As the minutes crawled on, however, he couldn't repress a tremor of anxiety. Mary was punctual. He couldn't recall ever having waited more than five minutes for her, but there was no sign of her in the doorway. Was it possible that she had been inside all along, simply waiting for a suitable moment to approach him? Perhaps he had been followed, and she, seeing that, was reluctant to confirm the link between them. Or . . . the suppositions grew darker and more violent, and it required real effort to wrench his thoughts away from tragedy and disaster. This was becoming a habit at the moment.

It was ten past the hour, and he could remain still no longer. James carved his way through the writhing mass of elbows, crinolines, and canes, and emerged into the almost wintry damp: a shock after the heat of all those bodies in the library. He chose a spot against the wall just a few yards from the main press of the crowds, yet which afforded a clear view of the entrance. Five more minutes, then ten. He was genuinely worried now, and wondered what on earth his next step might be. He was just weighing up the dangers of going to Mary's flat when a female figure trotted briskly down the street toward him and, despite the fact that he was a perfectly still and predictable obstacle, half collided with him at some speed. The book she carried slipped from her hand, somehow knocking his own volume, the *Memoirs*, from his grip. Both books fell to the ground, and there was the distinct sound of a spine cracking, stitches tearing. James flinched. He couldn't help himself.

As he bent to recover them, the lady scooped them both from the ground. "I do beg your pardon," she was saying—gabbling, rather, in nervous, anxious tones. "My fault entirely . . . dreadfully shortsighted . . . so sorry . . . no great harm done, I think—" She pushed a book into his hands and was off again: not into Mudie's, which James found peculiar, but directly past its entrance.

James stared after her, bemused. How shortsighted could a person be before she was considered blind? Then, automatically, he inspected the book for damage. It might have been worse: a few smears of dirt on the buff covers, one corner dented. It was also not his book. The volumes had been of similar size and color, and the lady had taken away his *Memoirs*. He now held a slim volume of John Donne's sermons.

Light dawned. James opened the cover and began to leaf through the pages. There, buried at its heart, was an envelope addressed only to "J" in a bold yet entirely recognizable pencil stroke that made his heart contract. He fished it out slowly, frightened that he'd drop it.

Dearest,

I am so sorry to miss our meeting; I was hoping for a chance to distract you again. I am following A. to a meeting with her mother. I think you are now involved,

too: Mrs. F. is trustworthy. In an emergency, write to
me c/o Miss Scrimshaw's Academy for Girls, Acacia
Rd.

    All my love,

        M.

It was pure Mary: brisk, teasing, practical. It made him want to laugh and cheer and spring into action, all at the same time. Truly, it was just the tonic he needed.

The assurance that Mrs. Frame was trustworthy didn't make him like the woman any better, but it did clarify his own plans. Only an hour ago, in his meeting at the Bank of England, the court of directors had resolved on an unprecedented course of action. The work on the vaults had originally been planned to begin in the new year. With the revelation that their detailed plans had been stolen, however, the most influential director, Mr. Bentley, had suggested that they act immediately: this very night, the Bank's entire store of gold would be removed from the vaults and sent by armored train to Paris for safekeeping. It was a radical plan, one that denied the thief time to make use of the stolen plans. It was also one that required the near-instantaneous summoning of England's most powerful men: permission wrung from the prime minister, the active cooperation of the chief of the Metropolitan Police, and the assistance of both army and navy. It was a perfect illustration of the power of money.

James had been assured, halfheartedly, that Easton Engineering was held blameless in the loss of the plans, and he need do nothing until construction was ready to begin in the new year. He had remained outwardly acquiescent. But Mary's letter affirmed his existing resolve. He turned into a convenient pub and scribbled a terse message to Felicity Frame, to be delivered by hand. Then he walked home to Gordon Square to prepare. He was far from satisfied. Mrs. Thorold had, even from a distance, managed to cancel his meeting with Mary. And Mrs. Frame's dark insinuations about Mary's new friend still troubled him.

However, the great removal was scheduled to begin tonight at eleven o'clock. He would be there.

Fifteen

Early evening, the same day

Regent's Park

Mary had spent the entire day in nerve-fraying stasis. After her frank but inconclusive conversation with Angelica last night, sleep had been a long time coming. Mary was still uncertain as to whether Angelica's deepest loyalties lay with her mother but decided that it was, for now, irrelevant. What mattered was that Angelica could still lead Mary to Mrs. Thorold. That was, after all, the point of her original assignment.

Infuriatingly, Angelica displayed no interest in being alone or leaving the Academy for the better part of the day. Mary had arranged for a second agent, in male guise, to shadow her. She asked that somebody convey a message to James at Mudie's. As it was essential that the messenger be able to recognize James, Anne had undertaken the errand herself — an enormous concession that Mary appreciated all the more, since it stole a precious hour from Anne's care of Ivy Murchison. Mary would also miss her appointment with Lang in

Leicester Square, but she was less concerned about that. Lang knew that it was quite likely, and his only real danger this evening was the loss of a sum of money. Yet after all that preparation and anticipation, Angelica and Mary and the shadow agent had loitered aimlessly about Regent's Park all the afternoon. Mary checked her small watch and groaned inwardly. She could have met James herself.

Patience, she counseled herself. *The longer you've waited, the more important it becomes to remain vigilant and sensitive.* Much to her relief, the nearby bells of St. Mark's Church began to chime. That gave her the excuse to stretch her limbs, stiff and cold from sitting on a park bench, and say to Angelica, "It's nearly the supper hour. Shall we walk back to the Academy?"

Angelica jumped. She had looked strained and anxious all day, as though the burden of her secret was consuming her from the inside. "Oh, you go without me, Mary. I'm not hungry. I might just sit here a while longer in the fresh air."

Mary glanced about. Dusk was creeping in, and the park was rapidly emptying of respectable ladies. It was far from unpeopled, however, and soon a different sort of woman would begin to make herself visible, beside lampposts and in the shadows near the railings. Surely Angelica was worldly enough to know what misapprehensions might befall a lady alone after dark?

Angelica seemed to resent Mary's hesitation. "Go

on!" she said vigorously, flapping her hands in a shooing gesture. "I can take care of myself in a genteel park. For heaven's sake, Mary, I'm traveling back to Vienna alone tomorrow."

Mary shrugged. "All right, then. I'll see you a little later." She set off casually along the graveled path, not looking back. Once her light tread was beyond earshot, she stepped onto the grass and behind the wide trunk of a convenient tree. A moment later, Angelica glanced about sharply — left, right, behind — then squared her shoulders and began to walk, purposefully, eastward.

Mary's pulse leaped. She forced herself to give Angelica as much distance as possible: it would soon grow difficult to see her in the semidarkness. In her plain mourning wear, Angelica would become as discreetly invisible as Mary herself. For the time being, however, it was simple enough.

They left the park and began to pick their way southeast, trailing through Marylebone in a sort of silent procession: Angelica in the lead, followed by both Mary and, somewhere out there, the shadow agent. Angelica walked steadily, but seemed unhurried. Apart from a certain sense of purpose in her bearing, this could have been yet another long stroll to pass the time. Yet Mary would have wagered a great deal that Angelica did, in fact, have a destination in mind.

Darkness gathered and thickened about them. There were still people aplenty in the streets: clerks and laborers trudging homeward, wagons creaking under heavy loads, and the occasional lamplighter with his ladder and lantern, struggling to create a bit more illumination amid the heavy fog.

They turned into Tavistock Place, and Mary wondered for a wild moment if they were going to her own flat. It was impossible, surely, for Angelica and Mrs. Thorold to know about that. Who could have told them but a member of the Agency, or perhaps James himself, under duress? She arrested her train of thought: that way lay panic and disaster.

Still, she felt a distinct sense of relief when they veered south instead, winding their way toward Russell Square. Angelica slowed her pace and began a sedate stroll around its perimeter. The foot traffic was thinner here: most passersby cut straight across the square, eager to reach their destination. As a result, each of Angelica's footsteps in the gravel was faintly audible, and Mary again turned onto the grass and gave Angelica more distance in order to remain unnoticed.

This sort of waiting is always difficult, thought Mary. It was a delicate push and pull between being poised for anything and eschewing undue haste. Although Angelica seemed entirely immersed in her thoughts, Mary felt increasingly conspicuous following her in what was merely a large circle. She chose a plot of bushes at the southeast corner of the square and disappeared behind it.

Waiting in stillness was harder yet. Mary had to be

vigilant, constantly turning her thoughts and anxieties away from James Easton, Anne Treleaven, Ivy Murchison. She had to have confidence that Angelica would keep to her established circuit around the square and not suddenly dart into a side street. Mary was not naturally a woman of great faith, and so the minutes oozed by, lethargic and grudging. Mary counted them slowly, while mapping the square in her mind, exploring its possibilities for exit and entrapment. When that exercise was exhausted—Angelica had now performed nine unhurried laps of the path—Mary breathed deeply, felt her stomach rumble. She'd eaten nothing since midday. She thought longingly of a nub of cheese, a small bread roll. A boiled egg. Better yet, a cold chicken leg. So intent was she upon this fantasy that she nearly missed the nautical sweep of a tall lady's skirt as it glided along the path.

A moment later, however, Mary straightened, spine tingling. The woman was veiled and dressed in simple dark raiment. Yet something about her bearing was deeply and alarmingly familiar, as it had been two days ago, outside the Bank of England. Mary rose from her hiding place and followed at a cautious distance. Sure enough, the woman walked with quiet confidence toward Angelica and took her by the arm.

To her credit, Angelica did not cry out. She jumped in surprise, then turned to face the woman. She spoke to her in a low tone—Mary was still too distant to discern any words—and, for answer, the woman raised her veil.

Prepared as she was, Mary had to bite back a gasp. Those pale, glittering eyes. That prominent jaw, made squarer by thin lips. They sat ill with the expression on the woman's face, which was of maternal pride and affection. But it was unmistakably she: Maria Thorold.

Mary's stomach turned over. Her eager hunger soured into nausea and her heartbeat felt violent enough to bruise her ribs. She fell back a step, then wondered if her movement had been too sudden. Yet luck was with her. The two women were focused only upon each other. A few moments later, the veil fell again, and Mrs. Thorold took her daughter's arm once more. They began to stroll.

Mary abandoned all notion of returning to her post behind the bushes. She had no intention of permitting Mrs. Thorold out of her sight now that she was really, truly found. A moment ago, she had been merely a vague threat, a sort of Agency bogeyman. Now she was here. She represented real danger, but she could also be apprehended. Mary realized how sound a decision it had been to stay quietly behind some bushes and risk Angelica's wandering off unsupervised. Mrs. Thorold would surely have been watching from afar to confirm that Angelica was alone. Had Mary been trailing her . . . She shuddered and stopped the thought there.

She was interested in the women's postures. Each held herself erect, at a cordial distance from the other. Yet Mary thought that even from her perspective she could discern Angelica's tense skepticism, her readiness to pull away. This was in contrast to Mrs. Thorold's uncharacter-istic eagerness: she seemed to do most of the talking, her head pivoted toward Angelica.

When Angelica next spoke, it was accompanied by a gesture toward a nearby bench. Mrs. Thorold demurred but eventually agreed, although she chose a bench near a corner of the square. It sat just within the yellow haze cast by a gaslight, and was ringed by open space. It was a good choice for privacy, and Mary bit her lower lip. How would she ever overhear a murmured conversation?

In daylight, it would have been impossible to get any-where near the Thorolds' bench. Tonight, however, the rapidly falling darkness was her accomplice. Mary left the square by the nearest exit, although it pained her to turn her back on the women even for a moment. Still, they would only feel confident in their solitude if it was genu-ine. She made a wide circuit around the square and, after several agonizing minutes, reentered at the corner behind the Thorolds. There was a wide, sturdy oak tree some yards behind the bench, just outside the circle of gaslight. It was far from ideal, but better than open ground. And, as Mary eased herself into a comfortable position against the tree trunk, she realized that luck was still with her: mother and daughter were speaking in normal conversa-tional tones, rather than hushed and secretive whispers. Even from her limited vantage point, Mary could catch enough words to fill in the gaps with confidence.

"Most mothers are commonly, unjustifiably proud

of their children," Mrs. Thorold was saying. "But you have accomplished much. I am proud of you, Angelica, although I can take no credit for your achievements."

Angelica's tone was pleased, confused, a trifle embarrassed. "That's enough about me, Mama. I am dying of curiosity to know more about you. Where do you live? What is your life like?"

An expressive sigh. "Oh, my dear. It's been a curious two years in exile. As you yourself know all too well, we fell from the heights of luxury and social advantage into lives as penurious outcasts. Your father's estate was forfeit, of course, as a result of the terrible crimes of which he was accused and convicted." A pause. "I do not say that he committed them, my dear. I find it impossible to believe that your poor father was capable of such evil. But he was convicted, and we have all paid the price.

"You will think that I left London because of the disgrace, and that part is true. But the main reason I live in France, my dear, is that I, too, was left penniless by the crime. Rural France is relatively inexpensive. I pawned my jewels and have been living on their proceeds ever since."

Angelica's intake of breath was loud. "Oh, Mama! I never even thought to ask—"

"And rightly so," said Mrs. Thorold. Her tone was perfectly pitched between maternal love and steely self-possession. "After the way I treated you. I am grateful that you are here at all, and willing to speak with me."

Another pause. "In any case, we have both survived the sort of disaster that would cast other women into the streets, or the poorhouse."

"Have you thought how you will live once that money runs out?"

Mary smiled at Angelica's practical bent. So much for cosseted debutantes and starving artists.

Mrs. Thorold sighed. "My money is almost gone, and that is why I'm back in England. I must confess, Angelica, that I haven't many ideas. I have no education to speak of, no conspicuous talents. My own parents are long dead, and their families dispersed. Even if they would own me after such a disgrace, I have been unable to find them. I am utterly without resources."

"Have you tried to find some sort of work?" There was genuine curiosity in Angelica's tone: she hadn't the faintest idea what the answer might be.

A puff of disgust. "Work! I am not above hard work, my dear. But tell me what I can do! It's not merely the lack of training that stands in my way: I am beyond the middle age, my dear girl, and for that reason, nobody wants me."

"Your age might be an advantage as a governess, or a paid companion." Angelica's voice was timid, as though she knew how weak this sounded.

Mary grinned in the darkness. There was a rich and satisfying irony here of which even Angelica must be uncomfortably aware.

"The difficulty of such work is twofold: first, one is

forced to depend upon the mercy and kindness of others, and obey their slightest whims. The second is that the paucity of the salary makes it impossible to save any money. Accepting such work will ensure that I must labor until I can labor no more, after which time I am certain to be destitute."

A silence. Then, slowly, Angelica said, "You speak rightly, Mama. I have recently been talking to a lady who is in much the same position, and while she seems resigned to her situation, she says no differently."

"And this lady is content with a life of threadbare servility, followed by the workhouse?" There was distinct contempt in those words: shades of the old Mrs. Thorold.

"If she has other ideas, she has yet to tell me of them."

"Well, not I. And in the same predicament, you would be no tamer, I wager."

"Ask me in ten years, when I'm no longer a young, aspiring musician." Angelica appeared to be thinking hard. "Have you any little store of capital left, Mama? You might try renting a house and taking in lodgers." She hurried on, knowing it sounded preposterous. "It needn't be seedy. There must be any number of genteel widows in reduced circumstances—"

"Like myself?" There was even the hint of a smile in Mrs. Thorold's voice.

"Well, not unlike you . . ."

"My dear, it's a promising plan, but I haven't enough

money to risk it. If I live carefully, I've enough for a few months yet. If I fritter it away on the lease of a house and cannot find sufficiently respectable lodgers, I am lost."

Another pause, and then Angelica said, "You sound as though you've considered all these ideas closely, Mama, and rejected them. Have you other plans in their stead?"

Instead of answering the question, Mrs. Thorold shivered dramatically. "The weather is cold this evening, is it not? Much as I used to love this city, I have come to prefer the heat and sunshine of my adopted home in the south."

"So you intend to return? Why did you come to London at all, Mama? Was it to see—" She seemed to choke on the end of her intended sentence.

"Your father?" Mrs. Thorold sighed. "I wish I could have seen him one last time. But as you know, I am still under suspicion. Impossibly evil accusations have been leveled at me. I could not run the risk of falling into the hands of the police."

"Yet if you are innocent, surely the truth will emerge? If you have not committed such crimes, how can they prove their case against you?"

"My dear, sweet girl." Mrs. Thorold's laugh was utterly mirthless, and disturbingly familiar to Mary. "You are still young enough to believe in grand ideas of justice and truth. But I am old enough to know of many instances of justice miscarried and innocent people irretrievably wronged. I cannot take that chance, Angelica."

She sounded suddenly fierce. "I will not risk my neck on the supposed intelligence and honesty of strangers. Not while I have a choice."

Angelica's voice was very quiet. "And what choice is that, Mama? If you starve, it matters not whether it is here or in France."

Again, Mrs. Thorold failed to answer Angelica directly. Instead, she picked up an earlier thread. "You said 'if' I was innocent. Are you so uncertain, Daughter?"

A pause. "I am largely certain."

"But a frisson of doubt remains?"

"Mama, I am not accusing you of anything."

"Yet you lack faith in me."

"Mama, I feel as though I scarcely know you. You were an invalid for years. I was brought up by the nurse, the governess, the finishing school. I met you at the dinner table, and scarcely elsewhere. I am not complaining of this, yet I ask you: how could I feel absolute confidence in your character, when this is the case?"

"Because circumstance is the key to this puzzle. As you say, I was an invalid for most of my adult life. I was only healed of my complaint after I moved to France, where the climate is so much more salubrious. A lifelong invalid might be able to plot criminal destruction, but carrying it out requires sustained physical vigor." In her fervor, Mrs. Thorold turned to Angelica and raised her veil. "I can't be guilty of those heinous crimes, Angelica, precisely because of who I was."

Mary could only admire Mrs. Thorold's stagecraft: dignified yet impassioned, emotional yet governed by logic. It was a tour de force.

"Thank you, Mama." Angelica sounded immensely relieved. "The accusations seemed impossible to me, too. But I am glad to hear the truth from you."

"I am both glad and relieved, Angelica. You are my only remaining relation; my child. I should like to know that our future is free of such shadows."

Mother and daughter sat in silence for a few minutes, still clasping hands. Their words, however, reverberated in Mary's thoughts. Angelica's doubts, and Mrs. Thorold's clever, circumspect denials, were oddly reminiscent of her own last interviews with her father. She was glad that he'd lacked the strength for such strategy, an eloquent succession of half-truths. Better to have a drug-addicted killer for a parent than a lying murderess. Or perhaps Angelica would disagree. Both Lang Jin Hai and Maria Thorold were criminals in the eyes of the government. Ultimately, that was all that mattered.

Enough. Mary bit her lip. Any superficial resemblances ended there.

Mrs. Thorold broke the lull. "Are you cold? Shall we walk?"

"I would prefer to go somewhere warm. Indoors. A coffee room, perhaps?" Angelica hesitated. "My treat."

"At this hour? My dear, your Viennese habits are showing. Any of London's coffeehouses willing to serve ladies—poor excuses though they are for true Continental cafés—are long since closed. Ditto for restaurants, if we could even afford one."

"I'd forgotten," admitted Angelica. "Well, I suppose there's nothing to do but to remain here in the park."

"I'd have thought you'd be inured to the cold, living so far north as you do."

Angelica shivered. "It's a different cold here. Damp. It gets into everything, and one's clothing is never quite dry."

"Terrible how one doesn't even notice it until one's been away, and suddenly it's insupportable." Mother and daughter laughed briefly, united in discomfort and expatriation.

"So tell me, then," said Angelica, emboldened by this renewed—perhaps brand-new—intimacy. "How much longer do you intend staying in town? There's no suitable work. You've no more jewels to pawn. How and where will you live, Mama?" A thought seemed to occur to her. "My situation in Vienna is little better. I lodge with my music teacher's family and share a bedroom with his young daughter, so I can't even offer you a roof over your head."

"That wasn't my secret intention behind our meeting," said Mrs. Thorold, sounding dry but unoffended. "I haven't much of a history as a mother, but the least I can do is not hinder your musical career by clinging to your petticoats."

"That's the third time you've not answered my

question, Mama. This refusal is unnerving. Why are you so loath to tell me about your future?" Angelica's voice held a new note of anxiety. "You are not planning anything . . . *extreme,* are you?"

Another pause, during which Mary's thoughts ran in an entirely new direction. She had always assumed that Mrs. Thorold's plans must include another large and audacious criminal scheme. But what if she'd been wrong? What if Mrs. Thorold intended self-harm instead, and this was her way of saying farewell to her daughter? It would be a shameful end to a stained and warped life, but it would, at least, be her decision. One couldn't say the same for the workhouse. And if Mrs. Thorold did plan to commit suicide, what was Mary's responsibility to stop her before she could take another life, even if it was her own?

Mary thought again of her father. Was a courageous suicide of more value than a dishonorable life? It was the Chinese way, yet he had not chosen it. Perhaps her father had been more English than she knew. He might have understood Angelica's bleak horror of the taboo of self-murder. The stigma that would attach to Angelica and any children she might have. The denial of burial in Christian ground. Above all, the endless, exquisite anxiety about how different things might have been.

"If by 'extreme' you mean destroying myself, then you may rest assured, my girl. There is yet too much fire in this old bed of coals for me to entertain the possibility."

Such are the complexities of family devotion that Angelica actually sighed with relief. Eventually, however, she said in a wary tone, "How else might one define 'extreme'?"

"How might others define the term, you mean?"

"You're prevaricating again, Mama."

"True," conceded Mrs. Thorold. "For I should not describe my plans as the least bit extreme. In fact, they seem rather apt to me, featuring a strong element of poetic justice."

Mary rolled her eyes. Mrs. Thorold had the most thoroughly fractured sense of justice she'd ever encountered. "Apt," from her, could mean anything at all, so long as it significantly benefited her.

"Mother!"

"Hush, Angelica. We are yet in public." Mrs. Thorold turned her head left and right, glancing behind the bench. Mary froze. The darkness was in her favor—by rights, the glare of the gas lamp ought to render blackly invisible anything outside the glowing circle—but she had a half-superstitious faith in Mrs. Thorold's powers.

"Mama, you are talking in riddles!" Angelica's voice was no less fierce for being a whisper.

Mrs. Thorold sounded amused, indulgent. "You were always very literal. Shall I unfold my scheme for you, then?"

"Anything, so long as you stop hinting and alluding in that portentous way."

"I am speaking entirely seriously now, Daughter. I can only take you into my confidence if you promise faithfully to keep my plans a secret, and never reveal what I am saying to another living soul. Are you able to make and keep that promise?"

Mary hitched herself forward very slightly, fighting to hear clearly over the sudden roar of blood in her ears.

Angelica was silent for a short while. Then, in a very subdued voice, she said, "Is it possible to make such a pledge without becoming part of the scheme? I can't promise to join anything blindly. Not even for you, Mama."

"That is wise, Angelica. And yes, so long as you swear perfect secrecy, I shall not ask you for a thing."

"In that case, I promise."

"Swear it," insisted her mother. "On your father's grave."

Angelica's voice was shaking now, but she said in a low, hoarse tone, "I swear on Papa's grave."

When Mrs. Thorold spoke, her voice was buoyant with satisfaction. "Thank you. I do not believe your confidence shall be misplaced, my dear, but I shall first explain to you the reasoning behind my decisions.

"As Englishwomen, I suspect you and I have always had an unthinking confidence in our nation. The excellence of our policemen, the protection of the common law, and the essential fairness of the judiciary were things we took for granted. So far as we deigned to think of them,

219

we were grateful to live in such an enlightened country, especially in comparison to the bloody violence that wracked the Continent less than a generation ago. For me—and, I suspect, for you—that illusion was abruptly smashed two years ago when your father was arrested, disgraced, jailed, and indirectly murdered by the very government we'd trusted." Mrs. Thorold paused here, but Angelica made no response. "It was this betrayal that left me homeless, and worse than a widow. The only thing that stood between me and utter destitution was the handful of jewels I'd managed to hide—illegally, of course. Even my journey to France, where I desperately sought to recover my health after such a brutal series of shocks, was considered against the law, for not content with obliterating my husband and his life's work, the police also sought to destroy me with their preposterous and utterly impossible accusations." She was panting now in her vehemence, and still Angelica remained silent.

"Now, on the brink of starvation once more, I must support myself. I do not seek the comfort and plenty to which I was born and to which I was accustomed, but merely to keep body and soul together. I find it impossible. There is no honest work I can perform, nobody who will employ me, no honest opportunity available to a lady of my age and education and talents. I have made up my mind, Angelica, that I cannot live in a country such as this; a country that sought to crush me under its heel;

a country that cast me to the dogs. And so, tomorrow, I depart its shores for the last time. I shall never return."

Despite her knowledge of Mrs. Thorold's true history, and despite her ready skepticism, Mary found herself somewhat moved by this florid speech. It was too easy to imagine a false accusation that would effortlessly destroy a life. After all, Mary had herself been accused, tried, convicted. The law had been just as harsh and unforgiving as Mrs. Thorold made it out to be. But she mustn't allow personal feeling to sway her judgment. As it happened, Mrs. Thorold was guilty of the crimes with which she was charged, and that changed the portrait entirely: from one of pathos and female disadvantage to one of an expert manipulator who would say, and probably do, whatever was necessary to achieve her ends.

"That does not surprise me, Mama," said Angelica in low, emotional tones. "I, too, find it easier to live abroad and alone because of what happened to Papa. But I remain entirely in the dark as to how you intend to support yourself in France. Surely the same obstacles exist in that country? Unless . . ." She suddenly swiveled toward her mother, voice rising in her excitement. "Unless you came back to London to retrieve some jewels or gold you had hidden away somewhere? Perhaps they are even in our house—the old house, I mean—in Cheyne Walk?"

"That would be apt in a fairy tale," said Mrs. Thorold. "And yet you are not so far from the truth. Are you certain

221

you wish to hear me out, Daughter? My tale is still largely untold, and you may go away from here as innocent as you came, if I stop now."

Once again, Mary couldn't help but hear an echo of her own life: the moment when Anne and Felicity asked if, as an agent, she wished to hear more about a case. The point at which she was entrusted with dangerous information.

Angelica's consideration was brief but agonizing to Mary. Much as she wished Angelica to follow her own conscience, this was the best opportunity Mary would ever have to learn how Mrs. Thorold thought. Finally, Angelica released a pent-up breath. "Yes, Mama," she said in an admirably steady voice. "I do."

"Very well," said her mother. She paused for a moment, and Mary was tempted to creep forward, beyond the protection of the broad tree trunk. What was Mrs. Thorold about to do? Half a moment later, she heard a swish of skirts, the crunch of a boot on gravel. She immediately shrank back against the tree trunk, trying to slow the pounding of her heart.

"Mama, where are you going?"

"I mistrust this spot. It's overlooked."

"It's the most open bench in the square," said Angelica, impatience in her voice. "There's absolutely nothing around us, all the way back to that tree."

"And behind the tree?"

Mary tensed, ready for flight.

Angelica sighed. "Mama, you are stalling again. Pray

222

do me the courtesy of speaking to me frankly, as an adult, instead of toying with my emotions."

Mrs. Thorold seemed to resettle herself on the bench with a sigh. "You remember your solemn oath."

"Yes."

"My intention is this: Before I shake the dust of this country from my sandals, I shall take what I need from its coffers. I shall perform an act of restoration to our family, of true justice. And in doing so, I shall ensure my future—and yours, too."

Angelica was swift to slice through such pompous rhetoric. "Mama, you are talking of *theft*?"

"It requires a certain Robin Hood morality, I grant you," said Mrs. Thorold, "but once one opens one's mind and sees things from all sides, it is the only possible solution."

"But how on earth . . . ? Mama, are you feverish? These are the ravings of a—a—a person who is unwell," Angelica finished limpingly.

"A madwoman or a lunatic? Oh, no, my dear. I promise you I am of sound mind."

"Then . . . how? How can a lone woman, without any experience or training, steal enough valuables to make such a colossal risk worthwhile?"

Mary could hear the smile in Mrs. Thorold's voice. "In being just that: a humble, underestimated lone woman." Again, that jolt through Mary's body, as Mrs. Thorold's wickedness mapped itself onto her own life, her own beliefs. The skill of the overlooked female: that was the central premise of the Agency, the reason for its many brilliant and unlikely successes. And now Mrs. Thorold was intent on exploiting it for criminal ends. Perhaps this ought to have come as no surprise, for she had done much the same thing two years earlier, as the apparently invalid wife of a rich merchant.

Mrs. Thorold reached into her pocket and retrieved something small and gleaming: a gold watch. "I shall not explain the details in this moment. Suffice it to say, I have a plan thoroughly worked out, and every confidence that it will succeed. I know what I want to take, where it is, how securely it is guarded, and its value as a stolen object without provenance. By sunrise, I shall be halfway across the Channel. And I shall be a free woman at last." She paused. "The question is, Angelica Maria Thorold, will you also be free?"

Angelica's silence was maddeningly ambiguous. Was she thunderstruck? Calculating? Tempted? Appalled? Mary scarcely dared breathe as she awaited a response.

Eventually, Angelica spoke coolly and quietly. "If you are asking for my help, Mama, I shall need to know more about your plans. I cannot possibly agree to help you blindly."

"I do not require help, child; I am entirely prepared to act alone. Indeed, I had expected to do so, until we so fortuitously met again. But as your mother, and a lady who understands the complexities of being alone in the world, I am offering you an opportunity. A business venture. A partnership, if you will."

"Thorold and Daughter, instead of Thorold and Son?"

"Just so." A brief pause. Then, "I need hardly enumerate the advantages to you, but perhaps I shall, in any case. An assured income, much larger than the present pittance you earn by teaching music. Independence in the world. An alternative to the stage, should you decide that such a life is not for you."

"That is all very tempting," said Angelica slowly, "but you omit what would be, for me, the greatest incentive."

"And what is that?" Mrs. Thorold sounded genuinely curious.

"Family. Not being entirely alone in the world."

A brief pause. "Then it appears that I have your answer."

"Not yet," said Angelica firmly. "As I said, I need to know more."

"What more would you know?"

"I need your solemn oath, Mama, that nobody will be harmed in this scheme of yours. I will not have blood on my hands. And I need to hear the plan, in detail, and satisfy myself that it is rational. If I am to risk not only my music and my career but also my neck, I must be a full partner in the scheme."

Mrs. Thorold took her time considering before she spoke. "All your requirements are reasonable. I give you my word that no blood will be shed. And I appreciate your caution: I expected no less. But to explain the plan, we must walk on." She rose, a little stiffly, and extended her arm to Angelica. "Shall we?"

Angelica hesitated for only a moment before standing and linking arms with her mother. "Yes. Let us go."

Sixteen

As mother and daughter returned to the graveled path, Mary stretched her arms and legs with slow, small movements. Mrs. Thorold wasn't the only one who felt the cold. Mary's first thought was of immediate action: Did she and her shadow agent have the strength to overpower Mrs. Thorold and bring her to a police station? They had the element of surprise, which they would need. Mrs. Thorold was almost certainly armed.

Yet it would be more effective by far to catch her in the commission of her next crime. If the old charges were dismissed for any reason, or if James's testimony was somehow void, it would be better to have fresh evidence against her. Furthermore, Mary didn't quite believe Mrs. Thorold's protestations that she was prepared to work entirely alone. It was possible, in fact, that Mary and her fellow agent had walked into a loose snare, and that the moment they moved against Mrs. Thorold, her collaborators would spring the trap. With her heart racing like this, all senses stretched to their limits, Mary sometimes found it difficult to distinguish between legitimate suspicion and rank paranoia.

She watched the Thorolds walk away at a dignified but steady pace, yet she continued to linger on the path in plain sight. Within a minute, she was joined by a person in rough trousers and sailor's peacoat. "I couldn't hear a word they said," was the first thing the stranger said, resettling her cloth cap.

"Mrs. Thorold asked Angelica to join her in a large robbery. Angelica is considering," said Mary.

"Where are they going now?"

The Bank of England, of course. And yet Mary refrained from leaping to such a conclusion. She'd had no further confirmation on that matter, from this evening's work. Once she had that knowledge, Mary could safely summon a constable, a squadron of constables, the whole bloody army, if that's what it took. Until she was certain, though, it was just four unaccompanied women trotting briskly down Montague Street on a Saturday night. "We'll follow them and see," said Mary. "When I give you the signal, report to the Agency as fast as possible."

The woman nodded and evaporated into the shadows once more.

At the end of Montague Street, Mary expected the Thorolds to veer eastward, to the City. The swiftest route to the Bank of England would take them through Holborn, past Newgate and St. Paul's. However, they instead turned west onto Great Russell Street. Mary's gut tightened.

After a minute, the Thorolds stopped before the museum's high, brass-spiked fence, mother pointing out something to daughter. Mary passed them at a brisk walk, staying silent and far enough away that she was only another pedestrian hurrying home of an evening. When she reached the corner of Museum Street, just opposite the main gates, Mary slowed her steps. There was a shallow doorstep a few yards down, the entrance to a tightly shuttered shop, where she could take shelter from the wind. And if the Thorolds turned eastward, as she still anticipated, she would be once more behind them.

Two minutes passed, and then five. Mary scanned the rest of the street, but it was a murk of shadows and fog. She was just about to set off in an easterly direction when a pair of women presented themselves before the immense gates. Mary caught her breath.

The museum was closed, of course. By four o'clock, all visitors would have been shooed out and the two enormous pairs of gates locked until Monday morning. Yet in the gloom, she could see the taller figure, Mrs. Thorold, in conversation with the turnkey. Mary frowned. This seemed entirely unorthodox, Mrs. Thorold's offering herself to a person's notice. She wasn't the sort who appreciated witnesses. And what on earth did she hope to accomplish at the museum after hours? But less than half a minute later, the guard unlocked the small, human-size entrance within the larger gate. Then, dragging his heels as though exceedingly weary, he locked the gate once more and collapsed into the guard's box, while the Thorolds vanished into the foggy courtyard.

Astonishing. Mary stared into the mists, as though seeing into the depths of the museum—not to mention Mrs. Thorold's mind—were merely a matter of concentration. What on earth . . . ? And then, quite suddenly, the answers tumbled into place in her cold and sluggish brain.

It wasn't the Bank at all.

Perhaps it never had been. Mrs. Thorold's sudden apparition outside the Bank, her perplexing disappearance from the hackney carriage—these now seemed part of a blind, a cunningly laid diversion . . . or, at the very least, a malign coincidence.

It was only Mrs. Thorold's meeting with Angelica this evening that had led Mary to the real target: the British Museum. Had Mrs. Thorold been able to resist recruiting her daughter . . . Mary shivered. Significant events so often turned on casual coincidence, sudden impulse. But this time, the good fortune was hers. She suddenly understood not only where and when, but the all-important how.

Mrs. Thorold must know the gatekeeper because she worked at the museum! It was an inside position that granted her frequent access to the museum's collections, the knowledge with which to plan a successful heist, and the leisure to pull it off when the building was closed to the public. The museum had a staff of curators and experts on any number of arcane subjects, of course, but as a woman, Mrs. Thorold could never hope to attain such a post. No, she had to be one of the domestics who lived on site: maids, cooks, housekeepers, a governess. *This* was what Mrs. Thorold had referred to when she spoke of being a humble, underestimated lone woman. And they were all housed in the vast, private wings of the museum.

Mary waited another minute, allowing the guard time to resettle himself. She saw no movement in the other sentry box, but assumed that it was manned nonetheless. She began to walk along Great Russell Street at a crisp but ladylike pace. As she passed through the yellowish haze of the nearest streetlamp, she raised her right hand and brushed it across the brim of her bonnet: a small gesture, the removal of a distracting hair or thread. It was also the signal for her colleague to report their location to the Agency.

As Mary tucked herself into the next available doorway, maintaining a clear view of the entrance gates, she felt a distinct sense of calm. It was now a little after eight o'clock. By her calculation, a good runner needed half an hour to reach the Agency's headquarters in Acacia Road, over slick cobblestones in the ill-lit streets. Then Anne Treleaven would have to present herself at Scotland Yard to explain the situation, and there would be a brief wait for a unit of policemen to be dispatched. Mary could expect to be here alone for at least an hour and a quarter, and likely a bit longer. Then there was the trifling matter of how they might apprehend Mrs. Thorold. For now, however, she pushed those thoughts away with fatalistic serenity. This was a case with exceptionally few certainties, but a fresh one now emerged: The end was in sight.

Seventeen

After roughly three-quarters of an hour, Mary became aware of footsteps in the middle distance. In the darkness and fog, her ears offered more information than her eyes: the sound came from a pair of steel pattens ringing unevenly on the cobbles. She was therefore not surprised to discern a woman, wrapped in a shawl, just inside the museum gates. She rapped briefly on the guardhouse and said quite loudly, "Coffee, Mr. Welland."

After a few seconds, the turnkey emerged. "Eh?" From his tone, it seemed that he had been napping.

"Coffee, you sorry beggar," said the woman. Her tone was impatient but fundamentally affectionate; an elder sister doing him a favor. "Don't say you couldn't use a little waking up."

"You're a savior, Mrs. Price," he muttered, cupping his hands around the mug. "Good Lord, I feel like death warmed over. What a night to be the only one on guard."

"What, they took Mr. Entwistle with them, too?" She jerked her head toward the other guard hut.

"Aye. Matter of urgency in the City, they said." He drank deeply of the coffee and groaned, but it didn't sound like satisfaction. "Oh. God. I swear, my insides are on fire."

"I told Cook them prawns was too far gone to be served at dinner," said Mrs. Price in waspish tones. "Do you think she'd listen to me? Oh, no: she'd as soon poison us all as waste a scrap of the upstairs leavings. You didn't eat any prawns, did you, Mr. Welland?"

"No prawns," he croaked. "I don't hold with foreign food." He raised the mug to his lips, then suddenly lowered it. "This ain't right," he said suddenly. "I never had food poisoning like this before."

"No call to be such a baby about it," retorted Mrs. Price. "I'm feeling half dead myself, and don't get me started on the state of that lot upstairs. They'll want nursing all night, and who else is to do it, I ask you?"

Welland raised his mug once more, with unsteady hands. He gulped, flinched, and clutched his abdomen. "You don't think it's the dysentery, do you? I seen that go through a building like wildfire."

"Don't say that." Mrs. Price shivered and huddled deeper into her shawl. Then, sharply, "You drinking that coffee or not? I got to get back inside."

The mug wobbled for a few seconds. The next moment,

Welland's body buckled. He gave a wordless cry, dropped to his knees, and began to vomit.

"Here, you! You never said it was that bad, you silly—" Mrs. Price sounded genuinely worried. "Why didn't you say you needed a basin?"

Welland was unfit to reply. He retched violently, repeatedly, his body tipping forward until his cheek was pressed to the slime and grit of the cobbles. Even then, he continued to vomit and writhe and moan.

Mrs. Price hovered over him, flapping her hands in agitation. "Welland, you oughtn't lie on the ground like that—you'll catch a chill. Sit up, why don't you?" After several minutes, Welland's agony weakened. His body continued to shiver, but these were smaller convulsions, quite different from the noisy, painful voiding of before. He was sobbing now.

"There, there," said Mrs. Price. "Let's get you inside. You'll have to stand, Welland—I can't help you. It feels like there's a knife in my bowels, and I'm for my bed, but we'll get you inside and cleaned up first. Whether it's the prawns or the dysentery I don't know, but it's bad, this." The two servants clung to each other and hobbled in stages back toward the museum, Mrs. Price muttering all the way.

Mary took a moment to absorb what she'd seen. The museum gates were currently unguarded, with Welland indisposed and his colleague called away on a "matter of urgency in the City." Illness was at large within the building, apparently affecting both servants and the academic staff. That left Mrs. Thorold and Angelica inside, free to do God knows what.

Mary peered through the palings, trying to discern movement amid the fog. It seemed bizarre that the courtyard would be unpatrolled. Yet if there was a guard on his rounds, Mrs. Price would have hailed him for help rather than force Welland to stand and walk on his own. No, the courtyard must be deserted.

What was Mary's best course of action? She had planned to remain outside the gates in order to brief Anne Treleaven and the police when they arrived. Yet what might Mrs. Thorold accomplish inside, while Mary waited in safe if chilly inertia? Besides, it had already been a full hour since she dispatched her fellow agent for help. The police would soon arrive, likely within the half hour.

There remained only the challenge of entering the gate. The railings were some fifteen feet high and too narrowly spaced to squeeze through, even had she been unhampered by a crinoline. Mary felt a twitch of resentment for the slow labor of picking locks. Luck continued with her, however: even as she reached for her unusually long steel hairpin, her eye caught a gleam of metal lodged in the muck. She smiled widely. Instead of bothering with the hairpin, she extended her umbrella between two palings, curved handle foremost. A moment later, she was holding a small ring of keys that could only have fallen from Welland's belt as he writhed on the ground.

Mary unlocked the gate and left it wide open: a sign of warning and invitation for the police. She stepped around Welland's pool of vomit, gleaming dark and viscous in the gaslight, and into the courtyard. She found a locked door, and then a key on Welland's ring that fit the door. Soon, Mary was inside the museum.

She was in an unlit passage, which probably meant she was in the servants' wing. Mary found it difficult to imagine that the corridors of the educated and affluent men who ran the museum would be so dim. She closed the door and stood still, listening in order to find her bearings. There was, first of all, a striking silence: a building at rest. Then, as her ears adjusted, a few sounds of habitation—footsteps, a voice or two—one floor above. The large doormat was muddy beneath her feet, and she saw a pair of pattens hastily kicked to one side. Mary glided forward, pausing to read the brass nameplates on each door she passed: HOUSEKEEPER. PANTRY. LINENS. She was in the right place. Each door had a faint aroma of olive oil and vinegar, the traditional components of wood polish. At the end of the corridor she found a stairwell with flights of steps leading both up and down.

There was no noise from below, but the smell of smoke, onions, and meat announced that she'd found the kitchens. It was quiet, rather to her surprise: even the washing up was finished, which meant that the museum staff dined early. Silence meant that Mrs. Price and Welland were above, with the other domestics. She turned away from the staircases, toward the central building. There would presumably be a set of connecting doors, sturdily locked, that led into the museum proper. She groped her way left, wishing it was safe enough to light a candle. It would be instructive to see, not merely feel, the layout of the building. However, the corridor made a ninety-degree turn and ended in a locked single door. It was much simpler than she'd envisioned, and in keeping with the neoclassical severity of the new building.

She touched her palms to the door. It was covered in baize, to muffle any domestic noise that might drift into the great public space of the museum. It was secured only with bolts at top and bottom, and a heavy brass lock in the middle. It occurred to her that there might be a guard on the other side of the door, so she put her eye to the keyhole. There was nothing conclusive: no perceptible source of light, for example, to indicate a human presence.

She didn't like it. The very serious disadvantage of this elegant floor plan was that it provided absolutely nowhere to go if her explorations were interrupted: no dogleg corner, no antechamber, not even a thick drapery behind which she could hide and hope. She turned carefully back toward the stairwell and descended halfway to the kitchens. Here was a promising spot from which to listen.

She had been waiting for only a few minutes when she heard footfalls: one—no, two pairs of footsteps. They were descending from the first floor, accompanied by the murmur of female conversation.

"I heard one of them say it's dysentery," said a familiar voice. "It's hardly surprising, living in a filthy city such as this, in such an unhealthy climate."

"I do hope you've not caught it, Mama."

"Don't worry about me, child. Since living in France, I've developed the constitution of the proverbial ox."

"Most unladylike." There was a smile in Angelica's voice that made Mary cringe.

"Indeed. In any case, they're settled now with their sugared barley water, and they ought to keep to their beds tonight."

A pause. "And so we begin?"

"We begin."

Only silence.

"Unless, of course, you have changed your mind. If that is the case, speak now, Angelica. For once we begin, we must stand together."

A deep breath. "Mama, you promised that nobody would be hurt, no blood shed."

"I did."

"Very well," said Angelica. Her voice shook, but only a little. "I am with you, Mama."

"Thorold and Daughter?"

"Thorold and Daughter."

Pact made, they lapsed into silence, making it easier for Mary to track their steps. Accompanied by a shimmering haze of lamplight, they walked down the long corridor that seemed to lead toward the main hall of the museum. There was a pause as they shot the bolts, and then the quiet scratch of a key inserted, the faint clicks of tumblers rotating. The door bumped softly as it closed once more, sealing Mary in darkness. She listened again. It was entirely quiet upstairs. Disconcertingly so, for a building supposedly full of domestic servants. After seeing Welland and Mrs. Price at the front gates, Mary thought she understood why.

She shed her cloak, making it into a neat bundle and pushing her reticule into its folds. She left these on the step and twisted the tip of her umbrella. It was specially adapted for the Agency's purposes and had a small but extremely effective blade concealed within the shaft. Her fingertips tingled, as did her cheeks. She felt light and pared down, ready for adventure, as she glided silently through the corridor. She paused before the baize-covered door, listening. Nothing—although the fabric would damp any noise from the other side, too. Blind entrances were always a risk: exposing oneself, moving into an unfamiliar space with no idea of who or what awaited. She rotated the knife in her palm and took a deep breath. There was nothing to do but keep going.

Moving swiftly, Mary opened the door and walked into the King's Library. She also walked directly into the expectant presence of Maria Thorold. "Close that door, please," Mrs. Thorold said, speaking over Mary's left shoulder.

Mary knew better than to turn her head. Besides, she couldn't tear her gaze from the neat black revolver pointed straight at her chest. It was her first time as the target of such a device, and what frightened her most was its power to send her mind whirling, fracturing her thoughts like the segments of a kaleidoscope. Mary snatched at them: fragments about James, Anne Treleaven and the Agency, Scotland Yard. But she could control none of them, pursue nothing to its rational conclusion. She felt pure panic, a dangerous pulse of undisciplined energy, and all she could do was stare at the gun.

"Mama," said Angelica, her voice full of fear, "you gave your word."

"Hush," said her mother, visibly irritated. "I know what I said." She stared at Mary with open dislike. "I underestimated you the first time. You and that silly schoolma'am. I shan't make that mistake again."

Mary swallowed, but her mouth was still too dry to permit speech. Just as well. She had nothing clever to say. Very slowly, she tucked her right hand into the fold of her skirts, hoping to conceal her blade.

Mrs. Thorold only sighed. "Angelica, take that stupid toy from Miss Quinn."

With trembling fingers, Angelica obeyed. She offered Mary's knife to her mother, holding it with the extreme tips of her fingers.

Mrs. Thorold didn't even glance at it. "Get rid of it, dear girl. We don't need brass when we've got gold." She waved the revolver under Mary's nose. "You've been quite the little friend to Angelica, haven't you? Comforting the grieving daughter, picking her brains about her mother's whereabouts, sneaking about town, keeping an eye on her. . . . How many of you are there? The Treleaven woman, of course. Any others?"

"You'd know," said Mary, her voice shaking. "What about the one you stabbed in the back?"

Angelica gasped.

"I don't know what you're talking about," said Mrs. Thorold with a delighted sneer. "Safest to assume it's every hag in that damned school, though. I'm tickled to learn that Scotland Yard is so exceedingly radical in its ideas. Women police constables! How thrillingly modern."

Suddenly, one of the tiny shards of the kaleidoscope clicked into place. "You're terribly confident," said Mary, "considering we're presently surrounded by policemen. There's a detachment of constables from Scotland Yard assigned to the museum; the old Military Guard; even the Fire Brigade. They all live on the premises, or very nearby. Are you quite sure you've chosen the right place to burgle, Mrs. Thorold?"

Mrs. Thorold smiled. "And how do you intend summoning all these fearsome bogeymen, Miss Quinn? You could scream, of course, but I'm terribly sensitive to sudden noises. Why, standing here with my finger on the trigger of this little revolver, anything at all might happen."

"Let us suppose I am not afraid. I scream. You shoot

me—breaking, incidentally, the promise you so solemnly made to your daughter not ten minutes ago. Let us further suppose that such a betrayal does not bother you, and also that I die. The noise from the shot will awaken the entire building. The place will be swarming with police and soldiers in less than a minute. How far do you think you can run in that time?"

"Such courage in the face of danger!" exclaimed Mrs. Thorold. "Shall we test your hypothesis, Miss Quinn? Go on: scream."

Mary stared at her, astounded. Had Mrs. Thorold in fact gone mad? Why on earth was she so willing to risk discovery, pursuit, an additional death on her hands?

The seconds ticked on, and Mrs. Thorold grinned, exposing a set of excellent teeth. "Where is your spirit of scientific inquiry, Miss Quinn? Remember: nothing ventured, nothing gained."

There was something nagging at her . . . evidence toward a theory for Mrs. Thorold's obscene confidence that she would not be caught. Something about the staff . . . in her memory, she caught an echo of the gate-keeper's helpless retching, the dark gleam of vomit on cobblestones: food poisoning or some other digestive upset, they'd all assumed. She also heard an echo of Angelica's voice saying dysentery, and of Mrs. Thorold delivering sugared barley water to the invalids.

Mary's eyes widened as she snatched the possibility and held it tight, examining it with incredulity. Could

Mrs. Thorold have engineered a museum-wide wave of illness? It had to be something sudden, which gave no time to send for a physician or sound an alert. Something that would affect an entire group of people who shared a source of food and drink, or who breathed the same air. It was straightforward enough to poison a hundred people sitting down to the same banquet, thought Mary, but what of many separate households, which was effectively the case within the museum? There would be different dining tables and menus with which to contend, and surely no one servant was involved with all those varied meal preparations. Besides which, that accounted only for the museum staff. The police, the Military Guard, the Fire Brigade . . . they would surely have separate living and dining arrangements. And dysentery was a closed mystery, spreading rapidly through an entire neighborhood while leaving the next street unharmed; one couldn't expect to harness a plague, or to pass untouched by it oneself. What did that leave as a possibility?

"I confess myself disappointed, Miss Quinn," drawled Mrs. Thorold, still smirking. "I thought you braver than this, more self-sacrificial." She lowered the gun. "Come, then, I promise not to shoot. For the time being, in any case. Will you now do me the honor of creating a ruckus?"

Mary swallowed, certain now of the situation. "How did you do it?" she demanded. "How did you disable so many people?"

Mrs. Thorold twirled her revolver and trilled a snatch

of song, a cheeky music-hall favorite from a couple of years ago. The choice of tune rather surprised Mary, although perhaps that was part of the point. The main idea, however, was soon exceedingly clear: although Mrs. Thorold was close to tone-deaf, her hard contralto voice rang out freely, up and down the considerable length of the King's Library. On finishing, all three women listened in silence for a response: footsteps, voices, anything at all.

Mary pivoted so she could see both women. "Are they still alive?" Her voice echoed harmlessly into the resounding silence. "Or have you already broken your promise to Angelica on a scale she could never have anticipated?"

Angelica's face blanched at the suggestion, and her eyes darted to her mother. She opened her lips as though to speak, but no sound emerged.

"And where are the police and Military Guard?" demanded Mary. "Why was there only one gatekeeper? Why is Mr. Entwistle on an urgent errand in the City?"

Mrs. Thorold waved her hand dismissively. "I am not here to answer your questions, Miss Quinn. Besides which, they bore me." She leveled the gun at Mary once more. "Now that we've established a sound reason for your perfect obedience, let's get on with it. Walk."

Faced with the gun's muzzle, Mary felt her pulse surge once again. She was relieved, however, to note that she was not quite so panicked as she had been a few minutes ago. She asked, in a voice that shook only slightly, "Angelica? Are you satisfied with such an answer?"

Angelica licked her lips. "Mama. Are they alive?"

"Do you think I would break my word to you?"

"That is not an answer." Angelica's voice was hoarse.

Mrs. Thorold sighed. She said with exaggerated patience, as though to an irrationally anxious child, "Yes, they are alive." She paused. "Do you believe me, or do you require ocular proof?"

"Forgive me, Mama. I ought to have had more confidence in you."

Mrs. Thorold dealt Mary a triumphant look but said only, "Then let us have no more second-guessing." She prodded Mary with the gun. "Walk."

They thus embarked on a nightmare tour of the museum, a party of three on a private viewing. Their only light source was Mrs. Thorold's paraffin lantern, which she gave to Angelica to light the way. This was in direct contravention of museum rules: artificial illumination of any sort—candles, oil lamps, the new gas lighting—was strictly forbidden, for fear of fire. As they progressed through the building, the lamp's yellow glare flickered and danced, creating monstrous shapes in the nearest shadows and transforming art objects: a marble sculpture became a flash of fractured bone; a bronze vessel seemed to gleam with unearthly light.

Mary strained her ears, listening for approaching footsteps. Close to two hours had passed since she had sent her shadow agent to summon help. Why had nobody yet arrived? What could have gone wrong?

They wandered past the natural history exhibits, bypassed Lord Elgin's infamous marbles. Mary suddenly thought of the spectacular Indian amulet she and Angelica had admired here just a few days ago. There was no inviolable chain of reasoning, but the object simply fit. It was extraordinarily valuable. Small, thus easy to carry and conceal. Mrs. Thorold might even have seen Angelica admiring it at some point. But the most compelling reason was Mrs. Thorold's own personal history with items such as this: Indian treasures raided and illegally traded by her dead husband. Taking this amulet represented both a return to form and a journey back in time. It also gave Mrs. Thorold the last word in the long power struggle of her marriage.

Mary slowed her pace imperceptibly, trying to create a little more time in which to think. She was outnumbered at the moment. Even if she thought she could best Mrs. Thorold in a physical struggle—an unlikely proposition, so long as the woman kept the gun trained upon her—Angelica was still apt to side with her mother. Mary's only small chance, going into this room, was Angelica's sentimental connection to her father. If she could somehow touch that raw nerve, Angelica might begin to yield.

They were in the right part of the museum now, moving swiftly through centuries and across continents. As they approached the Far Eastern exhibits (the Orient, the Middle East, the Asian subcontinent, and even Turkey were all jammed together into one category), Mary felt Angelica tense, evidently recalling the amulet and their conversation on that day. *Good. Let her remember.*

They swept past a large display of armor and made their way toward the jewel case. Angelica gulped, a small but distinct sound in the perfect silence. The women stared at the amulet, all three of them made still and reverent by its exquisite perfection. Even now, under weak artificial light, its ruby depths held fire captive and its fine gold filigree sparkled an invitation.

Mary counted to five and then said abruptly, deliberately, "You'll never sell this on the open market. You must have a private collector in mind; someone to whom you've sold similar treasures in the past."

Mrs. Thorold recovered quickly, but not before Mary saw a flash of irritation cross her face. "That's enough from you," she said, waving the revolver slightly in reminder. "Speak only when spoken to, Miss Quinn; there's a good girl."

Angelica blinked and shook her head. It was difficult to know whether she was troubled by the suggestion or merely irritated by Mary's efforts.

"Now, Miss Quinn, you may make yourself useful. Smash that glass, if you please."

"Don't you have the key to the case? I thought you'd be better prepared than this," replied Mary. In answer, the nose of the gun dug into her spine. Mary swallowed hard and thought of Ivy Murchison's back.

"Break the glass." Mrs. Thorold took two steps back but kept the gun trained upon Mary.

Mary thought longingly of the cloak she'd left in the residential wing: wrapped around her hand, it would have offered excellent protection against broken glass. Instead, she raised her arm and brought it down on the top of the glass case, using the back of her elbow like a hammer. The glass cracked. She glanced at Mrs. Thorold, who nodded, and she struck again. This time the glass shattered into tiny shards, some of which lodged in her sleeve and skin.

Mary stepped aside and watched Mrs. Thorold reach gingerly into the case for the amulet. She tucked it into a small velvet bag, which she then handed to her daughter. Angelica stared at it for a minute before looping it around her wrist.

Now they had each taken part in the theft. Mary had acted under compulsion, it was true, but the fact remained that she had smashed the glass. That violence now marked her body, a form of evidence against her. She did not permit herself to consider under what conditions her body might be found and that evidence interpreted. For the moment, her job was to keep trying to change the balance of power; to feed Angelica's doubt and uneasiness; to stay alive.

She turned to Mrs. Thorold and asked, "Where next?"

Eighteen

The same evening

The Bank of England, Threadneedle Street

It was better than the theater. This evening, in a cordoned-off triangle of the City of London, there waited the commissioner of the Metropolitan Police, an entire division of uniformed constables, an army platoon, a detachment of the Military Guard, a unit of the Fire Brigade, and the full court of directors of the Bank of England. They were all here to shift some gold.

James Easton stood at the corner of Threadneedle Street and Bartholomew Lane, insensible to the wind and the chilling drizzle that permeated his overcoat. He had no official role in this drama, of course, but had prevailed upon Mr. Bentley for permission to observe. Witnessing the transfer of the gold had some bearing on his design work and on his better understanding of the project requirements. But mainly it was because he could not possibly rest easy until the gold was safely removed and the risk created by the theft of the building plans therefore neutralized. It was, he also conceded, a magnificent logistical feat.

He checked his watch: ten o'clock. As if in confirmation, the bells of St. Paul's Cathedral began to chime. Weary of standing still, James began to pace up and down the street, listening and learning as he went. The removal of the gold was scheduled to begin at eleven, for reasons best known to the court of directors, but that now sounded optimistic. There was still a deal of organization remaining: officers to brief, men to instruct, a train of closed wagons to marshal. James was counting the people all around him, trying to work out where they belonged, when his gaze caught on a familiar-looking stranger. He was of middle height and build, with dark gold hair, and had a neatly trimmed brown mustache and beard. Handsome. He stood attentively under an umbrella, quite alone. James couldn't think where they might have met, yet found himself persuaded that he somehow knew this gentleman.

As though privy to James's perplexity, the man glanced over and winked at him. James's first impulse was to check over his shoulder, but there was nobody behind him. A faint blush rose to his cheeks. He didn't know quite how to respond, except to avert his gaze. When, a few moments later, he risked another look, the blond gentleman was deep in conversation with a police officer. James frowned. Not just any police officer: the commissioner himself. Where had he met this man? They weren't on amicable terms, he felt, but he couldn't for the life of him remember why. His memory was generally excellent, and this lapse troubled him greatly. The conversation concluded, the two men nodded briskly to each other, and then the mysterious gentleman was striding purposefully toward James.

James swallowed hard and stood his ground.

"Thank you for the note," murmured the man.

James blinked into feline green eyes and suppressed a gasp. He was silent for several seconds, absorbing the immense transformation that a beard, mustache, and manly bearing could effect. Then he cleared his throat. "Would you otherwise have known about this evening's plan?" he asked in a tolerably natural voice.

"Yes," said Felicity Frame. "But I appreciate the thought. I take it you've spoken to Miss Quinn about my bona fides?"

"She says you are trustworthy."

"I am honored," said Felicity. "I hope that this will be the beginning of a productive partnership between our firms."

James inclined his head noncommittally. "What name are you using at the moment?" he asked.

Felicity accepted the change of subject with grace. "Fiske. Frederick Fiske."

His next question—there were many—was interrupted by a small commotion at the western side of the cordoned-off street. A pair of burly policemen were pressing back a woman on horseback with limited success. She sat erect in the saddle, spectacles flashing in the gaslight. Her voice was strong and clear. "Constables, I must speak to Mr. Fiske. It is a matter of utmost urgency!"

At the first syllable of the woman's voice, Felicity drew an audible breath. Her head swiveled around, and her expression, always so elegant and impervious, sagged for a moment. Then she nodded to James. "If you'll excuse me . . ."

James watched her approach the horse, saw the female rider dismount with more speed than grace. They conferred for half a minute, heads close together. Then Felicity nodded, spun on her heel, and raced toward the commissioner of police. The rider was about to turn her horse when she caught sight of James. She paused. James still couldn't see her features, but anybody who received prompt obedience from Felicity Frame was a woman to reckon with. He ran toward her.

"You don't know me," she said, "but I have Mary's safety at heart. She is at the British Museum with Mrs. Thorold. Come with me now."

James stared at her for several agonized seconds. It was the perfect trick. What stronger appeal could a person make to him in this moment? What better way to lead him into the unknown? He searched the woman's expression: inscrutable gray eyes behind steel-rimmed spectacles, the jaw of a person accustomed to obedience. He glanced back toward Felicity, who was absorbed in animated conversation with the commissioner.

"If you haven't a mount, you may ride with me," said Anne, vaulting lightly back into the saddle. "I am Miss Anne Treleaven."

His hand was already on the pommel, his foot in the stirrup. "James Easton," he replied, swinging up behind her.

"I know. I have your library book."

It was exceedingly uncomfortable, riding on the hind edge of a lady's sidesaddle, but nothing could have distracted James from Anne's explanation. With the theft of the Bank plans from James's office, Mrs. Thorold had effectively diverted the entire security staff of the British Museum to the Bank of England. She was at the museum now, intent on robbery and assisted by her daughter. Mary had sent for assistance more than two hours ago, but when Anne first turned up at Scotland Yard, she had found only a skeleton staff. All the officials she knew—the ones familiar with the Thorold case, the ones inclined to trust the word of a lone woman who burst into the office and demanded a large-scale response at the peaceful-looking museum—were already at the Bank. Anne had thus been forced to ride on to the Bank to obtain help.

"And then you asked Mrs. Frame to relay the message?" asked James. "Why not tell the commissioner yourself?" Before Anne could reply, he twisted violently in the saddle behind her.

"What's wrong?" asked Anne.

"Let me down," he said. "I'll meet you at the museum."

Before Anne had fully halted, James was on the ground. "I'll meet you there," he said again. And then he was off, chasing after a figure walking eastward along Holborn.

"Wait!" called James. "Mr. Ching?"

The man turned slowly. "Who are you?" He remained in the shadows, and his posture was wary.

"James Easton." The name clearly meant nothing to the man, a fact that rankled. Nevertheless, this was not the time for misplaced vanity. "You are the prizefighter Mr. Ching, are you not?"

The man paused. "Why do you ask?"

James drew a deep breath. Now that he was about to phrase his question, it seemed like an absurd assumption. Felicity had mentioned Mary's sudden intense friendship with a young Chinese man, and he'd leaped to the obvious conclusion. This was an impulsive waste of time. And yet, here he was. Anne Treleaven was fast receding into the distance, and Mary was still alone. With Mrs. Thorold. James swallowed his pride and said, "In the name of Mary Quinn. You are close to her, I believe." No response. James wished he could discern Ching's expression in the darkness. "She is in danger. Will you come with me to help her?"

The man did not hesitate. "Show me the way."

The two men set off toward the museum at a run. Despite James's height advantage, Lang (as James was learning to call him) had a smooth, rapid stride that enabled him to keep pace. His fitness showed: as they ran, he was able to talk without difficulty, explaining not only his name but the fact that he'd expected to meet Mary that evening at seven o'clock. When she had not appeared, even after his prizefight had concluded, Lang's curiosity was piqued. He remembered her sudden urgency at the Bank of England the last time they'd met, and had thought to begin his search for her there.

The museum was less than two miles away, James calculated. Anne was riding at a moderate trot, the fastest speed possible without laming the horse on a dark night on the unevenly surfaced streets. If he and Lang could maintain this pace—and there was no reason they could not, unless one of them put his foot in a pothole—the three of them would arrive at roughly the same time, in twelve minutes or so. Felicity might need five minutes to communicate her needs to the commissioner, and another five for the marshaling of sufficient men. Then it might take the police half an hour, or a little more, to march quickly to the museum. Mary would have some help within the quarter hour, and a small regiment within the hour.

James could only hope that was soon enough.

Nineteen

The British Museum, Bloomsbury

In theory, Mary was worried, guilty, anxious, perplexed, and angry about tonight's events. She worried about being powerless to stop Mrs. Thorold, felt guilty for her own part in the theft of the amulet, was consumed with anxiety for the safety of others, was perplexed by the continued absence of any sort of police presence, and was absolutely livid that Mrs. Thorold seemed, thus far, likely to get away with her nefarious plan. In practice, however, Mary was merely numb. She followed Mrs. Thorold from display to display, watched her select only the most precious items, and listened with increasing impatience for any sounds of police arrival. Most of all, she waited, with small hope, for a chance to intervene.

Mary was also learning a great deal from this mistress of crime. Watching Mrs. Thorold at work was rather like an intimate and advanced tutorial in the art of theft. Mrs. Thorold had clearly researched the pieces she wanted to steal, selecting them as much for size and ease of concealment as for value. For how long had she been planning this heist and living amid the items she planned to take? Most of the prizes she chose were unique, valuables that were far more precious in their present state and would not reward melting down or recutting. This meant she had either one extremely rich and voracious client ready to buy from her, or else was connected to a network of antique dealers who specialized in stolen goods. And, of course, there was the question of how the Thorolds would escape. Mary was genuinely curious on this front, and she wondered if Angelica, in her tremulous acceptance of the present venture, had yet considered its complexities.

"Tomorrow is Sunday," Mary mused aloud as they trotted along. Mrs. Thorold had been silent for some time, and Mary had an obscure sense that they were nearing the completion of her tidy project. "There are few trains running, and those that do are merely local lines, for the benefit of working people on their Sunday excursions. There are no steam packets, of course, or regular ferries across the Channel. Is it possible that you're planning to go into hiding in England with all your booty?" She watched Angelica from the corner of her eye as she spoke, but Angelica failed even to blink. She'd not spoken for nearly an hour, ever since accepting Mrs. Thorold's assurance that the museum staff were alive. What was going through her mind?

"Do you really think I'd forget to provide for something as essential as our escape?" asked Mrs. Thorold. She sounded amused rather than offended. Possibly she, too, was finding the silence wearying and welcomed a little light banter, so long as she was in charge of the subject matter. "I thank you for your concern, Miss Quinn, but we shall manage very nicely, even on the Sabbath." They rounded a corner, and she led them steadily on toward an exterior doorway. She transferred the revolver to her left hand as she unlocked the door with her right, then returned it to her dominant hand and ushered Mary outside into the freezing drizzle.

The air smelled of mud and rain, and Mary breathed deeply of it. She'd not realized just how claustrophobic she found Mrs. Thorold's dark, silent museum of the unconscious until this moment. Mrs. Thorold closed the door behind them, then pointed Mary down a narrow flight of stairs that took them below ground level. Mary remained still and unwilling. Nothing good could come of descending those steps.

"Quickly now, Miss Quinn," said Mrs. Thorold briskly. "Nothing to be afraid of. It's one of the underground storage chambers. There are one or two more items I must retrieve before we are on our way."

Mary couldn't tear her gaze from the solid wooden door, the neat brickwork arch that framed it. Her every instinct resisted the idea. "If Angelica and I precede you down," she said slowly, "there won't be room for you to open the door."

Mrs. Thorold frowned, but soon saw that Mary was

correct. "How thoughtful of you to observe that. I must confess that when I made my calculations for this evening's entertainment, I failed to anticipate having a tourist along on the journey." She considered her choices, gazing for a long moment at the beautiful, expressionless face of her daughter.

Mary held her breath. In this unscripted moment lay her only chance. Perhaps.

"Angelica," said Mrs. Thorold, "pray take these keys and unlock the door."

Mary swallowed. It would have been much better had Mrs. Thorold given Angelica the revolver, but that was too much to hope for. The present arrangement was still deadly, with the gun firmly in Mrs. Thorold's hands, but it might be the best opportunity she would get.

After a brief hesitation, Angelica took the key ring from her mother's upturned palm and descended the half-flight of steps to the locked door. As the lantern bobbed down into the stairwell with Angelica, Mary remained still but slid her gaze toward Mrs. Thorold. It was more difficult to read her expression in this new degree of darkness, but Mary clearly saw her attention flit toward Angelica, checking on her progress. *Good.*

"Your turn, Miss Quinn," said Mrs. Thorold. Her parlor voice sat oddly with the gun she waved in Mary's direction, but Mary was growing accustomed to the paradox. She turned to follow Angelica, who was apparently finding it difficult to manage both lantern and keys. One step, and then another. Each tread was slick with mud, moss, mildew. Mrs. Thorold was directly behind her.

Mary was midstride, descending to the third step, when Angelica gasped and the keys fell to the ground with a surprisingly loud jingle. Here it was: the decisive moment. Mary pivoted on her left foot and twisted her body around, seizing the thick folds of Mrs. Thorold's skirt and pulling with all her might. Mrs. Thorold's feet lost purchase, she slipped onto her back, and the gun fired, lodging a bullet high in the stonework of the museum's exterior wall. Mary leaped onto Mrs. Thorold's prone form, scrabbling after the gun in the near darkness.

Mrs. Thorold kicked wildly, tangled in the cage of her crinoline. She seemed breathless and disoriented, but instinctively held tight to the gun. Mary caught her weapon hand and struck it hard against the stone steps. The gun discharged again, at close quarters this time, deafening them both and blasting brick dust into their eyes and noses. Coughing and crying from the dust, Mary seized Mrs. Thorold's hand in both of hers and banged it a second time, then a third, against the stairs. She felt a sudden, sharp pain in her forearm and realized that Mrs. Thorold was biting her. Mary raised her uninjured left elbow and did what she ought to have done earlier: she knocked Mrs. Thorold unconscious with two decisive blows. At last, the gun clattered out of Mrs. Thorold's grasp and bumped its way down the steps. Mary snatched at it, but it was too dark: she could hear, but not see, its downward journey.

She abandoned the woman with a prayer that she remain unconscious and dived down the steps in search of the weapon. Whoever held it also held the future. But just as her fingers found its cold barrel, she felt it whisked from her grasp. She spun around and tried to stand, but was immediately pressed back by the glare of the lantern, so close she could feel its warmth. Its bright rays danced along the barrel of the gun, and she could smell the sharp warmth of hot metal from those two very recent bullet blasts. Mary swallowed.

"Sit," said Angelica. Her voice shook, as did the revolver.

"Angelica, please," said Mary, in her calmest tones. "Let me help you."

"I said, *sit!*" It was a shriek now, the voice of a person confused, desperate, distraught. A person capable of almost anything.

Mary obeyed. As the lantern retreated and rose higher, Mary was able to see Angelica's form and work out what she wanted: she was looking at her mother.

"Is she . . . dead?"

Mary's tongue felt too large in her mouth. "No. Unconscious," she said. Not for long, either.

Angelica appeared to fall into a trance. A minute passed, and then she began to mutter something under her breath. It was rapid and soft, but after several seconds, Mary caught it: she was asking, repeatedly, *What shall I do? What shall I do? What shall I do?* Still she remained motionless, staring down at her mother's body.

Just as Mary thought she might risk movement, Angelica abruptly stumped back down the steps. She held her right arm stiff, and the gun swung wildly in Mary's general direction. Mary tried not to flinch. Angelica passed her and, putting down the lantern, opened the door she'd worked so hard to unlock. Its hinges groaned, and the sweet aroma of damp rot floated out to envelop them. "In here."

Mary blinked. "But . . . your mother?"

"Bring her in here."

"I'll need help."

"I suspect you are stronger than you look."

"Truly, I'll have to drag her. She's heavier than I."

Angelica remained stone-faced. "Fine."

Mary set to work. She had no idea what Angelica was thinking, feeling, planning. Likely Angelica herself didn't, either. Mary clasped Mrs. Thorold under the arms and lifted. That itself was manageable, but once she pivoted to descend the steps, she struggled against the dead weight of the larger woman's body. She got stuck midway and said, "Angelica, you'll have to help."

Angelica stared at her. Her fingers tightened around the revolver.

"If it's about the gun, you can put it down: I promise

not to try to take it." It was a daft thing to say and an even madder thing to promise, since Mary intended to keep her word. "But I'm going to drop her if you don't help." She paused, the slumped body growing heavier in her arms by the moment. "It's up to you, of course."

Angelica set down the lantern, tucked the gun into her handbag, and grudgingly took her mother's legs. Between them, they managed to hoist the unconscious body through the doorway without too many bumps and scrapes, and set it clumsily onto the floor. As soon as she was able, Angelica retrieved both lamp and weapon. She seemed calmer, with one in each hand.

For lack of anything better to do, Mary studied the underground room in which they found themselves. It was a low brick cavern, strongly reminiscent of the sewers beneath Buckingham Palace, which she and James had explored a number of months ago. The room in which they stood had two tunnel openings in addition to the door. One appeared to lead toward Great Russell Street, and the other seemed to run at a right angle to the first.

"What is this place?" asked Angelica. She sounded panicked, suspicious. Not at all the sort of person who ought to have her finger on the trigger of a revolver.

Mary tried to sound reassuring. "I believe this passageway is used to walk from the museum's entrance to the Reading Room."

Angelica shivered. "No loot to collect, then."

"Not in this room."

"So my mother lied to you about the reason for coming down here." Both young women looked at Mrs. Thorold's body, sprawled on the floor. There was a bruise already forming on her temple.

"I suspect she has lied about a number of things," said Mary in studiously neutral tones.

"What do you think she planned to do down here?"

Mary took a deep breath. "I think she intended to kill me, and somehow frame me for the thefts." Their gazes once again returned to Mrs. Thorold.

"You don't believe her promise not to shed blood?"

"As it happens, I do not." Mary paused. "Do you?"

"I must, if I am still to consider myself her daughter." It wasn't a proper answer, and they both knew it. "As a dutiful child, I ought to carry out her plan," said Angelica. "I don't know how to frame you, of course, but I could still leave you here to take the blame."

"If I were found alive, I would surely give evidence against you." Mary kept her voice calm and quiet. "You would have to kill me, if you wanted me to take the blame."

"So I would." Angelica carefully lifted the revolver and pointed it at Mary. "Do you think I could kill a woman, Mary? Or a man, for that matter?"

Mary swallowed hard. "Only you know that, Angelica. But there is another choice open to you at this time."

This time the gun did not waver. "Really?"

"Yes. You could leave now. Go back to the Academy, pack your trunk, and return to Vienna as you originally intended. Your mother is here, and I am here, but there is no reason for your name ever to be mentioned. Your choice this evening is not yet irrevocable."

Angelica's eyes widened. "I hadn't thought of that," she whispered. "All this time, I thought my fate was sealed."

Mary watched the gun, watched her hands. "There will still be disgrace, of course; that is inevitable, no matter what happens tonight. But there will also still be music, work, and a future."

"I am accustomed to disgrace," murmured Angelica.

"But I am not," said a third voice, sudden and biting and cold. Mary and Angelica both jumped to face Mrs. Thorold, who was even now raising herself slowly to hands and knees. "I expected no less of you, Miss Quinn, wheedling for your life. But you are a Thorold, Angelica, and you have made your choice. There is no turning back, at this point."

Angelica nearly dropped the weapon in her surprise but managed to recover it. "Mama!" She set the lantern down on the ground.

"Who else?" demanded Mrs. Thorold, rising unsteadily to her feet. "Angelica, you may give me the gun."

Angelica looked at her for a long moment, her expression unreadable. Mrs. Thorold held out her hand expectantly. And then, very slowly, her own hands shaking, Angelica raised the revolver. She pointed it at her mother. "Not yet, Mama."

Mrs. Thorold froze, an expression of pure incredulity

on her strongly marked features. "Don't be absurd, Angelica. Give me the gun." But her voice was hollowed of its usual command, and her pockmarks suddenly stood out on her chalk-white skin.

"Answer me first, Mama. Were you planning to kill Miss Quinn?"

A sly look. "I gave you my word earlier, did I not, Daughter?"

"So you did. But you have not answered my question."

"And if I did think to leave Miss Quinn here? She was not part of my original plan; I cannot be held to account for variables such as this."

"I thought as much," muttered Angelica. "And the museum's security staff that she asked about earlier: the Military Guard, the police, and I think there was a third group?"

"The Fire Brigade," said Mary helpfully.

"Shut up," snapped Angelica, but she kept the gun trained on her mother. "Answer the question, Mama."

"Oh, they're all fit as fleas and jumping about London," said Mrs. Thorold lightly. "I give you my solemn word: they're all fine."

"Then why haven't they roused to the sound of those two shots in the courtyard?"

"They're not here," replied Mrs. Thorold. "There's a tricky little operation going on this evening at the Bank of England, and they're all buzzing about it like flies on a dunghill."

Mary swallowed hard. So that was the reason for such a delay: Anne would have had to go all the way to the Bank, via Scotland Yard, to sound the alarm. Mary made a rapid mental calculation. Allowing for time to send policemen back to the museum, they ought to be here soon. Within the next half hour, probably. Although at that point, they might be entirely too late.

Angelica seemed to calm a little. "And the domestic staff? The academics? They've no reason to be away. Why are they all still asleep?"

"They are alive, if somewhat indisposed. You saw that with your own eyes."

"I asked you earlier if they were alive, and you said they were. What I ought to have asked—what I was too afraid to ask at the time— is this: Had you anything to do with their indisposition?"

Mrs. Thorold adopted a simpering maternal expression. "Angelica, my darling . . ." She took a step toward her daughter but promptly froze when Angelica cocked the trigger. Fury and disbelief chased rapidly across her face.

"Answer me, Mama."

"You saw me make that batch of barley water. Did you see a poison bottle in my hands?"

Angelica's voice was tight and small. "Not as such."

"Well, then?"

Silence. It was bulky and almost palpable, a fourth presence in the room. Mother regarded daughter.

Daughter stared at mother. Mary strained her ears, trying to hear something—anything—above the thundering of her pulse, but she could discern nothing with certainty. She might have heard a distant patter of footsteps; she might simply have wished for them.

Angelica took a deep breath, clearly trying to calm herself. She softened her grip on the revolver but did not lower its muzzle. "Then answer me this, Mama: Will all the museum staff be alive come morning?"

Mrs. Thorold sighed. "We are wasting precious time, Daughter. I shall answer all your questions fully and completely once we are embarked on our journey."

"Yes or no, Mama!" Angelica's voice rose to a shriek. She braced the gun with two shaking hands. "Answer me!"

Mary tensed, ready to spring. That gun would fire at any moment, and there was no telling where.

Mrs. Thorold's features twisted into a smirk of fear, bravado, contempt. "No."

A deafening explosion.

Mrs. Thorold staggered, then launched herself toward Angelica. Mary's stomach plummeted: the bullet had missed its mark. She forced herself to pause, to assess. The Thorolds were locked together on the floor, struggling for control of the weapon. It was impossible for Mary to see the gun, clutched close between the bodies of mother and daughter. After several tense moments, Angelica cried out. It was a sound of surprise and pain, and Mary interpreted it to mean that Mrs. Thorold had got what she wanted. Although the eldest woman in the room, she was the most ruthless. Mary leaped at Mrs. Thorold's back, and all three women went tumbling, a tangle of elbows and crinolines and fury, the ground cold and gritty beneath them. Another discharge, but it sounded muffled, as though the revolver had been pointed directly into the dirt floor of the tunnel. *How many bullets remain in the chamber?* wondered Mary as she clung grimly to Mrs. Thorold's neck and shoulders. She was the smaller woman by several inches and perhaps four stone, and she struggled to keep her grip in this strange embrace.

Mrs. Thorold staggered up and backward, smashing Mary hard against the brick wall with the full weight of her body. "Two bullets left, so don't get your hopes up," she hissed. Mary grunted as all the air left her lungs. For answer, she locked her arms tighter about Mrs. Thorold's neck. As her vision cleared, she noted the revolver bobbing in Mrs. Thorold's right hand, while the left clawed at Mary's hold, twisting her fingers, seeking to break their clasp. Mary felt no pain, heard only Mrs. Thorold's increasingly labored gasps for breath. All she had to do was hang on.

But where was Angelica in this melee? It was only when Mary scanned the room, deliberately searching, that she saw something sprawled carelessly across the floor. It was Angelica's body. It didn't move. Something primal blossomed within Mary, and she squeezed harder still across Mrs. Thorold's windpipe. The gasps became choking sounds, and the gun soon crashed to the ground. Mary ignored it. She didn't need it anymore.

With immense effort, Mrs. Thorold staggered forward and then back again, once more using her body as a weight to crush Mary against the wall. It was a weak effort compared to the first, however, and in response, Mary squeezed tighter. She envisioned the air leaving Mrs. Thorold's body, expelled by the force of her struggle, leaving only a dark vacuum. It was in the grip of this fierce delirium that she first saw the change in the room. One moment there were three bodies; the next there were four. The new arrival was male and darkly silhouetted in the doorway.

Mary blinked and almost slackened her grip, so startled was she by this sudden apparition. "You!" she whispered, a ragged scrap of breath she could ill afford to waste. Half a moment later, she caught her error and renewed her crushing grip across Mrs. Thorold's throat.

Mrs. Thorold emitted a strangled roar.

James sprinted forward, fear and anxiety etched across his face. "Move your arms!" he said, low and tense, as he reached Mary. She scarcely had time to absorb his meaning and react before he added his weight to hers, slamming Mrs. Thorold facedown to the ground. He twisted her arms up and behind with swift precision, making her bellow in the process, and knelt at the center of her back.

Mary was panting, her arms aflame. As she slid off Mrs. Thorold's struggling form, she could think of nothing to say other than, between gasps, "Well. Hello."

James cracked her a grin. "Hello, yourself. Is that a gun I see, just beside us?"

Mary nodded, crawled toward the revolver, and picked it up. "Best check her for other weapons," she said.

"I'd not gotten that far."

"You surprise me."

"It's been rather a hectic evening."

"Would you do the honors?" he asked, looking suddenly squeamish. "It's, er, rather an intimate thing."

Mary stared at him for a long moment. "Only you would worry about propriety at a time like this."

"Well, I'd hate for her to think I was enjoying it."

"You stupid, vain, vapid, smug, self-satisfied, sneering little brats," said a voice like a lash. "I might have known that you were in league. I should have guessed it the moment she turned up this evening."

James blinked down at the body wedged beneath his knee. "Who asked you?"

Mary sighed and began to pat down Mrs. Thorold carefully. It was a delicate task, made additionally challenging by the woman's prone position and her rather complicated structural undergarments. Eventually, Mary said, "I can't do a thorough job like this. She'll have to stand up." She slid the gun to James. "Here."

They positioned Mrs. Thorold with her hands on her head. James stood several feet away, taking careful aim with the revolver. "Remain perfectly still," said Mary. "As you said, two bullets remain." She began at Mrs.

Thorold's back, working slowly and carefully. The devil was, as ever, in the details, and women's undergarments were nothing if not rich in detail: the structured layers of whalebone, steel, leather, string, brass eyelets, padding, and ruching could conceal nearly anything. She moved to Mrs. Thorold's left side, which yielded a thin, long-bladed knife tucked into a garter. Mary slid that carefully across the floor toward James, who whistled low. "Nasty."

"Yes." Mary had seen just what its sibling could do.

"My arms are growing numb," complained Mrs. Thorold.

Mary rolled her eyes but didn't reply. She moved to the woman's right, where she discovered an old-fashioned pocket strapped between overdress and petti-coat. It held a large roll of banknotes, a door key, and a French bank-account book in the name of Mme. Robert Downsby. It also contained a broken vial of white pow-der, which Mary examined for a moment. "Arsenic?" she asked, but received only a snarl in reply. Mary wiped her fingertips and replaced the vial in the dusty pocket. That was work for the police. And speaking of which . . .

"It's always lovely to see you," said Mary, turning to James, "but are the police also on their way?"

James half smiled. "Any minute now. They were about a quarter hour behind me."

"Well, I'm glad you're here now. Even though I already had things in hand."

"I beg to differ," said James casually. "You were

strangling Mrs. Thorold in self-defense. It's thanks to my intervention that she's alive to face trial."

As he uttered the last word, his face twisted in alarm. It was the only warning Mary received before she was jerked roughly upward and a muscular arm wedged itself hard against her throat. A gritty chuckle filled her left ear, making her pulse leap. "Sloppy sideshow amateurs, the pair of you. Too busy flirting to do it right."

James leveled the gun at the two women, but it was a meaningless gesture, and they all understood that. Mary and Mrs. Thorold were locked once again in close embrace, this time with Mary in front, struggling for breath. He couldn't possibly shoot at one without hitting the other.

"Now," said Mrs. Thorold, relishing each word, "who said anything about a trial?" She began to edge backward, keeping Mary between her own body and the gun.

Mary gulped. Mrs. Thorold was squeezing her airway, true, but her real fear in this moment was their destination: the dark tunnel that bisected the present room. It was neither the route to the museum's front hall nor to the outdoor steps they had first used. This was an entirely new direction, one that seemed to lead into the storage catacombs that snaked below the museum's vast footprint. It was a direction she'd completely neglected to consider.

James pivoted slowly, following their progress. His expression was perfectly neutral, and Mary felt a helpless spurt of anger and despair. She adored this man.

She hated that she'd permitted that adoration to sap her concentration, to taint her work. This was not how she wanted to die: a tragicomic footnote in the Great Museum Robbery of 1860.

"Put down the gun," said Mrs. Thorold. She continued to retreat toward the mouth of the connecting tunnel.

James hesitated.

"Or I'll snap her neck like a chicken's," sneered Mrs. Thorold. "It's not much thicker."

James swallowed visibly. "All right," he said, his voice hoarse. "I'm putting it down."

"Don't—" began Mary, but Mrs. Thorold squeezed her throat tighter, choking off her protest. They were in the shadows now, poised to vanish into the brick labyrinth.

"Now kick it toward the door."

James obeyed with slow, steady movements, never taking his eyes from Mary's.

Mary stared back at him, willing her gaze to convey all the things she felt and had neither time nor breath to utter. As she and James stared at each other, she noticed a subtle change in his expression, from grim neutrality to desperate affection to a tiny flare of . . . triumph?

A moment later, Mrs. Thorold emitted a small, brief gasp. Instantly, the crushing pressure at Mary's throat fell away and she stumbled backward, suddenly deprived of the support of Mrs. Thorold's body. She tripped on something and struck out blindly, furiously, before crumpling to the floor, desperate for air.

"Mary!" James was instantly by her side. "My God, Mary."

For several seconds, all she could do was sputter and choke. The fetid air of the tunnel flooded her throat and lungs, and with it the stinging sensation of life returning. She sobbed and shuddered some more, and feared that she couldn't possibly get enough air. As her senses spun and tilted, she caught the thread of James's voice. "How did you do it?" he was asking.

Mary tried to protest that she'd done nothing. Then she realized that he was speaking to a third party: a slender, black-haired man with a quizzical gaze.

"Pressure to a precise spot on the throat," the man was saying. "I will show you, another time. For now . . ." He pivoted to welcome a new element to the conversation—a figure who emerged briskly from the shadows, coiling a hunting whip.

"Well done, sir," said the fourth person, in tones that were slightly husky. "I, too, should be glad of a lesson at a future time, if you would be so gracious."

Mary struggled to sit up in the cradle of James's arms. This couldn't possibly be a hallucination. She simply hadn't the imagination to contrive a meeting between these two people in her fancy. "Lang?" she croaked. "And Miss Treleaven?"

Anne tried for her usual prim smile, but her lips trembled and a rapid pulse was visible in her throat. "My dear, I came through the readers' tunnel."

Mary nodded. Speech was painful.

Lang only smiled at Mary mildly, pleasantly, as though they'd met by arrangement. "Hello, Cousin."

James looked astonished. "Cousin?" he echoed. "No, don't try to talk; tell me later." The next moment, they felt the tremor of rapid, synchronized footsteps one floor above: a phalanx of policemen, marching into the museum. James smiled. He glanced at their audience of two, then kissed Mary gently on the lips. "Much later, I think."

Twenty

Monday, 22 October

The streets of London

The joint directors of the firm Quinn and Easton, Private Detectives, were in conference once again. Their office today was in Russell Square, a location chosen specifically for its evocative associations. It was eleven o'clock in the morning, and the weather was, as usual, cold, dark, wet, and generally abysmal.

"It seems especially unfair," said James, "that although you were the principal in this case—all the work and all the risk were yours, in the end—you were still excluded from the police interviews. I thought Chief Inspector Hall would be more enlightened than that."

"He was probably just embarrassed by how effective Mrs. Thorold's diversion strategy was. It took forever and a day for Scotland Yard to arrive."

"It's still unreasonable of him to blame that on you, however indirectly."

"I'm feeling philosophical today," said Mary. "If Chief Inspector Hall prefers to believe that you did most of the work, and I was simply another busybody female who got involved at the last moment, it leaves me free to work more discreetly in the future."

"He seems to have wrapped his brain around the idea that Mrs. Thorold planned and executed a large-scale crime."

"Precisely. We'll let him grapple with that enormity first before opening the door to a whole parade of female freaks."

"Otherwise, what might come next? Women owning property in their own names! Women at university! Women who vote!"

Mary grinned. "Witches, succubi, and vampires."

"Speaking of vampires, how is your arm?"

"Sore, but the physician thinks it ought to heal. The bite wound is not too deep, thanks to the very thick wool of my sleeve. I'm to flush it regularly, keep it well dressed with honey, and rest it for a few days."

"And your throat?" His gaze hovered at the high collar of her dress, as though he wished to peel it away.

"Black and blue and nothing more."

"You were fortunate."

"We were both fortunate. Have the police linked Mrs. Thorold to the attack upon you?" Mary shivered. James had told her of it in a minimal, offhand fashion, but she could picture the gleaming knife only too clearly.

"Not yet. I doubt they will unless she makes a full confession."

Mary frowned, knowing how very unlikely that was. "What about her inside contact at the Bank of England? Has he said anything useful? It seems astonishing to me that she could bend somebody so powerful to her ends."

"I don't think there was much bending to be done. The man in question, Mr. Bentley, is well-known as a businessman and even better known as a collector of antiquities. His collection of ancient currency pieces is especially admired. I think so long as the Bank's holdings were never in real danger, he was happy to assist with her project. It was simply another way of augmenting his collection."

"Is there any evidence that he and Mrs. Thorold have worked together in the past?"

"Not yet, but Chief Inspector Hall is optimistic."

Their boots crunched in the gravel, and Mary indicated a particular bench, currently occupied by a nurse and her two small charges. "That's where Mrs. Thorold laid out her plan to Angelica, and promised to shed no blood."

James frowned. "She never had the slightest intention of keeping her word. Even at the time she made that promise, she had administered an initial dose of arsenic to everybody at the museum. That's about forty people."

"It was definitely arsenic?"

"Chemical tests show that large quantities of arsenic were mixed into the sugar, flour, and salt stores in the pantry at the museum. Although the different households at the museum have their own cooks and dining rooms, they all obtain their supplies from the same storeroom. By ensuring that all the dry staples were contaminated with significant quantities of arsenic, Mrs. Thorold was able to ensure that every person, no matter his or her appetite or dietary preferences, consumed some of the poison."

"She mentioned a run of dysentery among the staff," said Mary. "I shouldn't be surprised if she'd tinkered with the process before Saturday night. She is meticulous enough to want to know whether such a delivery system would be effective. In fact, she may have toyed with it for a few weeks, as a way of accustoming the staff to putting up with moderate amounts of digestive upset. That way, on Saturday evening, they would have been less inclined to call for a doctor at the first signs of illness; they'd have thought it was more of the same minor complaint."

James nodded. "Very likely. Museum records show that she was taken into employment about a month ago. It would be interesting to chart her time at the museum against recurring illnesses among its members of staff."

Mary was silent for a moment. "How many have died thus far?"

"Nine, with more likely to succumb."

"Arsenic is a bit of a cliché," mused Mary. "So many of the most infamous poisoners are women. I wonder why she chose it?"

"Perhaps because it's relatively subtle. She may even

have dosed herself with a small amount on a couple of occasions, to produce convincing symptoms of illness. It would certainly throw others off her trail."

"And it's still easy to procure, even with the new restrictions."

"Yes. The police are now at work searching for her trail of purchases."

"Everything else seems straightforward enough," said Mary. "After all, she was caught in the act with a bag full of loot."

"The dictionary definition of 'red-handed.' Although what's distinctly complicated is Angelica's role in the affair. And how is Angelica? Do you know?"

Mary nodded. "She wasn't shot, as I'd feared. In hindsight, I think Mrs. Thorold must have struck her unconscious with the butt of the revolver, which then discharged into the ground. She is recovering, although it was a nasty blow to the head. She's still feeling very shaky."

"Where is she?"

"At the girls' school in Acacia Road." Mary paused. "I believe you met the head teacher, Miss Treleaven."

"Yes." James hesitated. "For now, let's continue talking about Angelica. Did she really seek to prevent her mother's crimes?"

"It is her current story, and I confess to planting its seed that evening. It goes like this: Angelica initially sought a reunion with her mother for all the usual reasons—last remaining family member, seeking her mother's blessing for her new life as a music student, that sort of thing. Then, when Angelica first realized that her mother was up to something criminal, she knew she couldn't go through with it. But she pretended to participate, in the hope that she could dissuade her mother from wrongdoing and prevent harm to others. And when Mrs. Thorold threatened my safety, Angelica was forced to act against her." Mary smiled and made an equivocal gesture. "It's fairly close to the truth. Not bad, I think, considering that Angelica suffered a significant injury and thus hasn't had a great deal of time to work out a coherent story."

"If that narrative is so close to the truth, why bother with fiction? Not for the sake of mere moral posturing," James added hastily. "Only it's more difficult to keep track of a story. Besides that, the truth won't land Angelica in jail."

"Angelica thinks it necessary to protect her reputation for the sake of her future career as a musician. There might be a certain sensational value in having been a burglar, however briefly, but nobody would invite her into their homes to give a concert after that. And," added Mary, "I don't know precisely what the truth is, and I doubt Angelica does, either. Motives are murky, confusing things. Once you add family loyalties and a sense of obligation, they are prone to change minute by minute. Perhaps Angelica seriously embraced the prospect of a life of mother-daughter crime; perhaps she was only playing at it, waiting to see what happened; perhaps she genuinely hoped to dissuade her mother from the thefts. I suspect all those theories are true, depending on the moment in question."

James nodded, and they walked a turn of the square in silence. "Is she off for Vienna, then?"

"Scotland Yard has asked her to delay her departure by a fortnight, in case of further questions. But yes, she'll return to the Continent as soon as possible. I doubt she'll miss London much."

"She'll miss you. You seem to have been the closest thing she had to a friend."

"A friend with an agenda." Mary shivered. "This sort of work is always so morally compromising. Even when one begins with the best of intentions."

James looked at her keenly. "Does it put you off?"

Mary thought about it. "Sometimes. Not enough to stop doing it, I don't think. Not yet, at least. But enough that I need these sorts of conversations, to remind myself of who I am and what I believe." She thought for a moment of the Agency and the debriefing she was missing. It was the denouement she would never get: the meeting where she made a final report to Anne and Felicity and heard the full case from their perspective. Mary missed the closure that a formal report seemed to confer, and yet she didn't. It was simply another interpretation, another lens through which to see the events that had transpired. Here was a new measure of her independence, now that she was the person creating the narrative, the author of her own case report.

"This is a good time to explain to you about Mrs. Frame and Miss Treleaven," she said after another brief pause. She wasn't surprised by James's delicacy in not asking directly about the Agency. He was too observant to miss her hesitation there, her obviously conflicted loyalties. "I've wanted to tell you about them for some time now, but never felt able: their secret was not mine to divulge. Now that you've met them, however, and seen them in action, it's only reasonable to fill you in." She paused for a moment. "You know—I've told you—what happened when I was twelve."

Nearly a decade later, it remained difficult to articulate. Her almost-fate was hedged around with words, mere words, yet each time, those words caused her to relive the nightmare of her conviction for housebreaking, the despair of her prescribed fate at the gallows.

James nodded. "I know. Don't pain yourself with the details."

Mary drew a deep breath. "It was Anne and Felicity who saved me. From Newgate, I mean. They brought me to the Academy, where I lived and was educated. They were essentially my foster-mothers. I shall never cease to be grateful to them both, for the innumerable things they have done for me." Her voice shook slightly, and James stroked her hand. They walked for a minute in silence.

"When I was seventeen, they revealed to me that they had a second, hidden life: they were the leaders of a secret detective agency staffed entirely by women. Its rationale is that because women are so habitually dismissed as foolish, vain, and frivolous, we are therefore well positioned to exploit that stereotype as spies. Who would suspect a servant or a female clerk? They invited me to join the Agency, and they trained me. My first assignment was as a lady's companion to Angelica Thorold, in Chelsea."

James looked startled, bemused. "That night we met, in the wardrobe?"

Mary smiled. "I should never have tried to search Mr. Thorold's study. I was embarrassingly inexperienced and desperate to impress Anne and Felicity."

He squeezed her hand hard. "I'm so very glad you did."

She returned the pressure. "A little over a year ago, Anne and Felicity began to have some significant differences of opinion about the future of the Agency. I hoped desperately that they would manage to resolve them. Instead, nine months ago, they parted ways. Anne continued to operate the Agency as a female-only establishment; Felicity founded a new firm, in which she planned to employ both men and women."

"She asked if I would like to work with her again," said James.

"What did you say?"

"Nothing yet. But it occurs to me: that explains why, when Miss Treleaven arrived at the Bank on Saturday night, she spoke only to Mrs. Frame. Mrs. Frame was already there, and known, in male guise."

Mary's surprise was brief. "Yes. Anne would have wanted to preserve her secrecy as the female head of the Agency. And it would have been easy enough for Felicity to explain away her appearance: a female clerk, or perhaps an upper domestic, charged with a message." She paused. "And that small act of collaboration explains what I saw yesterday, when I called upon Anne on a related matter." It had been both a relief and a surprise to hear that Ivy Murchison's wound was not yet infected. If things continued as they had begun, Miss Murchison might live. "I was extremely surprised to see Felicity there, at the Agency. She and Anne seemed to be in the middle of a long conversation, and the atmosphere in the room was . . . intense. Intense and far from hostile. I think they miss each other more than they would ever admit. To a third party, anyway."

"Do you think they might reconcile?"

"It's far too soon to say. They are both incredibly stubborn."

"So are we."

She grinned at that. "And as we know, anything's possible."

They walked in silence for another full turn of the

square before Mary said, "I don't suppose Mrs. Thorold deigned to explain to Scotland Yard how she planned to escape with her loot on a Sunday morning?"

"I don't think she's said anything at all. Do you have any theories?"

"Nothing so grand as a theory, but an idea. She was working as a domestic, and may have taken part in a Sunday excursion or two. She could have mingled with a group of Sunday holidaymakers and thence made her way to the coast. From there, I don't know. She could have waited for a steam packet on Monday morning. Or possibly she had a boat waiting for her in one of the port towns."

"The police may like to investigate that. I'll pass it on." He squeezed her hand. "I'll be sure to tell them it came from my lady associate."

She laughed. "Only if something comes of it; if not, they can think it was your harebrained conjecture."

"Speaking of associates, is Lang really your cousin? And how far removed?"

Mary laughed again. "He is my father's sister's son. And his tale is so entirely incredible that I don't really expect you to believe it."

"Try me."

"Disowned by his father, trained as a rebel soldier, wanted by the Imperial Army in China, seeking his long-lost uncle in London?"

James whistled softly. "Your family doesn't believe in half measures, does it?"

"Apparently not."

"What are his intentions in England? Does he plan to settle here?"

"I don't know. I'm not sure he does, either."

"He might be a useful addition to Quinn and Easton."

"I haven't any idea whether he'd be interested, but we'll certainly meet again. I hope to become much better acquainted with him."

James hesitated. "I'm embarrassed now to confess that I am somewhat jealous of him."

Mary shot him an incredulous look. "Of my cousin?"

"I didn't know about the family connection; Mrs. Frame simply told me that you were 'intimate' with a young Chinese man."

"That's cheap emotional leverage. You know better than to fall for that."

"In theory, of course. But it's quite different when it actually happens." He paused. "Besides, cousins often marry."

"Well, despite the continued popularity of first-cousin marriage, it holds no interest for me."

"No? He's handsome and strikingly talented. And he could offer you the exciting life you so enjoy. Just think: you could wear breeches every day and never see my housekeeper again."

"It sounds terribly appealing, when you put it that way," said Mary, "but I'm afraid I'm still rather partial to you."

"Partial!" He feigned a wounded look. "One is *partial* to jam, or to three-volume novels."

"Fond?" she offered with a smile.

"Of a puppy, or a distant uncle?"

"All right." Mary swung around to face him, taking both his hands and halting him midstep. "James Easton, I am fervently, passionately, utterly, scandalously in love with you."

He went perfectly silent and still.

After a few moments, Mary laughed nervously. "James? A response would be nice."

His voice was half strangled. "You've never said that—anything like that—before."

"I didn't think it needed saying."

"It didn't. But I'm beyond glad you did." The hitch in his voice made her tremble. "As for a response, all I can think to do is kiss you blind, here in the middle of the street, until we're arrested for public indecency."

Every nerve in her body rose up. Her skin prickled with heat. After a moment, she managed to say, "All our hard work. Propriety and formal courtship and such."

"Please, Mary, I want nothing more than to marry you. I want us to be one. How much longer must we wait?"

Mary paused. "'Man and wife'?"

James caught the slight edge in her tone. "Yes, 'man and wife.' And therein the difficulty lies."

Mary clasped his arm, and they resumed walking. "It's not a difficulty with you," she said. "I'm unreasonably confident that, as my husband, you will continue to treat me with respect. You will not impose your opinions upon me—"

"As if such a thing might be possible," interrupted James.

"—or expect unquestioning obedience."

"I would never have such fantastical delusions of my own power," he murmured.

"Hush!" said Mary with a laugh.

"I hear and obey."

"You didn't! You spoke!"

James smiled and sealed his lips with a dramatic gesture.

"My difficulty is with the legal arrangements," said Mary. "Why should all my worldly goods automatically become yours upon our marriage? More importantly, why should we be *man and wife*, with me as yet another of your household chattels?"

They walked in silence for a few minutes. At last, James said quietly, "I haven't good answers to those questions. I suppose I could promise always to treat you as an equal and to take utmost care with your possessions. But that doesn't address the real difficulty. Mary, I'm keenly aware that if you choose to marry me, you are taking all the risk. I receive all the benefit. I retain all the power. And as such, I have no right to press you on the subject.

"This is but a weak answer, for there is no strong position I can take. But it is my hope that together we can create the sort of marriage that will, one day, be usual and customary. We will respect and advise and assist each other. We will be equal partners.

"If you can find it within yourself to trust me, in such an effort . . ." James stopped and took both her hands in his. "Mary, you know I hope you will. But I can also see how, as a woman who prizes her hard-won independence, this may be too great a sacrifice. Perhaps I am asking too much." His gaze was somber; his hands gentle. "All I can ask is that you give it your consideration. And I promise that I will accept your decision without complaint."

Mary blinked back a tear. "Thank you, James. I will consider it . . . for the next ten minutes."

James looked visibly surprised at this time constraint, but seemed not to trust his voice. He offered her his arm, and they continued to walk, leaving the confines of Russell Square and pacing silently up Woburn Place. They looked precisely like what they were: a courting couple taking the air of a late morning. They also looked nothing like what they were: a pair of radicals, quietly at war with their society.

After several minutes, Mary stopped walking. She turned to face James, who looked at her with very real trepidation. "Well?"

"I ought to be asking you that question," said James. His voice was husky.

"What's in your pockets?"

He obediently performed a small inventory. "Handkerchief, penknife, pencil, billfold, two shillings and six, a penny stamp . . . and this." He pulled from his breast pocket a thick sheet of paper covered with spidery handwriting. He showed it to her, and Mary saw, with a pang, that his hands were trembling. "A marriage license. I, er, got it this morning. Before coming to see you."

"Wasn't that a trifle presumptuous?"

He offered her a shadow of his usual arrogant grin. "Optimistic, I'll grant you." He presented it to her. "Well? Aren't you going to tear it up?"

"Have you noticed where we are?"

James blinked and looked around him. They were standing at the foot of the steps to St. Pancras Church. He smiled weakly. "Mary? Are you planning to torture me for much longer?"

She looped her arm through his once again, and lightly tugged him up the first step. "I suppose it depends upon one's definition of 'much longer.'"

He followed her warily. "And yours comprises . . . ?"

She gave him her sweetest, sunniest smile. "How about the rest of our lives?"